BIDING MY TIME

A CAMBRIDGE MYSTERY

MARTYN GOODGER

This book is a work of fiction. The story and characters are wholly the product of the author's imagination. Any resemblance to actual persons, living or dead, businesses or events is entirely coincidental. For more information about the background to the book, please see the author's Afterword.

In memory of my late mother, Thelma Anne Goodger

1

Friday daytime

I was annoyed with both Helen and Max before the meeting was even halfway through.

Annoyed with Helen because of some of the questions she was asking. I wished now that I had insisted on leading the meeting. I was by four years the more senior lawyer. I had only let her lead because, deep down, I knew that she was better than me at the exchanges of pleasantries which were usual when meeting a new client for the first time.

And annoyed with Max because of the way he kept looking at Helen. I could have guessed what he was going to be like from the way he was chatting up our pretty young receptionist when we came down to meet him. The receptionist had been laughing at something he must have said, looking quite different to the person who gave me a cursory painted-on smile when I arrived at the office each morning.

If it had been down to me, I would have gone straight to the meeting room, leaving Helen to bring Max up on her own. But that wasn't how we did things at Doveley's. It might have given Max the impression that I felt I was too important to come down to meet him in reception. And, although I wasn't always finding it easy, I had good reasons at the moment to try to do things the firm's way.

So I had stood patiently behind Helen while she swapped horror stories with Max about the Cambridge traffic. She was good, I had to admit that. Max would have thought that meeting him was the highlight of her professional day.

Finally, she introduced me. 'Max, this is Alan Gadd. One of the firm's most experienced commercial solicitors. Once you and I have talked through the purchase of your new office, he can advise you on the other things you mentioned.'

I was possibly being over-sensitive, but it had sounded to me like Helen was downplaying my role in the meeting.

However, I had made all the right noises and then followed Helen and Max to the lift, noting with irritation how his eyes watched the wiggle of her buttocks under her skirt. It would have been quicker to take Max up the back stairs, but the unwritten rule was that these were only to be used by staff and contractors.

Helen and Max continued their small talk up to the first floor. Helen was looking forward to having a friend over from Northern Ireland in a couple of weeks' time; someone I hadn't heard of before. Max was recommending the tasting menu at a new French restaurant that had just opened in the city centre. Neither of them made any attempt to draw me into the conversation.

The doors to all of the meeting rooms were windowless. This was deliberate. If you were a client, you wouldn't want your closest business rival, in for a routine meeting with their regular employment lawyer, to see you sweating in an adjacent room with one of the firm's top restructuring and insolvency specialists. However, once you were in a meeting room, you had a glorious view out over Parker's Piece and, beyond that, towards the heart of the city which was still dominated by the centuries-old buildings that belonged to the colleges of the University of Cambridge.

I couldn't fault the way that, once we were seated and coffees had been poured, Helen had moved seamlessly from social into business mode. She was dressed in her usual office combination of dark suit, with the hem of the skirt just below the knee, smart plain top and modest heels. I could tell from his body language that Max found her attractive, with her mop of dark, deliberately dishevelled hair which tumbled down to the top of her neck, and her round, slightly mischievous face.

'So, Max, which restaurant in Cambridgeshire is hardest for you to get your clients into at short notice on a Saturday night?' she asked.

Max named a place I had never even heard of, apparently out in the sticks rather than in town. But, going by her smile and nod of her head, Helen clearly knew it well. 'Though I've never failed yet to get a client in,' he added. 'Ignore what they say on their website about their limited number of covers. They always have enough flexibility to make space for two more if it's me on the phone. Sometimes space for more than two if I can promise that my clients will dig deep into the wine list.'

Only a couple of years after graduating from university, Max Blake had set up a business in the city, providing personal concierge services to cash-rich, time-poor clients. Want a last-minute reservation at a top restaurant? Or a pair of tickets for a sold-out concert? Or a bespoke round-the-world trip for your zero-ending wedding anniversary? If so, Max was your man. Many of his clients had made their fortunes with one of the many technology companies that were all over Cambridge, often spin-outs from the city's famous university.

'And now you are planning to buy an office in the heart of Cambridge, rather than continue to rent space on the Business Park? That's a big step-up,' Helen said.

Max gave her the kind of winning smile that he no doubt practised in the mirror each morning. Dressed in a dark navy blazer, white open-necked shirt, light brown chinos and shiny classic brogues, he could have stepped out of the smart casual pages of a catalogue from any upmarket Cambridge menswear shop.

'My business is rapidly expanding,' he said. 'For the first eighteen months we pretty well just acted for wealthy individuals. But now I'm also targeting the corporate market. Firms of lawyers and accountants. Financial services companies. Technology companies, obviously. They all have a lot of well-paid employees who don't have the time to do routine things for themselves, but who probably couldn't afford to sign us up as a personal concierge service. So my new growth area is for their employer to hire us, with us then providing ad hoc services to the employees as a perk of their job. The employees love it, and it's all very tax-efficient too for both the individuals and their employers. The Business Park was OK when we were doing most of the business remotely, but now I am meeting more clients and I want somewhere in town which will impress them.'

'OK, that makes sense. But buying rather than renting? That's very unusual for a relatively new service business such as yours. May I ask why?'

I wasn't entirely sure that this was any of Helen's business, but Max didn't seem to mind. 'I'll benefit from any increase in value,' he said. 'Property prices in Cambridge just keep going up. I can re-brand the office anyway I like, without having to get permission from a landlord. My rent won't keep getting increased every year. And I can stay there as long as I like.' He shrugged. 'It seems a no brainer to me.'

'But you are making a huge capital investment,' Helen persisted. 'Twenty-five per cent of the purchase price up front as a deposit, according to the heads of terms you have agreed. Can your business afford that? I haven't read your accounts, but ...'

'It's nothing for you to worry about,' Max said quickly. 'Business is good. I've done a few deals. I'm on a few promises. And I've got the deposit already gathering dust in the bank account. Honestly, Helen, I'm grateful for your views, but financing the purchase is the least of my problems. What matters is that you progress the legals as quickly as possible, because until we exchange contracts I can't give notice on my present lease.' This time he smiled at Helen in a slightly condescending way, as if she was a waitress making a pig's ear of taking his order.

I toyed with the idea of giving Helen's leg a nudge under the table. I thought she was asking too many unnecessary questions.

But my intervention wasn't needed; she seemed to come to a decision.

'That's fine, Max,' she said. 'It's a commercial call, of course, not a legal one. I'll review the contract package as soon as I get it from the seller's solicitors, and request the property searches.' She ran through the various steps that would take place before exchange of contracts and completion. 'Now,' she continued, 'Alan can deal with the other things. Alan?'

Objectively, it was over-kill to have us both at the meeting, given our usual eye-watering hourly rates. Helen had to meet Max, of course, as part of routine client due diligence. My bits, though, could have been dealt with efficiently enough by e-mail and phone. But there were good reasons on this occasion for us both to meet Max in person.

'Thank you, Helen,' I said. 'Now, Max, if I understand you correctly, you want advice on three things. A restrictive covenant in the existing employment contract of someone you want to hire. Your new data protection policy. And your new terms of business. Is that right?'

It was. The restrictive covenant was easily dealt with, once I had seen the employment contract. I told Max that the current employer wouldn't be able to stop the person jumping ship to work for him. Data protection was one of the most boring subjects I advised on. In my experience, the only lawyers who actually enjoyed data protection work were those who were too unimaginative to make a success of anything else. But advising Max on the necessary changes to his new policy was straightforward. The drafting of some new terms of business for his corporate clients was more interesting, even though I would probably farm the grunt element out to my trainee.

This was the part of the job I enjoyed most. Giving clear, pragmatic advice to clients. None of this wishy-washy 'On the one hand ... on the other hand ...' stuff that too often I had seen other lawyers give. I may not have been the sort of lawyer the firm liked to parade on tenders in front of big new potential clients, but once the work had been brought in I certainly knew how to deliver.

After five more minutes the meeting was over. Helen – doing things by the book as usual – summed up what each of us was going to do after the meeting, and within what time scales.

Outside, the morning rush hour had come to an end, but the road that ran past our office building towards the Catholic church at the Hills Road crossroads was still busy, as much with the city's ubiquitous cyclists as with cars. Right beneath the window, an energetic-looking cyclist in fluorescent green Lycra was over-taking a middle-aged woman who had a small child in a rickety trailer behind her bike. Typically for Cambridge, none of them were wearing helmets.

As Helen led Max back along the corridor towards the lift, he was turning the charm on again. He mentioned being able to get her a ticket for a James concert that had long sold out. He made a couple of gently flirtatious remarks. I knew that I wasn't going to enjoy working for him. It wouldn't surprise me if he tried it on with her at some point.

'I'll say goodbye here, Max,' I said when we reached the lift. 'It was a pleasure to meet you. Helen will show you out. Don't forget to return your visitor's badge to reception.' I was pleased with the last two sentences, reminding Helen that she was junior to me, and Max that he was still very much an outsider. Helen and I had tried to behave professionally towards each other since we had split up, but I did still have some pride.

I shook hands with Max, then hurried up the back stairs to the second floor, using my swipe card to let myself into the staff area where my desk was. I was curious to see if Jeff had left me another message.

2

When I'd first joined Doveley's, as a newly qualified solicitor down from the North almost ten years ago, I'd had my own office here on the second floor. OK, I'd actually had three different offices over the years, and they had always been shared with someone else. First, with a more senior lawyer than me, to supervise my work and for me to learn from. Then, after a couple of years, with a lawyer of about my own seniority, both of us able to work unsupervised but not yet sufficiently experienced to supervise juniors. Then, for the last few years, with whichever trainee was passing through the team at the time. But each of the offices had been my safe space, with four walls and a door which could be closed to keep the noise, and other people, out. And since I had invariably worked longer hours than whoever I was sharing with at the time, the unspoken agreement with my room-mate had always been that I could have things in our office just the way I wanted.

But times had changed, and the firm had decided that everyone would prefer to work open-plan. More collegiate. Easier to communicate. No hierarchy of offices. Obviously, nothing to do with the fact that more lawyers could be crammed into the same floor space. The reality that it was almost impossible to work undisturbed, whether by phone calls or just general gossip, in a large open-plan area for any length of time was of no concern to the decision-makers. These were the firm's most senior partners who had largely given up legal work anyway in favour of vaguely defined stuff such as client relationship management, which seemed to consist mostly of wining and dining the firm's most profitable clients at the city's top restaurants. In practice, it meant that I often found myself saving my most complex work for when everyone around me had gone home for the night. Something which would no doubt have been considered another point in favour of open-plan working by the decision-makers, given that like all of the firm's lawyers I wasn't paid any overtime – the work that landed on my desk just had to be done, and it was my problem if I was unable to finish it during normal working hours.

My desk was one of a pod of four, near the centre of the second floor which was where the firm's large Commercial team (my team) was based. I shared the pod with Lucy, my current trainee; Hayley, the secretary who worked both for me and for the partner who headed up the team; and Rosemary, a middle-aged professional support lawyer.

Rosemary wasn't due in until the afternoon, but as I approached my pod after the meeting with Max, I noticed that Hayley and Lucy were having a whispered conversation. They were both in their twenties and, although quite different in looks, background and personality, seemed to get on well together. However, I suspected that part of this was due to Lucy not wanting to make the classic trainee mistake of rubbing the support staff up the wrong way. There were legendary stories of trainees who had arrogantly offended the people in reprographics, and who had then mysteriously found no one to help them at 4 p.m. on a Friday afternoon when completion documents had to be printed, collated and bound before they could go home for the weekend.

'He said *what*?' I heard Hayley saying as I slid into my chair. But a fraction of a second later she and Lucy both spotted me, so I never found out what Lucy's reply would have been. Lucy dipped her head and pretended to concentrate on her computer screen. I guessed that either they had been talking about me, or there was some other firm gossip they didn't want me to hear about.

'Good meeting, Alan?' Hayley asked, in her usual cheery way.

Working class Cambridge born and bred, Hayley was the antithesis in background to someone such as Max, even though they had both probably gone to school within a few miles of each other. She lived with her brickie boyfriend and their young son in Abbey, one of the most deprived wards of Cambridge. Because of my own northern roots, I sometimes felt we should have an affinity in the middle-class professional Cambridge world in which we both worked. But although she never showed any sign of disliking me, I occasionally had the feeling that I amused her for some reason.

'Yes, thank you, Hayley,' I said. 'Helen's letter of engagement to Max will cover the work we are both doing for him, so there's no need for you to do a separate letter from me. I'll be dictating you an attendance note though.'

Attendance notes were all about covering your arse, one of a lawyer's most prized techniques. The attendance note was supposed to be a record of advice given, not a record of advice which with hindsight you wished you had given. But the difference between the two could be a fine line, and most experienced solicitors were sufficiently skilled in the dark arts to make an attendance note do the job they wanted.

'I've got some work out of the meeting which I'll be supervising Lucy on,' I went on. 'Please can you find a slot in our diaries so that I can brief her.' Automatically I looked over at Lucy as I said this. There was a flash of interest on her face, but also something else which I couldn't quite make out, almost as if she felt she knew something which I didn't.

'Consider it done.' Hayley wasn't the most attractive of secretaries, with her dull-looking straight dark shoulder-length hair, minimal make-up and plump figure. But she was one of the most efficient on the second floor and I relied on her a lot to ease my administrative tasks. 'By the way, Alan,' she went on, 'I couldn't help but notice that you'd had an e-mail from Jeff while you were in your meeting. I was checking your in-box in case the new client you met last night had sent through the paperwork we need for the injunction. It's the third time today Jeff's contacted you. He phoned during your meeting and told me that he'd already left you a voice message first thing this morning which you hadn't yet got back to him about. I asked if I could help but he said he would send you an e-mail instead, which he must have done straightaway. Do you think it's an urgent client matter?'

I looked hard at Hayley but she had only a look of helpful innocence on her face. I noticed Lucy smiling as she stared at her screen. 'I'll deal with it,' I said.

I scanned the e-mails which had come in while I had been away from my desk. There was the usual rubbish from the non-legal support teams on the first floor - marketing, HR, IT, finance, and so on - trying to justify their relevance. There were some routine e-mails in from clients, but nothing which couldn't wait. There was also an automatic reminder of my meeting later in the morning with Sam Snape, the partner who headed up the Commercial team. My boss, in other words. I had done all my preparation for this meeting last night so I could forget about it for now.

And there was an e-mail with a blank subject line from Mr Nosey Parker himself up on the third floor: *Alan, can we have a word please. Give me a call when you get out of your meeting. Jeff.*

I was fairly sure what this was about. I didn't particularly want to speak to him, but he clearly wasn't going to leave me alone until I did. He answered the phone straightaway.

'Alan,' he said. 'I'm sorry, but I've got to be frank about this. Helen's moved on. I know it's not easy for you, but you have to accept it.'

'I don't know what you are talking about,' I said. I started doodling on a notepad, as was my habit when feeling uncomfortable. I was aware that neither Hayley nor Lucy was using their keyboard, although I didn't dare look directly at them to see if they were watching me. Fortunately, I knew from experience that as long as I kept my voice down, they wouldn't be able to overhear me over the whirring of the office printers behind me and the general noise of the second floor.

'Look, mate,' he said, in a low voice. 'We've all been there. I can understand you being pissed off with me. I'd feel the same in your position. But it's nothing personal, you know. Helen and I haven't done this to hurt you. It's just happened. So you can't blame me, and you certainly can't blame Helen. You can't keep on bad-mouthing me to anyone who will listen. It's not professional and it's not going to change anything.'

That was quite a speech, I thought. I wondered idly if he'd jotted down what he was going to say beforehand. 'I haven't bad-mouthed you,' I said quietly.

There was a deep sigh. 'Really? Jeff and the Boneheads?'

'That was a joke,' I said.

'Well, it's not the sort of joke you should make to a group of trainees when they are asking for advice about applying for a seat in the Corporate team. You made it sound like you think we are all cowboys up here. What do you think Sam would make of it, if he knew what you'd been saying?'

'Have you told him?'

'No, Alan, of course not. Unlike you, I'm not mixing work and play. What goes on outside work stays outside work as far as I'm concerned. Or at least that's how it should be. But we both know that's not the only time you've said something like that about my professional abilities.'

I decided to ignore that last bit. 'Anyway,' I said as quietly as I could, 'I'm not blaming Helen.'

'What about today? The first thing she did when she got back from your meeting was to call me. She said that you had been sulky again and had tried to put her down in front of a client.'

'No, I didn't. I just suggested she showed the client out.' I kicked myself mentally as soon as I'd said this. It would be obvious now that my slight had been intentional.

'We both know what you were doing. So does she. She also said that you had deliberately left her to pour the coffee as if she was a trainee. And that you were huffing and puffing when she was asking Max how he was going to finance the purchase of his office.'

'Well, she hasn't complained to me.'

'Alan, Helen's a good sort. She knows you were upset over the break-up of your relationship with her. She understands that you find it difficult working alongside her, as you have to do from time to time. She agonised for ages over whether to invite you to provide the commercial support in her meeting today with Max. She could just have easily have invited someone else from your team, but she wanted to give you the opportunity to get in with Max right at the start. But she does struggle with your attitude, both towards her and towards me. So think on, mate.'

Fucking think on yourself, you bastard, I thought, as I put the phone down without saying another word. I wasn't going to be taken in by Jeff's show of reasonableness. It hadn't taken him long to make his move on Helen after we had split up. OK, after she had suddenly dumped me, almost ten weeks ago now, in the run up to Christmas. Although they had both denied it, I was convinced that Jeff had had something to do with her decision. Helen and I had been together for nearly a year, and even though we had never made each other any promises, I had started to assume that we would be together for the long-term. The relationship had seemed to suit us both, especially during her illness. We had not moved in together, but because we worked for the same firm, I could see her whenever I wanted. And although I was the more senior lawyer, doing broader and more complex work than Helen, the fact that we were both in the same profession meant that we could lend an empathetic ear to each other's problems. I had never found it easy to open up to people, but I could remember many evenings when she had listened for hours as I talked about the things that were bothering me.

Jeff himself I had known for more than six years. He'd had a six-month stint as a trainee in the Commercial team when I was still relatively junior. I hadn't therefore had to supervise him myself, but I'd had plenty of opportunities to see him in action. Both work-wise and women-wise.

Work-wise he was good enough with clients and always got praised in reviews for being 'very commercial'. But I had noticed that he didn't seem to care much for the detail of the law. I hadn't been surprised, therefore, when he decided to accept an offer on qualification to join the Corporate team up on the third floor. Corporate lawyers were notorious for enjoying doing deals without bothering too much about getting the technicalities right.

And, women-wise, well what could I say? When out drinking with other men, he hardly played down the 'Jack the Lad' side of his character, not denying the rumoured number of his sexual conquests. The gossip was that he usually managed to sleep with at least one of the female trainees in each year's intake. But he had the habit of saying something like 'a gentleman never tells' if someone probed him for details of who he was sleeping with. When talking to women, though, he became the good ol' West Country boy, courteous and attentive to their every whim. I could never stand his hypocrisy, even before he started sniffing around Helen. He had worked with her last autumn on a number of big property finance deals. He had even come into the office one weekend to help her, when her assistant was sick and she was struggling to put together the paperwork for a big completion on the Monday. I remembered asking Helen if he fancied her, and she had just laughed it off.

'What if he does? It's not a crime. And if it helps me get the work done, I'm not complaining.'

'Would you find him attractive if you weren't with me?' I had asked. It was a perfectly reasonable question, I felt, but perhaps with hindsight her response had been revealing:

'You do go on, Alan. Look, can you honestly say that you don't fancy anyone else in the office? How about Lucy, your trainee? I'm not saying you would shag her, I know you wouldn't. But there's no harm enjoying looking at her, and you never know she may be flattered.' She had then giggled, although I wasn't sure why.

So, while I had been shocked to find out that Helen had taken up with Jeff within a few weeks of our break-up, I can't say with hindsight that it was a complete surprise. She had been very open with me about her new relationship, and we had agreed that it wouldn't affect how we behaved to each other in the office. But, my God, how I loathed that man. What made it worse was that everyone else seemed to like him, and to accept that he and Helen were now an item.

I must have spent a few minutes mulling things over after I had ended my call to Jeff. When I looked down at my notepad, I saw that I had filled a complete page with a series of random circles which I had then all viciously crossed out. I tentatively raised my eyes to see if Hayley and Lucy had noticed anything amiss, but to my relief both of them appeared to be hard at work and concentrating on their computer screens.

3

'Any plans for the weekend, Alan?'

Sam and I made the usual small talk while we walked down the stairs to the staff meeting room that Hayley had booked for us on the first floor. Staff meeting rooms were at the opposite end of the floor to the client meeting rooms, and could be accessed without having to go through the client area. This meant that we could use them without having to first make sure that we were 'client respectable', as the firm's staff handbook put it.

As partners went, Sam Snape wasn't the worst. Now in his mid-forties, about ten years older than me, he had been made up to partner, and become my boss, when I was still a relatively junior solicitor. He was ex-City of London, of course, like most of the male partners at Doveley's. The usual pattern was for them to move out of London around six to eight years after qualifying, claiming to have done so in order to achieve the so-called work life balance. In a highly competitive legal market such as Cambridge's, though, this typically still only meant having a chance to get home in time to read bedtime stories to the kids on a couple of nights a week. It was almost invariably kids in the plural, often three or four. There seemed to be something about the anal qualities needed to be a partner which meant that they often over-compensated by impregnating their wives on a regular basis. In the old days, it was often their secretaries that they impregnated too, but after a few high-profile scandals that had escaped from the legal press into the broadsheets and even the tabloids, most partners were now a lot more careful about not dipping their pen in the company ink.

That was the male partners. The firm had some female partners too, although a smaller proportion of the overall partnership than you would expect if you had been relying on the publicity pages of the firm's glossy new website. At the junior level, the quality of the female lawyers at a firm such as ours was usually higher than that of the males. This was because the best women coming out of law school often plumped for a regional firm from the outset, not feeling the need to prove themselves in a cock-waving contest by working hundred-hour weeks in the City of London. Many of the female partners chose to work part-time, however, and I had heard more than one of them openly boast on a drunken team night out that they had stopped taking the pill the day they got made up as a partner.

'Nothing special, Sam,' I replied. 'I might play some tennis on Sunday if it's fine. But I've got nothing else planned.' The unspoken words 'as usual' hung in the air between us, so I hurriedly changed the subject. 'I've got some new work out of my meeting this morning with Max. All pretty straightforward and no reason why I won't be able to bill all my time. Just a shame that he's a bit of an arsehole,' I added flippantly.

I realised straightaway from Sam's reaction that it wasn't the brightest of things to say. The problem with Sam was his face. Not so much his fleshy jowls, Buddy Holly glasses and mop of thick wavy brown hair, which to my mind just made him look like a middle-aged pop impresario. Rather, it was his habitual smirk which made you always think that he was either about to crack a joke himself or was expecting one from you. So my experience of him over the years was that either I kept things serious and then worried that I was boring him to tears, or I said something jokey and then found out that he was actually having a bad day. I could never get it right. But, needless to say, the secretaries and junior female lawyers loved him. Fortunately, even though my pod was within his eyeline on the second floor, I was able to avoid having much to do with him on a day-to-day basis, as I didn't need his supervision and I was able to generate most of my own work.

'So why do you say he's an arsehole?' he asked deadpan, as we sat down in the meeting room. In design and decoration, it was no different to the client meeting rooms at the other end of the first floor. But here there was no tray of coffee and biscuits, and there was a whiteboard on the far wall covered in a flow diagram with names such as 'NewCo', 'OldCo' and 'TopCo'. The deal-doers from Corporate had obviously been in before us, planning yet another company restructuring, and as I had come to expect, they hadn't bothered cleaning up after themselves.

I felt my face redden. 'I was only joking,' I said. 'He's all right, I suppose. He's just a bit full of himself.' I didn't think it would help things to say that he had been making eyes at Helen.

'Don't you think he's got every right to be full of himself if that is indeed the case? He's only in his late twenties and he's built up a very successful business from scratch. He's got some clients we would kill for to have as our clients, including the founders of some of the most successful technology companies in Cambridge. If we do a good job for him, he may even refer some of these to us. Maybe not for their private equity work, that will probably still go to London, but there's lots of other work we could profitably do for them.'

Such as 'wealth preservation' work, I thought. Making sure that their clients never had to do a day's work in their lives ever again.

Sam paused before going on. 'Plus, there's his father. He owns businesses throughout East Anglia and is one of the firm's longest-standing clients.'

And plays golf with our firm's managing partner, I suddenly remembered. But this was typical of Sam. I'd lost count of the number of times I had heard him refer to clients in much more unflattering terms than the one I had used. It was one of his pet ways of currying favour with juniors who he was planning to beast over a weekend. Get them to think that while he was making them cancel their weekend plans, he was really on their side and that it was all the fault of the totally unreasonable client.

'You're right,' I said. 'I wasn't thinking.'

'Look, Alan,' he said, 'I'm on your side. I really want you to get promoted to partner in this year's round. There's no one else in my team who's in the frame. Plus, and I shouldn't really be telling you this, if you don't get it then the partnership slot on our floor will probably go to one of the, er, guys in the Tax team.'

This time there was a definite smug smile on Sam's face. However, I wasn't going to risk making the mistake of cracking a joke about the type of lawyers who spend their professional lives advising on the legal aspects of taxation. I had a sudden image of Sam, home with his attractive GP wife Julia and two teenage children, joking about which of the two candidates in contention on the second floor for this year's round of promotions to partner was more of an oddity.

'I want to get made up, too,' I said. 'You know I've worked for it. My figures are the best in the team. Some of the best in the firm, in fact. Chargeable hours, billed hours, realisation, cash – I've more than hit every financial target. And client feedback on the big deal that closed last week was that I was outstanding.'

That was the company takeover that had ended in a big night out in London with the client's top brass. The celebration had begun with a photograph for the legal press of our client's CEO shaking hands with the CEO of the target company at 4 p.m. on the previous Friday. There had been a single bottle of unopened champagne on the boardroom table, to keep the picture editor happy. Then, with the official publicity out of the way, the favoured few had gone on somewhere to have proper drinks, then elsewhere for dinner, then ... well who knows. I certainly didn't. Even though I had sweated blood on that deal, providing commercial law support to the partner from Corporate who was in overall charge, I hadn't been invited to the post-completion celebrations. Something had been said to me about the firm having to be careful not to go over the top in view of the latest anti-bribery guidance, so that only those actually needed at the completion meeting were going to be invited to the drinks and meal afterwards. The next morning, however, I had overheard Lucy and Hayley laughing about one of the Corporate trainees who had been sick in the ladies' toilets after getting home from the festivities in the early hours.

'You've done great, Alan,' said Sam. 'I wish I could hit my targets like that. And, yes, the client on that deal was massively impressed with your work on the documents.'

My work on the documents, I thought … Here's where he starts on about me needing to work on my softer skills …

'Corporate were also amazed at how quickly you turned your drafts and how efficiently you dealt with all the commercial law issues. So, er, well done, Alan!'

I would have sworn that his natural smug smile broadened, and – God - he even did one of his notorious thumbs-up at me. Fortunately, I resisted the temptation to do one back, as the next moment – smile still in place – he was moving onto what I knew he really wanted to say. 'But, look, you know that all the partners here have different strengths. There are finders, minders and grinders. The finders bring new work in, the minders keep the existing clients happy, and the grinders, er, actually do the work. No one can be equally good at all three or – ha ha – they wouldn't have settled for being a partner at a firm like this. But, as you know, every partner has to show a certain minimum competence in all three categories.'

Well, he certainly wasn't going to ask me to become more of a grinder … Sam leant forward, a move out of the best management textbooks to try to show that we were on the same side.

'I've been discussing your business case with the other partners,' he said. 'Everyone's really pleased that you feel ready for the next big step in your career. And your written business case is excellent. Great outline of your current practice, check. Convincing proposal to grow your practice over the next three years, check. Impressive marketing plan for the next twelve months, check. All backed up where needed with facts and figures.' I half expected him to give me another thumbs-up. 'And pretty well the only question mark that's been raised – and not by me obviously – is whether you yet have all the skills to implement everything that's in your business case, in terms of bringing future work into the firm. Remember you need to convince the other partners that you can help to feed others if you get made up, as well as feeding yourself.' Partners like Sam liked this type of transatlantic jargon, which often involved imagery of sharks or great beasts of the jungle. Firms such as ours were always said to be 'circling' when other firms were in trouble, or 'swooping' to recruit star performers who were unhappy at their current shops.

'Is there anything in particular the other partners are questioning?' I asked rather superfluously. I knew where this was going.

'Well, take your marketing plan. You say you want to increase awareness of your practice in the Cambridge area so as to bring in new clients, rather than relying on repeat work from the firm's existing big clients. You even provide a list of local prospects, which is great. But most candidates for partnership in your position would already be taking the initiative here, not just making promises of what they will do if they are made up. What sort of things have you been doing in Cambridge recently to win new clients?'

Now wasn't the time to complain about being landed at the client summer party with the bearded techie guy that no one else wanted to speak to. 'Er, I don't go out in Cambridge much at the moment,' I said through gritted teeth. 'I usually work too late during the week to get to anything. And no one I know ever seems to invite me to things at weekends.' Even to my own ears that sounded pathetic. But that was what always happened in these conversations with Sam. I felt like a mediaeval knight whose chain mail armour was being unpicked link by link, until I was left naked and unprotected. I did wonder whether he knew I had overheard Lucy thanking him for that 'lovely dinner' at his house a few Saturdays ago, when she and her long-time boyfriend had apparently had such a 'fantastic evening' with Sam and Julia. It went without saying that I had never been invited round to his house, not even when I had been going out with Helen.

It seemed like Sam was reading my mind. 'Of course, I know that you and Helen are no longer together,' he said. 'I hadn't wanted to mention it before, for obvious reasons. It must be very sad for you personally, but perhaps it might now give you an opportunity to put yourself out and about in Cambridge? To take your mind off things?' He raised his eyebrows inquisitively.

'I suppose so,' I said. I could see that Sam was curious to ask more, a bit like a ghoul wanting to pore over the remains of a murder victim. But I really didn't want to talk about it. So I stayed silent.

But now that Sam had finally broached the subject, he seemed unwilling to let it go. 'The break up must have come as a blow to you,' he said eventually. 'Though of course you are doing well to be able to work amicably alongside her when you have to.' I was irritated by the way he assumed, without asking, that it was Helen who had broken it off. After all, why would someone like me dump someone like her? I remembered having overheard last year a fragment of a conversation on the stairs between two of the Property secretaries. One of them had said something about Helen playing down a couple of divisions, and the other had replied that she must feel sorry for him. I hadn't realised at first that they were talking about me, but their sudden silence and reddened cheeks when they saw me had made it clear that this was the case. I had wondered sometimes why Helen had chosen to go out with me, and she had said once that something in me reminded her of your younger self, a time when she was less confident and doubtful as to whether she had any true friends.

'We wanted different things,' I replied. That was true. I had wanted her. She hadn't wanted me anymore. But I wasn't going to discuss it with Sam. There was a silence, and in order to distract myself I silently started counting the seconds. I had reached ten when Sam broke the silence, obviously realising that he wasn't going to get my side of the story.

'Well maybe try some of the networking meetings that are held after work, often in a pub in town, or on the Science Park. Find a couple that no one else from here goes to. Meet people, take an interest in what they do, let them know what you do, maybe even buy them a drink if you're meeting in a pub.' His smirk widened, no doubt at the thought of me buying someone a drink in a pub. 'In fact, there's one on Monday evening that might suit you. I was thinking of going with Lucy, but you'd be doing me a favour if you could go in my place. But remember, don't over-sell yourself. No one is going to instruct you on the basis of one or two meetings. Coming from a firm like ours, they will take it as a given that you are a good lawyer. You need to show you are their kind of guy … '

*

I had five minutes more of this stuff before the meeting was over. We had these 'one-on-ones' every month or two, to discuss the process of my application to become a partner. I really hated them, because I always came away with the impression that Sam was looking for an excuse not to see me made up, all his apparent encouragement notwithstanding. Of course, if that was the case, he wouldn't want to tell me so directly, in case I started thinking of a move to a rival firm. I was one of the best technical lawyers at our firm and I knew that I would be difficult to replace.

Sam and I exchanged small talk again on our way back upstairs to our desks. Sam's pod, which he shared with a junior solicitor and two paralegals in the Commercial team, was in the far corner of our floor. Unfortunately, this meant that I was within his line of sight the whole time, whereas I couldn't see him without turning more than ninety degrees to my left. It had always made me feel like a naughty schoolboy under the eye of the teacher, which I knew was ridiculous but I couldn't help it.

Once I had sat down at my desk, I saw that I had missed a call from Helen.

4

Helen wasn't at her desk up on the fourth floor, even though I called her back straightaway.

So I went out to grab a sandwich, taking the stairs down to the ground floor. It was quicker to do this than to use the lift, especially at lunchtime, but most other people didn't seem to mind hanging around in the corridor in a group and making small talk while they waited for the lift to arrive. As was usually the case, no one had asked me if I wanted to walk into town with them to get something to eat, and I hadn't wanted to ask anyone myself.

As I reached the ground floor reception, Lucy was walking out of the front door with Rachel, the young solicitor who worked for Helen in the Property team. Our office building is flanked by the swimming pool on one side and the sports centre on the other, and the two women crossed the road and headed off across Parker's Piece towards the city centre. In the summer the large green common would have been busy with people enjoying a lunchtime picnic or maybe a kick around with a ball. But on a cold February day such as today, the only people on the common were cyclists, joggers and pedestrians following the tarmac paths that run diagonally across it. This was the quickest way into the city centre, so I crossed the road as well and continued a short distance behind the two women. They walked in step with each other, their heads almost pressed together. 'The witches', was what Helen jokingly called them, having pointed out once that they seemed to be able to communicate with each other without the need for speaking. Rachel was professionally a year ahead of Lucy, having qualified as a solicitor the previous September, but she still lived in her house share with Lucy and two trainee solicitors from another of the many law firms in Cambridge.

At first, I maintained the same distance behind Lucy and Rachel, trying to match their own fairly slow pace, but this made me feel as if I was walking in slow motion so I decided to overtake them. As I drew level, I increased my pace still further to avoid overtaking too slowly, and realised with some embarrassment that it looked like it was turning into something of a walking race. I said a polite hello as I went past and saw them simultaneously stop their conversation mid-sentence when they recognised me. I had the uncomfortable feeling that they had been talking about me.

*

I bought a ham and something sandwich in town and decided to walk the slightly longer way back to the office, along Regent Street and then left at the Catholic church crossroads. While still on Regent Street, I spotted Helen and Jeff sitting at a table by the window in one of the independent shops where you can grab a coffee and a bite to eat. They were engrossed in conversation so didn't see me as I walked past. Jeff was leaning forward with the open expression and half-smile he often put on when trying to demonstrate to women what a good listener he was. On the spur of the moment, I turned back and walked more slowly past the window to try to catch Helen's eye. There was a rare flash of annoyance on her face as she noticed me peering through the window. I pointed a finger first at her and then at my ear, to show that I was referring to her attempt to reach me by phone. She said something to Jeff, got up and joined me outside: 'Yes, Alan, what is it?' she said.

'You wanted to speak to me?'

'It could have waited. I'm having lunch with Jeff. We've got something to discuss.'

'I'm sure you have,' I said.

She let out a deep breath. 'Alan, the lunch is work-related. I've got a problem that I wanted Jeff's advice about. It's got nothing to do with you and me. But, yes, about my phone call before lunch, I just wanted to ask you in the nicest possible way to have a think about how you have been behaving. Your body language this morning in the meeting with Max was embarrassing. You clearly didn't like the way he was looking at me or talking to me. You were discourteous to me in front of him when he was leaving. I know you are under a lot of pressure at the moment, going for partnership and all that, but please do make more of an effort when we are at work. I didn't have to invite you to the meeting, you know. I was trying to help you, by giving you a chance to get work from a new client.'

'You didn't have to get Jeff to do your dirty work,' I said, referring to the phone conversation I'd had with him that morning.

'I didn't.' She paused for a moment before continuing. 'Look, I did tell him straight after the meeting with Max what you had been like. But he was going to speak to you anyway. He's annoyed about you slagging him off to anyone who will listen. And I don't blame him, to be honest. He could easily make a thing of it with HR, but he's a nice guy and doesn't want to.'

I glanced through the window and saw Jeff watching me with an expression of mild interest on his face. He could have been watching a couple of animals at a zoo, rather than his new woman and her old boyfriend discussing his own new relationship with her on a Cambridge pavement. 'I could tell you a few things about Mr Nice Guy,' I muttered. However, I could see this wouldn't go down well and decided to change tack. 'That work thing you are talking about with Jeff. If I can help, just let me know. I assume it isn't a complicated legal point?' I didn't add what I was thinking, namely that it couldn't be anything of a complicated legal nature if she was wanting to talk it over with a lawyer from Corporate. That sort of comment about Jeff's professional abilities hadn't gone down well in the past.

To my surprise, Helen smiled the way she had done just before I had kissed her for the very first time, over a year ago now. At the end of an evening out together in Cambridge the previous January, first in an Indian restaurant on Regent Street and then in a quiet pub just across the road. I had walked her back to her house afterwards and kissed her for a long time outside her front door, half expecting spotlights to come on at any moment and a watching crowd to burst out laughing at the ridiculousness of me having believed she would want to kiss me for real. 'That's kind, Alan,' she was saying now, 'but, really, it's OK. It's just something Rachel has done. I need a second opinion from Jeff.'

That threw me. Helen liked and rated Rachel, so I couldn't understand why she would want to discuss with Jeff something that Rachel had done. Jeff knew even less about property law than me. The fact that they were discussing it privately at lunchtime, and not in their cosy love nest in the evening, suggested it must be something important. I racked my brains in case anything occurred to me, but it didn't.

As I walked back to the office, I wondered for a few moments if I should ask Lucy. But even if Lucy knew what was going on, she wouldn't tell me unless she thought Rachel would want me to know. The witches' pact, I thought. I made a mental note to try to find out more.

5

The rest of the afternoon passed by in a similar way to most Friday afternoons at the office.

I sat at my desk, concentrating on the drafting of a complicated patent licence, but breaking off every now and again to read or send an e-mail on some other matter. If I am honest, I was in my element. No one else in the firm could do what I was doing as well as me. And, despite the reputation of Cambridge as a hub of legal excellence in the technology sector, I reckoned not many other lawyers in the city could do so either.

On my left, Rosemary, our professional support lawyer (or PSL), was working her usual Friday 2 p.m. to 5 p.m. shift. We got on well enough with each other even though we never socialised away from work. Like many PSLs at the larger regional firms, she was a middle-aged, ex-City of London solicitor, who had done all the deals and seen all the sights in her younger pre-child days. She was divorced, but her two kids were now at secondary school and could mostly look after themselves. However, she still wanted fixed working hours without any client responsibilities. So she drafted and updated our template commercial contracts, wrote briefing notes on legislative changes, and circulated regular snippets on important cases that might impact our area of work. And she got paid about two thirds of what she would get if she was doing fee-earning work.

'My God, Alan,' she had told me at that year's team Christmas night out at a city centre Italian, when the table was groaning with the weight of empty wine bottles, 'you have no idea, no idea at all, how fucking boring this PSL job can be.'

Her use of the word 'fucking', for the first time ever in my hearing, had excited me slightly at the time. She was normally very quietly-spoken, a bit like a plump mouse in her practical dark suits, usually hunched over her keyboard as if wanting to isolate herself from the rest of the office. Briefly, I had imagined myself naked on top of her, driving her wild with a passion that she would undoubtedly not have experienced for years, but as was usually the case with me it had remained nothing but a fantasy. 'If you don't ask, you don't get,' had been the motto of a trainee I had had the previous year, in relation to women. I had never liked him, and had recommended that he wasn't offered a permanent job on qualification: a recommendation that I had been pleased to discover had been acted upon. The last I heard he had gone in-house to a company on the Science Park, no doubt boasting of his wish to get 'close to the business', as if all that we private practice lawyers did was to pontificate in isolation from the commercial realities facing our clients.

But I knew that Rosemary respected my ability, and I admired her for not being distracted by the waves of gossip that were always ebbing and flowing around the building. I liked to feel that she wouldn't have been one of those who gossiped about me and Helen.

'How did your meeting with Sam go?' she asked at one point when I got back from the printer with a completed first draft of my licence. Lucy and Hayley had gone off somewhere and no one else was within earshot. Rosemary wasn't stupid. If she had looked in my electronic calendar, she would have seen the meeting scheduled as another in a long series of regular one-on-ones with no subject matter listed and with no client files being taken to the meeting room. For someone in my position, that meant either that I was being managed out to make room for younger and cheaper blood (which even my worst enemy wouldn't have believed), or I was being considered for promotion to partnership.

'So-so,' I said non-committally.

She gave me a sympathetic smile. 'Do be careful, Alan. I've seen plenty of people in your position get turned over. People who do their jobs well and who deserve to get on. But for whatever reason, their faces don't fit. So they get strung along with promises of jam tomorrow, while working ridiculous hours to prove they are up to it. But however hard they try, there's always something that has to be done better, some new work that needs to be brought in ...'

She hadn't mentioned the word 'partnership', but we both knew what she was talking about.

'And sometimes,' she went on carefully, 'they can't even trust the person who is supposed to be championing them.'

We both understood this was a reference to Sam. It was no secret that he didn't much care for her. Nor she him. This had nothing to do with who was the better lawyer. It was more to do with the fact that, unlike Sam, she cared nothing for the firm's politics, working hard when she was in the office, but then clocking out mentally as soon as she had finished, just as if her job was no more important than stacking shelves in a supermarket. That said, I had recently had the impression that there was something more personal in her dislike of Sam. Nothing I could put a finger on, but I had noticed a distinct frostiness in her normally kindly expression when he came over to speak to Hayley about some administrative task or other.

'So come on, Alan, what did he say you have to do?' The unspoken words 'in order to get partnership' hung in the air.

'Socialise a bit more, show my face at some marketing events, get matey with potential clients. That kind of thing. All the stuff I hate, and which I know I'm no good at.'

'And are you going to?'

I laughed. 'Well, I'm going to The Drum tonight. Five o'clock sharp. Just like everyone else who doesn't have enough work to do.'

5 p.m. Friday drinks in the city centre pub just over five minutes' walk away were a tradition of the firm. One year, when the firm had made record profits, the partnership had

announced that the first round of drinks each Friday for the next month would be free. I had complained in a team meeting that the people who had actually brought in the money would be too busy at that time to go to the pub, and had suggested instead that the free drinks should be available from 7 p.m. on each of the Fridays. That way the fee earners who stayed late to do the client work would be the ones to benefit. The logic of this had seemed inescapable to me, but it hadn't gone down well. Nobody had even laughed. There had just been an embarrassed silence, punctuated with a smirk from Sam.

Rosemary smiled at my remark. She didn't even need to say 'rather you than me'. But I knew that was what she was thinking.

*

On Fridays no one other than me on our floor seemed to do much work after around 4.30 p.m. The secretaries started tidying their desks, making it silently clear to any non-partners that they didn't expect to get asked to do anything more until Monday. I could see Lucy smiling at an e-mail on her screen, and continuing to smile as she typed a reply. Obviously, nothing to do with a client. The only client e-mails that came in late on a Friday afternoon were those demanding that something urgent be done in time for Monday. Usually coming from a client who had been sitting on the matter for a few days and realised with a panic that they needed to off-load the problem to someone else before they went home for the weekend.

Rosemary logged off a couple of minutes before 5 p.m. and, with a sympathetic smile and nod at me, hurried through the security door out towards the lift, closely followed by Hayley.

None of the fee earners was stupid enough to charge for the exit, or even to openly log off, on the dot of 5 p.m. But they started stretching, looking around themselves, catching the eyes of their friends, and over the next ten minutes their computers were switched off one by one.

Normally I would have been head down at this point, looking

forward to the sweet spot between 5 p.m. and 7 p.m. when the noise had stopped and I could really concentrate on my work. But today I was on the lookout for a group heading for the pub together that I could latch onto. I tried without success to catch a few people's eyes but, preoccupied no doubt with their own plans, none of them seemed to notice me.

'Goodnight, Alan, have a nice weekend.' By the time Lucy's farewell had registered she had already turned away from her desk and was heading towards the door. I hadn't particularly wanted to turn up at The Drum with a trainee, but that option was now closed to me.

Ten minutes later, I had logged off myself. I went to the toilets to brush my teeth, and checked my nostrils in the mirror for any escaping hairs. I noticed that my glasses were slightly lopsided so I adjusted the earpieces to correct this. It was only a couple of weeks since I had had my last 'number 1' haircut, so my hair was still short and pretty smart.

I then walked on my own to The Drum. It was a strange place, with two completely different categories of customers. During the working week, at lunchtimes and in the early evenings, it was full of lawyers and other professionals from the nearby offices. At other times, it was a haunt of members of the Cambridge low life.

The most noticeable thing about the pub was how much more spacious it was than it looked from the outside. Like a Tardis, everyone used to say. At the front there was a line of larger tables, with a view out onto the street, which were used for more formal eating. This evening, looking completely out of place, there was a small group of tourists, probably American, having an early supper at one table, cameras and bags on the chairs alongside them. Beyond these tables was where people went to drink. The bar ran almost the full length of the left-hand side of the room as you looked towards the back of the pub, stretching further back into the interior than would have seemed possible from outside. There was plenty of free space near the bar for people to stand, drink and mingle in small groups, and further away there were also lots of smaller tables, some with two chairs and some with four, for more settled conversations to take place. Overall, the pub had a very modern look with chrome and polished light-coloured wood everywhere.

Already there were well over a dozen people from the firm in the pub. I could see two partners, though not Sam, each of them holding court to an audience of a small number of mostly female trainees or junior solicitors. The partners were clearly loving the attention. Where else would late middle-aged men, with paunches and bad hair, have pretty young women hanging on their every word. Certainly not at home, if rumour about these two partners was to be believed.

Lucy and Rachel were in conversation by the bar with a couple of male trainees from the Corporate team whose names I couldn't remember. I decided to join them. Side by side, Lucy and Rachel looked quite different. Lucy was wearing her customary immaculate make-up, her long dark hair with highlights reaching half way down her back. As usual, her face was quite expressionless, as if she was scared that laughing or scowling would crease her make-up. In contrast, Rachel looked as if she had tumbled out of a night club. She had a wicked smile on her face, was reaching out flirtatiously with one hand to the trainee she was talking to at the time, and had her other hand resting on the side of the short, tight skirt into which she had managed to squeeze her bottom. Helen had told me that on at least one occasion HR had had to have a gentle word with Rachel about what was appropriate office attire for a qualified solicitor.

'Anyone like a drink?' I asked in the sudden silence that descended when I joined them.

There was a round of polite 'no thank you's. I noticed a bit too late that they must have just ordered their drinks, as their glasses were still all mostly full.

'Everyone had a good day?' I persevered.

The two trainees smiled and nodded politely. I caught Rachel throwing Lucy a sideways look. 'Yes, thank you, Alan,' Lucy said. 'How about you?'

I realised a bit too late that it had been a bit stupid of me to include Lucy in my question about whether everyone had had a good day, given that she had spent it mostly sitting just opposite me.

'I've had worse,' I said. 'But it's good to finish on time for once. I haven't been to The Drum for a bit. I'd forgotten how nice it is. Do you lot come here often after work?'

'Only when I get time,' Lucy said. There was a pause as she waited to see what I was going to say next. Rachel and the two trainees stood silently by her side. I racked my brain for something witty to say. There was a raucous laugh from one of the nearby partners, echoed by the admiring circle around him. I wondered why he found it so easy, and I was finding it so hard.

Just then I saw Rachel's eyes shift away from me and focus on something behind me. She didn't seem to like what she was seeing.

'Hello, Rachel.' It was Helen. Lucy and the two trainees all gave her a welcoming smile and moved slightly away from each other as if to invite Helen into the group. I couldn't help but notice that their reaction was different to what it had been for my arrival.

'Hi, Helen,' Rachel said. 'Can I get you a drink?'

'No, thanks,' she said, 'I'm not staying. I'm cooking this evening for someone, so I need to get home. I just wanted to check that you are in the office first thing Monday morning, Rachel. We need a chat about the Ely file. And I'm out from ten o'clock on Monday. So how does nine o'clock sound?'

'That's fine.' However, Rachel didn't look happy. I wondered if she was due a bollocking. Helen was one of the most supportive supervisors in the firm. Someone to whom a junior could always turn if they were struggling with their workload, or simply just didn't know how to deal with an issue. But Helen also wouldn't take any crap.

With her arrangement for Monday sorted, Helen left. The space in the group which she had occupied immediately closed, and I was very much left standing on the outside. I decided to take the opportunity to leave too. I hadn't even bought myself a drink, let alone bought one for anyone else. As I walked to the exit, I imagined people watching and giggling at me, but when I glanced back as I opened the door, I realised that no one was paying me the slightest bit of attention. Lucy and Rachel had separated themselves slightly from the two trainees, and were in what Helen would have called 'full witch' mode, heads together and whispering to each other.

I walked away from the city centre, towards the multi-storey car park not far from the office where I had a season ticket for parking my Toyota Prius hybrid. I then drove back to my apartment on one of the new developments just south of Cambridge. Coming in early and leaving late as I normally did, the journey would typically only take fifteen minutes. But tonight, the Cambridge rush hour was still in full throttle and it took me over half an hour to get home.

6

Friday night and the weekend

I hated weekends at the moment. To be honest, I'd never been that keen on them ever since I had started at Doveley's. Everyone I worked with always seemed to disappear off into their own world at weekends. I had spent a lot of time thinking about this over the years, even when I had been going out with one of the few previous girlfriends, none from Doveley's, that I had had in Cambridge. I was never entirely sure whether the people from Doveley's were with family or with friends from outside work, or whether they were meeting up with mutual work colleagues without me getting to know about it.

When I had first started going out with Helen, we had been invited to dinner a few times at the houses of her friends from the firm. Friends of hers with whom I had also worked for many years. It had felt strange, going round to their houses for the first time, realising that Helen must have been there many times previously without me. Little things irritated me, such as how Helen would know without asking where the toilet was, or the way she would sometimes pick up what had clearly been an unfinished conversation with the friend's partner from an earlier visit. Sometimes there was an uncomfortable silence when everyone realised what I must have been ruminating over.

I had done my best to make these evenings a success, but I admit I always found it hard to talk about my work in a way that non-lawyers found interesting. Helen had gently suggested a few times that I should try to show more of an interest in what the husbands or boyfriends of her work friends did.

'Being a good listener,' she'd said once, 'doesn't just mean asking a series of one sentence questions and then sitting there silently when they answer you. Remember that although their work or their hobbies may not particularly interest you, it's an important part of their lives and you should try to engage in a proper conversation with them about these things.'

But most of these evenings had ended up the same way: Helen laughing and joking with her friend from work, and me and the friend's partner sitting silently listening to them. After a while, and without us actually agreeing anything, we had drifted into a situation where Helen would meet up with her work friends without me.

I had hoped that when I had bought my new apartment in the autumn that Helen would move in with me. Especially after she had started showing signs of unhappiness over the summer: losing interest in some of the things she used to enjoy doing, and becoming tearful at times. I had had visions of us spending most evenings together on our own, snuggling up on a sofa in front of the television or maybe just talking, telling each other that we didn't need anyone else in order to be happy. We had viewed the flat together, and Helen had said that she had liked it, but with hindsight I should have noticed how careful she had been to refer to it as 'your flat' and to have asked about things such as how I would get into work in the mornings, whether I would drive and pay for a parking season ticket, or take the Park & Ride. Although she had never expressly said so, I could now see that the implication had been that most days she still saw herself walking to and from work from her own house in the heart of Cambridge. Looking back, it was around the time when I started to try to persuade her to move in with me that she had first shown signs of withdrawing from our relationship.

Helen had never talked much about her diagnosis of depression, not even telling me at first that she had been seeing her GP. I had looked up the condition on the Internet, and been careful not to tell her to snap out of it, but I had found it hard to understand why she should have her low moods. On paper, everything seemed to be going well for her. Everyone at work seemed to like her, and as far as I could tell she was performing professionally at an appropriate level for her seniority. But there were times we spent together when she just went very quiet and I really didn't know what she was thinking. Then, the next day, I would see her laughing and joking with friends at work as if she didn't have a care in the world.

Since I had broken up with Helen, the weekends had been particularly difficult for me. Sometimes I found myself making the effort to have a brief conversation with a checkout girl at the nearby Waitrose just so that I wouldn't have to remind myself on the Monday morning that I hadn't spoken to a single human being since Friday.

*

That Friday night, as I parked my Prius neatly in my allocated parking space on the development, I looked up at my apartment block with my usual mixed feelings. There were a dozen flats on the first and second floors of the block, all identical from the outside, each with its little inset balcony with glass balustrade and space for two chairs and a small table. All looking very new and pristine. But all also looking quite characterless. My block was at the centre of the development, and whichever way I turned I could see rows of other similarly coloured and shaped buildings, some split up into flats and others built as proper houses, but all equally impersonal. It had gone dark and most of the flats and houses were showing lights, but there was hardly a soul on the street outside my block.

My flat had been described in the agent's particulars as a bright and spacious contemporary apartment. What this meant in practice was lots of LED spot lights, an open-plan combined kitchen, dining and living room, and a variety of greys and other off-white colours in all of the rooms. I still thought of the main bedroom as mine and Helen's. I had tried to personalise it with some water colours of country scenes that I had brought down with me from the North and which had hung on the walls of the various rental properties I had previously lived in. The second bedroom had always been intended to be an office, and I also used it as a dumping ground for everything too big to go in cupboards and which I didn't want on display.

I followed my usual Friday evening routine. I took off my suit jacket and swapped the trousers for a pair of jeans. I wasn't really into clothes, but if I spilt any food on my work trousers or jacket it would just mean another unnecessary trip to the dry cleaners. I opened a bottle of Mud House Sauvignon Blanc from Waitrose which I had put in the fridge to chill before leaving for work that morning. I put a Charlie Bigham ready meal, this week a fish pie, in the oven, and sat down to watch Sky News while it cooked.

An hour later I had finished the food and the wine and was mulling over the events of the day. I was still annoyed about Jeff Parker's phone call. It was none of his bloody business what I said to Helen. I hadn't liked the way Max had looked at Helen either. I wouldn't be surprised if he tried to wangle another meeting with her soon, no doubt without me there. I was also a bit cross with Helen, for having said something about me to Jeff. And I had certainly noticed how Lucy had kept her distance from me in The Drum. And then there was Sam Snape. I thought about what Rosemary had said, and realised that it made complete sense. I had a horrible feeling that he was going through the motions of supporting me for partnership, while looking for an excuse to have me turned down in such a way that his hands would be clean.

All in all, it was a not untypical Friday evening for me at the moment.

*

I had a shower and went to bed at about 11 p.m., falling asleep almost immediately. As was happening increasingly often at the moment, I woke up in the small hours. Normally I managed to get back to sleep fairly quickly, but tonight I made the mistake of starting to go over in my mind what had happened the previous day. Inevitably I began to think of Helen and Jeff, and wondered what they were doing just then. Was he the 'someone' whom she had been rushing home to cook for that evening? I assumed so, otherwise she would surely have mentioned the person's name. Was she now asleep in his arms, exhausted and covered in dried sweat after spending half the night shagging in every conceivable position that Nosey Parker had in his repertoire?

After Helen had started going out with Jeff, I had asked her once if it was serious with him. She had seemed amused. 'Not particularly,' she had said, without elaborating further. I hadn't dared to follow up by asking her if she was with him just for the sex, but the thought had of course been there. I had tried very hard to make our sex life enjoyable, buying a book on how to improve one's sex life, and trying something new every time I spent the night with her; but I had never been entirely sure how successful this was, and I had never asked.

In the end I realised that I wasn't going to get back to sleep that night. It was now 4.30 a.m. I had to know what was going on in Helen's life. I did a quick calculation. It was more than eight hours since I had finished the wine. I had drunk about nine units. So even if I was breathalysed as soon as I got into my car, I would be very unlikely to be over the limit. I got up, threw on the first clothes I could find, and went out to my car. The night had been cold, but not cold enough for the windscreen to ice over.

At this time of the morning the roads were almost empty. There was a thin drizzle falling out of the darkness, so everything glittered in the streetlights and in the headlights of my car. I was in the centre of Cambridge in less than ten minutes, going past the Botanical Gardens on the right and then turning right at the roundabout onto Lensfield Road. I went straight through the Catholic church crossroads, past our office on the right, sandwiched between the swimming pool and sports centre, and then turned right at the next crossroads into Mill Road. Mill Road is loved by many of the Cambridge liberal set, with its small independent shops selling the type of things these people are perpetually fawning over – secondhand books and clothes, bicycles, food from different nations, and so on. It had always reminded me however of the slightly rundown streets you find easily enough in Moss Side in Manchester, and if it hadn't been for Helen I would never willingly have set foot in the place.

Very soon I was turning off Mill Road, first in one direction, then the other, and finally onto the road that led to Helen's house. It was a tiny two-up two-down terraced house that would have been worth less than my annual salary if transported to a Coronation Street-style road in north Manchester. But because this was central Cambridge the house was probably worth ten times as much. A bequest from a grandparent had enabled her to pay the deposit soon after she qualified as a solicitor, and she loved living within walking distance of the city centre without the hassle of having to use public transport or the multi-storey car parks.

It was never easy to navigate the maze of narrow roads around Helen's house, and although mine was the only moving car both sides of the roads were crammed with parked vehicles. I drove carefully, because the last thing I wanted was to clip someone's wing mirror and have to make the split-second decision whether to put my foot down and drive on or to leave my name and address under their windscreen wiper.

Helen's black VW Golf was parked in its usual space outside her front door, underneath a street light. On the occasions I had spent the night at her house she had lent me a visitor's parking permit so I could park my car right behind hers. So now I was dreading, but expecting, to see Jeff's metallic red Audi A7 Sportback parked in what had used to be my place – just the sort of phallic car, I had often thought, that a specimen like him would drive.

But instead of Jeff's car, I saw a large blue Toyota Land Cruiser with a personalised number plate that I knew very well.

I just managed to avoid swerving into one of the cars parked on the other side of the road as I slowed right down and stared in horrified disbelief.

What the fuck was Sam Snape doing parking outside Helen's house overnight?

7

The rest of Saturday passed much too slowly. The only thing I wanted to do was to get back into the office on Monday morning to try to find out what the hell was going on.

When I had first arrived home after my trip to Helen's house, I was still in complete shock. After a while I tried to distract myself by tinkering with my partnership business case. I had promised Sam that I would update it to take account of our last meeting. He would then circulate the updated business case to the other partners before they made their final decision in the next month or two on whether to offer me partnership. So I added some waffly bits to emphasize what Sam would no doubt call my soft skills, and gave various undertakings to increase the amount of business development work I would do, throwing in some optimistic projections for new client work I expected to bring in. I couldn't throw off an uncomfortable feeling, though, that it might all be a charade. I suspected, from what I had seen happen to other senior solicitors in my position, that if they wanted to make me up to partner, they would do so pretty well regardless of what was in my business case; but that if they didn't, they would have no difficulty in finding some hole in the business case which they could point to as a good reason not to make me up.

And, of course, the more I thought about partnership the more I thought about Sam.

So after an hour or so I tried something else. When leaving the office on Friday, I had put in my briefcase a copy of the first draft of the patent licence I was working on. I now settled down on my sofa with a red pen to read it through and make any necessary amendments. Most junior lawyers seemed to do everything on screen these days, but I still found it easier to spot things I'd missed if I had a paper copy to work on. I tried not to broadcast this too widely though. The few times I'd mentioned it I could see slight smiles and exchanges of glances from other younger lawyers who obviously felt I was a bit of a dinosaur.

I was pleased with what I had drafted on this occasion. I was acting for a university in another part of the country which had invested a lot of academic time and money in developing and then patenting their innovative concept. However, they didn't want to commercialise the invention themselves; the further costs, commitments and potential liabilities were too great. Instead, they wanted to take a passive role, licensing another company, a leader in the field, to commercialise the invention while they enjoyed a long-term royalty stream. On another day I would have taken pleasure in the royalty clauses I had come up with. I had proposed a chunky up-front payment from the company that was going to take the licence of the patent; minimum royalty provisions for each year of the licence; and a mouth-watering percentage of all sales of products which incorporated the university's invention.

But it was no use.

My mind kept wandering back to the sight of Sam Snape's car parked outside Helen's house at five o'clock that morning. I was so tempted to drive back into Cambridge, park my car in its usual multi-storey car park, and take the short walk to the top of Helen's road to see if Sam's car was still there. But I just didn't have the nerve. I was scared of what I might see, and I was also scared of being seen.

I kept telling myself that things were seldom as bad as they looked and that I had an over-imaginative mind. But I couldn't think of any legitimate reason for Sam to be there so early on a Saturday morning. I'd never been to his house, but I knew it was several miles away from Helen's, in one of the leafy suburban roads on the west side of Cambridge where even the cheapest houses cost a seven-figure amount. So he must have been at Helen's for a specific purpose. If I had seen his car parked there later in the morning, I could perhaps have explained it away to myself as him having had to drop off or collect some documents relating to some pressing client matter that they were both working on over the weekend. I didn't know very much about either of their current workloads so that would have certainly been possible. But I did know that nothing would have blown up so suddenly on a Friday night that Sam would have had to call at Helen's before dawn the following day.

I couldn't stop myself from drawing the obvious conclusion as to why Sam had been there. Last night I had been tormenting myself with thoughts of Jeff having sex with Helen. Now I was picturing Sam in her bed, the same bed that I had spent nights in. I wondered if even now they were curled up in her bed together, perhaps reading the Saturday newspapers while they got ready for another round of frenzied love-making.

For a moment I toyed with the idea of sending Helen a WhatsApp message, but what on earth could I say?

The only thing that gave me any grim satisfaction was the thought of Jeff, and of Sam's wife, finding out about Sam's secret visit.

I imagined Jeff arriving at Helen's house to surprise her, and finding Sam tucked up in her bed instead of him. You wouldn't be telling yourself to be reasonable then, would you Mr Nosey Parker, I thought. I wondered for a few minutes if I could find a way of getting Jeff round to her house before Sam left. But I didn't have his personal mobile number. And even if I had had it, I couldn't think how I would have been able to persuade him to go round without admitting what I had been up to. In any event, because of my cowardice, I didn't even know if Sam was still there. Much too late, I wished now that I had stopped my car and taken a timed and dated photograph of Sam's car parked outside Helen's house. I could then have found a way of getting that photograph to Jeff without him finding out who had taken it.

I had similar thoughts involving Sam's wife. I had never been introduced to Julia, but he had mentioned her enough times over the years and I had seen her at a few firm events, usually dropping him off or collecting him. Once she had even come into The Drum on a team night out to have a drink with Sam and some of the other solicitors, but he hadn't bothered to bring her over to meet me. As was the case with a lot of GPs nowadays, she only worked part-time. If what I read online was true, she would still make more money than many full-time solicitors at Doveley's – without, I suspected, the same amount of stress.

Like many lawyers, I didn't really care for doctors. I had worked just as hard as any doctor to get where I was, but for some reason I was not accorded the same kind of public respect as they enjoyed. My experience was that a doctor only had to mention their profession at a social gathering for everyone else to be fawning all over them. It really rankled with me that I never had the same reaction when I announced what I did. Occasionally, people would ask me something about criminal or family law, or about wills, no doubt hoping for some free legal advice. But they quickly lost all interest once I explained that I practised exclusively in a weightier area of law.

I fantasized for a few minutes about Julia turning up at the firm's offices after finding out the truth, making a fuss in reception and demanding that Helen come down to explain what she was up to with Sam. That would wipe the self-satisfied smile off your face, matey, I thought. I imagined the pleasure I would take in watching him having to chair one of our weekly team meetings, aware of everyone knowing what he had been up to and judging him for his betrayal of his wife. At one point I found myself rubbing my hands together in glee at the thought of this.

But, in the end, nothing could alter how I felt about what I had seen that morning. I moped around my flat for the rest of the day and evening, browsing intermittently on the Internet and trying to find something on the television that would take my mind off things. Fortunately, I was very tired, having not slept well the previous night, and when eventually I went to bed at around 9 p.m. I fell asleep almost straightaway.

*

I felt a little better on Sunday morning. I was a member of a small local village tennis club, and enjoyed turning up for the social doubles' sessions held on Sunday mornings. I actually preferred playing singles, so that I didn't have to rely on anyone else, but recently I had found it difficult to find a regular partner. I had played a few people at the club who were weaker than myself, and enjoyed making them run all over the court. However, I had found them reluctant to play again even though they could have learnt a lot from me. I had also tried to get games against some of the stronger players at the club, by watching them play other people and then trying to analyse their games with them afterwards in the club house. But they almost always seemed to have games already lined up with other members when I asked them.

The social doubles' sessions operated a peg board system, which wasn't ideal. Everyone had their own 'peg' (actually a lollipop stick) with their name written on it. The pegs were then placed name downwards on a tray, with someone then choosing four pegs at random, to select each 'four' of doubles players. There would be a new draw every hour, so that everyone had a different selection of partners and opponents throughout the session. However, the drawback of the system was that I had often found myself being paired with, or against, members who were not up to my standard. I had therefore had the idea of secretly adding a small black dot to the blank side of my peg, so that I could identify it as mine when the draw was being made. I tried then to make sure that I did the draw myself every hour, usually with some jolly comment about seeing what fate would have in store for us all this time. I would draw three pegs at random and then, depending on whether or not I thought they were a suitable match for me, either pick my own peg to join them or pick some random other person's peg instead. I wasn't entirely proud of myself for doing this, but I justified it to myself by saying that this way I didn't waste other people's time just as much as they didn't waste mine. The problem was that many of the other players on a Sunday were elderly or unfit, or often both, and so couldn't offer much in the way of a challenge. All round I felt it was probably better if they stuck just to playing each other.

Today, however, I wasn't able to control the draw the way I would have liked, as someone else decided to choose the pegs. In the first one-hour slot, I was paired with an elderly woman of about 70, who had clearly played the game to a decent standard in the past, but who could now hardly break into a canter. Opposite us was a middle-aged guy of not far off my own standard, plus a younger sporty-looking woman I hadn't seen before.

'Goodness, Alan,' said my partner, 'we're going to have our work cut out today. Look at how that new lady hits the ball. So much top spin on her double-handed backhand.'

Fortunately, we managed to come out on top. I essentially played single-handed, taking every ball that was anywhere between me and my partner, shouting 'mine' at her if I thought she might go for it herself. Other than when she was serving, or receiving serve, she barely touched the ball.

'It's not Wimbledon you know, Alan,' she said mildly after I had just rushed across court to smash an overhead winner from a ball that had bounced close to her. 'You don't have to try quite so hard.' I did wonder for a moment whether she was suggesting that I was doing something wrong, but she spoke with her usual pleasant smile so this seemed unlikely.

Our opponents were hardly gracious losers though. The young woman had decent ground strokes, as my partner had indicated. But she was less strong at the net, reacting slowly the first time I drove the ball hard straight at her and playing a purely defensive volley back over the net that I was able to hammer away for a winner. After I had spotted this weakness, I decided to repeat the tactic whenever the opportunity presented itself. Once, she didn't react quickly enough and the ball hit her in the middle of her stomach.

'I'm sorry,' I said automatically, adding my usual jokey, 'Don't worry, I'm not good enough to do that on purpose.' But instead of making the customary conciliatory reply about it all being part of the game, the woman just gave me a long stare and turned away without comment.

After that, our opponents seemed to give up, as if they weren't really interested in the result of the match. We won the set 6-3 and this put me in comparatively good spirits for the rest of the club session.

My good mood started to wear off once I got back home. Try as I might, I couldn't stop thinking about Sam's car being parked overnight outside Helen's house. I can't now remember exactly how I spend the rest of the day, but it was a mixture of Internet browsing, television watching, reading various of my true crime books, and planning ahead for the next week at work. I stayed up as late as I dared, not wanting to have a sleepless night, and fortunately when I went to bed at last after midnight, I was able to enjoy a deep and uninterrupted sleep.

8

Monday

For most of the weekend, after I made my discovery, time had passed much too slowly. On Monday morning, though, the opposite was true.

While part of me wanted to investigate what was going on as soon as possible, I was scared about what I might uncover. And I realised that once I was in the office, I would have no excuse not to start my investigations. After getting up, therefore, I tried to delay the time when I would have to get ready for work. I made my usual cafetiere of strong black coffee and two slices of toast with butter and honey, then sat down to watch the recording on iPlayer of the highlights of the weekend's football. Normally this was something I could get really involved in. But, today, if after watching the first main match I had been asked what the final result had been, I wouldn't have had a clue. It was no good pretending that I could find a distraction. I switched the television off, had my usual piping hot shower, and got into my work clothes.

I had two suits, one navy blue and one light grey, which I liked to alternate daily. In order to add variety to my look, I had five shirts. One white, one check, one dark blue, one light blue, and one in the kind of bold stripes popularly favoured by barristers in television dramas. For a long time, I had worn each of my shirts in the same order each week. But after once hearing a secretary say to another with a giggle, 'Alan's in light blue so it must be Wednesday,' I had changed the order each week.

Normally I got into the office early, to beat the Cambridge rush hour, but today it was 8.45 a.m. when I walked into reception. Sub-consciously, I seemed to have taken a bit longer over everything that morning. I still wasn't entirely sure what I was going to do. I had chickened out of sending Helen a WhatsApp over the weekend to ask her what Sam had been doing at her house so early on Saturday morning. So I could hardly now march up to her desk on the fourth floor to ask her the same question. I suppose, if I had been put on the spot, I would have said that I was hoping to keep an eye on both her and Sam in the office, but what exactly that entailed I hadn't yet decided.

At least the first bit was straightforward. 'Have Sam and Helen got in yet?' I asked the receptionist. She wasn't laughing today, but then I wasn't Max, I couldn't help thinking.

'Not as far as I know, Alan.' she said. 'Do you want me to call their desks just in case though?'

'No, it's OK thanks. I was just, er, wondering. I need to catch up with them both later.'

Sam came and went at all sorts of times, as you would expect from a partner who liked to think of himself as a rainmaker. But Helen usually arrived just a couple of minutes before 9 a.m., being able to time to perfection her short walk from her house near Mill Road. I decided to hang around the back stairs until she arrived. This was done easily enough, as most people took the lift up to their floor, either through laziness or through wanting to delay the moment when they were officially at work. I had to walk up and down the first flight of stairs a couple of times when someone else chose the same route, to avoid looking suspicious, but in less than ten minutes I saw her familiar face and figure through the window of the door to the stairs.

'Hello, Helen,' I said, crossing reception and catching up with her as she got into the lift and pressed the button to the fourth floor. 'Have you had a good weekend?' I pressed the button for my second floor as well.

If there was any guilt on her face, I didn't see it. 'Yes, thank you, Alan. How about you? Did you play tennis on Sunday?'

'Er, yes, I did. And how's Jeff,' I said as innocently as I could, 'did you see much of him at the weekend?'

This time I got a puzzled look. 'He's fine, thank you. But, as it happens, I didn't see him at all. He was on a boys' weekend away. Why do you ask?'

I would normally have made a sarcastic crack at the reference to Jeff being on a boys' weekend. But I was thinking in other directions today. If Jeff was away, it would have been safe for Sam to spend the night at Helen's. My God, I thought, perhaps even the whole weekend. How I now regretted not having had the courage to make another foray in my car to the Mill Road area over the weekend. I felt sick at the thought of Helen spending the whole time, day and night, in bed with Sam. I looked her closely in the eyes to see if there were signs of tiredness, but I had to admit she looked no different to any other Monday morning.

'Just wondering,' I said, in an attempt to sound disinterested. Then a thought struck me. 'You're meeting Rachel now, aren't you, about the Ely file? You mentioned it in The Drum on Friday night. Is that anything to do with what you were talking to Jeff about at lunchtime on Friday?'

The lift door to my floor was now opening, and there were a couple of people waiting to join Helen on the ride up to the fourth floor. One was Rosemary, who gave her a warm smile which I noticed was reciprocated. That surprised me because I hadn't realised that they were particularly friendly. I will never know whether Helen would have answered my question properly if we hadn't been interrupted. As it was, she just nodded a yes and added a 'Bye, Alan, have a good day.'

*

As I walked to my pod, I noted that, as the receptionist had said, Sam was not yet in. But Hayley and Lucy were at their desks, and standing between them was Jeff, head bent forward conspiratorially towards them. I felt a stab of anger, and I confess jealousy, as I saw the two women laughing at something he was saying. Whenever I said something funny, Lucy's and Hayley's laughs always seemed to have a forced element to them. But here was Jeff, oozing his customary combination of old-fashioned courtesy and flirtatiousness, clearly having them hang on his every word. They all became aware of my presence at the same time.

'Hello, Alan,' said Hayley. 'How was your weekend? Did you win at tennis?'

As usual her voice and expression were cheery, her accent that peculiar mix of estuary and Fen English that you could still often hear outside the middle-class enclaves of Cambridge. But there was something in the way she always asked me about the tennis that rankled, almost as if she was teasing me. Jeff was a rugby fanatic, still regularly turning out for one of his club's lower teams on Sunday mornings, and I would bet my last pound that she wouldn't have asked him 'Did you win at rugby?' when she first saw him on Monday mornings.

'Yes, I enjoyed my tennis, thank you,' I replied. 'Is Sam not in yet?'

'No,' she said. 'He probably won't be in until late morning. He was away at a conference all weekend, so wants to catch up on some client stuff at home for a few hours where he can work without being interrupted all the time.'

Away at a conference all weekend. It all made sense now. Jeff had been safely off the scene, and Sam had simply told everyone that he was away too, with the result that he and Helen could spend the weekend together undisturbed. So obvious and so easy. But what on earth did Helen see in Sam? They had of course known each other for years. I thought Sam may have even mentored Helen when she was a trainee. But what was she doing carrying on with a married man with kids? Especially a married man like Sam, with his carefully styled hair, oh-so-fashionable glasses, and habitual self-congratulatory smile. At least Jeff had no wife, present or past, or kids. Or, rather, as I had heard him joke on more than one firm night out, no kids that he knew of.

I looked at Jeff. He seemed to be waiting for his turn to speak to me. You smarmy git, I thought, wouldn't you just love to know what I saw on Saturday morning.

'Alan,' he said, 'I hope I'm not being too presumptuous speaking to Lucy. But there's a new corporate job just come in on which we need support from the Commercial team. Our client is buying a local manufacturing company. So it's mostly due diligence, reviewing the target company's contracts to spot any red flag issues for our client. Knowing what we do about the target, there are unlikely to be any major issues, certainly none that would sink the deal. I thought Lucy would therefore be perfect for this, especially because she is due to do her next seat with us in Corporate. But, of course, she's your trainee so I knew I had to clear it with you first. I hoped there would be no harm though in me coming down first thing just to check on her capacity and whether in principle she was able to assist?'

As always with Jeff, it all sounded so bloody reasonable. I really didn't want him leering over Lucy at will, it was bad enough him doing that over Helen. But he was right, it was the kind of job that trainees usually did rather than qualified solicitors. It was important work, but clients wouldn't pay hundreds of pounds an hour for someone of my seniority to flick through pages of largely irrelevant contracts on the off-chance that I would spot something problematic. If Lucy saw anything, she was sensible enough to ask me for a second opinion. It would then be my neck on the line if I let something go through that I shouldn't have done.

I couldn't help but notice that Lucy was looking at me with a hopeful expression on her face. Although she was a hard worker, she was never that openly eager to take on new work from me.

'That's fine, Jeff,' I said. 'And thank you for clearing it with me first. If you can let me know what your budget is for the Commercial support, I will make sure Lucy doesn't exceed it without checking with you beforehand.'

Jeff sauntered off in his usual cheery manner and I logged on to my computer. I noted that Hayley had booked a slot at 9.30

a.m. that morning for me to brief Lucy on the work I was going to give her on Max's matter. I checked my e-mails. There were no surprises, but I did notice that Helen had copied me into an e-mail she had sent to Max. That meant that I was supposed to read it, which I did. Scrolling down, I saw that Max had actually sent the first e-mail in the chain, late on Friday evening, thanking Helen for her time and saying he looked forward to leaving the purchase of his new office in her *'very capable hands'*. I hadn't been copied into this e-mail. Helen had sent a brief reply, and then bugger me Max had sent her another e-mail on the Saturday wondering if she would like to combine a coffee the following week with a quick look at the outside of the office *'just so you know exactly what I'm buying.'* Helen had politely suggested that they wait until she had received and reviewed the draft contract package and received the results of the searches, and then they could decide if and when a meeting was advisable. This time she had copied me into her reply. I had been right about Max. He wasn't wasting any time trying to get in there. Helen would know from experience how this would make me feel, but to be fair to her she was probably copying me in more for her own protection professionally than because she wanted to annoy me.

*

I could have briefed Lucy at my desk, but I preferred to use one of the breakout spaces at the end of the floor. Just a table and two hard chairs, all brightly coloured to differentiate them from the standard office desk and chairs we used at our pods. The main advantage for me was that I could avoid being distracted by my desk phone and by new e-mails pinging onto my computer screen within my line of sight. There was nothing internally confidential about what we were discussing, so no need to book a meeting room downstairs.

As always, I felt on most comfortable ground with Lucy when able to focus one hundred per cent on a legal matter.

I explained Max's business model to her and gave her a paper copy of the precedent terms of business which I was suggesting she work from. They were a good starting point, but I needed to summarise for her the issues which would be of most importance to Max, so she could check that they were adequately addressed in what she drafted.

'Remember who these terms of business are for,' I said. 'They are for his corporate clients, businesses such as ours who want to give the perk of a personal concierge service to their employees. So what do you think is one of the first things to address?'

Lucy looked as inscrutable as she always did when talking to me. I wondered for probably the hundredth time what the real Lucy was like under that perfect make-up and composed office manner. I had had occasional glimpses of another Lucy, away from her work in the Commercial team, but nothing I could really get a grip on. However, although I couldn't warm to her as a person, I had to admit that she was bright.

'I assume the main thing is that he doesn't promise anything he can't guarantee to deliver. If his corporate clients give a perk to their employees, and then the employees get let down, they aren't going to be happy. They will complain to their employer, who in turn will complain to Max. So he doesn't want to get sued if, for example, he says he can get someone a ticket to a sold-out concert in London, then they go all the way down there and get turned away on the door because the ticket was transferred contrary to its terms and conditions. Is that right?'

'Quite right. So he can promise, for example, to use his reasonable endeavours to provide his concierge services as advertised to the employees, as long as he isn't in breach of his terms of business if he doesn't actually fulfil them. That wouldn't work for every supplier of business services. Sometimes their clients will insist on something being delivered by an agreed deadline. But it's the nature of what Max does, being dependant on third party suppliers, that he can't make any absolute commitments.'

'Even though,' Lucy said, 'he won't last long if he does keep letting people down?'

'Indeed. But that's not a concern of ours. Max will know that better than us. Our concern is that he isn't prejudiced legally if he fails to deliver a service that the employees are expecting.'

We covered the other main issues such as how long the corporate clients would be asked to sign up for, and how long a notice period they would have to give if they wanted to end the arrangement.

'When do you want to see my first draft?' Lucy asked at the end.

She knew the score all right. All the best trainees did. Always carry a notepad and pen when going to see a fee-earner. Check. If you don't understand something, don't be afraid to say so. Check. Always ask when the fee-earner wants you to do something by. Check. Always then do the work by the deadline. Check.

The very best trainees could hit a few different notes as well. Such as how to play mummy against daddy. For example, saying how much they would love to do a particularly boring piece of work for solicitor A, but first they would have to check that some existing task for partner B could be de-prioritised. Would solicitor A like to ask partner B, or should they … ?

Lucy had pulled this trick too, name checking Sam a few weeks back when I had wanted her to trawl through some patents relating to seed varieties for one of our agribusiness clients. But she was clever enough to save this kind of thing for when she really didn't want to do the work. She was just the type of fashionable young woman who would love to do a fairly straightforward piece of work for a high-end concierge business such as Max's. She would probably hope to get a perk out of it herself, and from what I had seen of Max already I was sure he would be only too happy to oblige.

'Is by close of business tomorrow OK, Lucy?' I asked. 'It's not urgent, but it shouldn't take long and you'll probably find it easier to do it while it's all still fresh in your mind.' Lucy was accompanying me to a networking event that evening, the one which Sam had on Friday suggested that I go to in his place. There was therefore no point in asking her to produce her first draft today, as I wouldn't be able to stay late to review it.

'That's fine, Alan, thank you. I'll have it with you before I go home tomorrow. If I have any more questions, I can ask you on our way to the event tonight.'

*

Nothing much else of note happened that morning. Sam came in at around 11.30 a.m., but disappeared for lunch before I could pluck up courage to speak to him about his weekend. It turned out that he would be out for the rest of the day.

'Shall I tell Sam that you want to see him?' asked Hayley, when I casually enquired about his movements.

'Er, no, it's fine, thank you. I wouldn't want him to think it's anything important. I'll catch him tomorrow.'

After lunch, I was copied into an e-mail from Helen to the partner who was the firm's MLRO, or Money Laundering Reporting Officer. She was forwarding to him her earlier exchange of e-mails with Max, and had added a new short paragraph:

Dear Tom (cc Alan)

Can we have a quick word please about this new client?

Alan and I met him last Friday to discuss, amongst other things, his proposed purchase of a new office in town. We verified his identity of course, but I am slightly concerned about why he is buying an office (rather than renting one), and where he is getting the money from. It doesn't make much business sense to me, and his accounts don't seem to support the proposed expenditure.

He is a very charming man on the surface, but he got quite defensive when I raised my concerns. He has also been asking me out for a coffee, he e-mailed over the weekend (see below) and he phoned again this morning. I was away from my desk so my secretary took the call, but apparently he's going to phone me again this afternoon! Very persistent!! So just wondering what I/we should do next?

Thank you,
Helen

9

'So, tell me, Piers, what exactly do you do?'

Lucy had been reading a crib sheet of networking tips for lawyers on our drive over to the Science Park. We hadn't bothered trying to avoid the Cambridge rush hour. Whatever time we left around the end of normal office hours, the roads leading out of the city centre were bound to be rammed. So we crawled past the Grafton Centre on our left, took the causeway over the River Cam, and after a long while turned right onto the slightly shabby looking Milton Road which heads towards the big A14 roundabout.

The networking event was just the kind of thing I hated. A hired glass and chrome room on the Science Park full of mostly young Cambridge men sporting beards or some other kind of facial hair arrangement that they thought made them look cool. 'Cambridge men' meaning that they either worked in the city of Cambridge, or had a past or present connection with the University of Cambridge, or in many cases did and had both. Most of their businesses depended on the value of their intellectual property and were in sectors such as the life sciences or computer software. Many of the businesses wouldn't yet have turned a profit, so typical subjects of conversation with each other were where the next round of funding was coming from, as often as what were the most recent technical developments in their field.

Although I was perfectly capable of advising these businesses on most of the commercial law issues they would face, I never really enjoyed it. I much preferred advising businesses which produced things you could see, feel and pick up, or which provided services which gave pleasure to customers rather than just made wealthy people even wealthier.

You could sum the whole event up as lots of people trying hard to make valuable professional connections. Almost no one having fun.

Lucy and I were hunting as a pair. No one looks more needy than a lawyer on their own at a networking event, and no one worth talking to wants to talk to someone who looks needy.

After a few false starts, we had pounced on Piers because he was standing on his own near the refreshments table. A much easier target than trying to break into a closed group of people who for all we knew may have been enjoying sharing horror stories about their lawyers. The refreshments were of the usual kind: passable red wine (think Rioja rather than Zinfandel), bottles of cool Eastern European beer, fruit juices, mineral water, and the usual mixture of nibbles that wouldn't make your fingers too sticky.

'Well, Lucy,' Piers said, taking a swig from the bottle in his hand, 'when I'm not drinking beer and talking to beautiful women, I spend most of my time staring at a computer screen.'

Dear God, I thought. Why on earth does a fat, sweaty guy like him think a woman such as Lucy is going to respond positively to that sort of comment.

But Lucy just laughed. 'So you don't wear a white coat and spend your day peering into test tubes then?'

'Not at all,' said Piers. 'Most of our experiments are conducted by robots nowadays. We do have lab technicians of course, but I don't get my hands dirty any more. I work on our computer models and analyse the results. For example ...'

And off he went, with Lucy making a good stab at showing some real interest.

We learnt that Piers had started off as an ordinary academic somewhere else in the country, but had been one of the named inventors on a biotech patent which had been protected in all the main markets around the world. He was now one of the owners of a company which had been set up to exploit the patent commercially, in collaboration with a big pharma company. They had just signed a lease on a new facility near Ely, the small cathedral city north of Cambridge, for further researching and developing their product.

'That's fascinating, Piers,' Lucy said eventually. 'I love listening to clients talking about their businesses. Especially when they are as enthusiastic as you. It really helps me as a trainee solicitor when I am trying to make things possible for them legally. Tell me, I know that in a perfect world you would never have to deal with lawyers, but since we aren't in a perfect world what exactly do you most want from them?'

I had to admit she was good. She probably only understood half of what Piers had been saying, but she had him eating out of her hand. My experience of talking to people like Piers on my own was that they seemed to spend most of their time scanning the room over my shoulder looking for someone else to talk to.

'My perfect lawyer, Lucy,' Piers was saying, 'would be one who offered me a freebie, perhaps in the hope of getting a lot of lucrative work later.' He ran a fat tongue all the way around his lips after he said this.

To my surprise, Lucy laughed again, reaching out to touch him lightly on the forearm with her fingers. 'I'm just being pimped out by my bosses, Piers, I'm afraid. You would have to discuss fee arrangements with them. But, seriously, if I was your lawyer, would you see me as being there just to help with legal technicalities, or would you regard me as a trusted business adviser as well?'

After five more minutes of sweet-talking Piers, Lucy showed how well she had learnt from her crib sheet of networking tips. 'I'd love to hear more about your plans, Piers,' she said, 'but I've just spotted someone that we have to speak to before they leave. Will you please excuse us? Let me give you my business card, though, and if you'd like to give me yours as well, then we can keep in touch with each other. Alan, shall we have a chat afterwards about how we might be able to help Piers?'

'That's a great idea, Lucy,' I said, trying not to look like someone agreeing to a dentist pulling out a rotten tooth without any anaesthetic. 'Piers, it was a pleasure to meet you and to find out more about your business. I hope we can talk again soon.'

Piers glanced at our business cards on their way to his pocket, then did a double take. 'Doveley's,' he said. 'Funnily enough we've just used your firm for the first time, for our new lease near Ely. I know one of your solicitors. Jeff Parker. He introduced me to your property people. Helen and Rachel were the ones dealing with the lease. You must know them?'

It was my turn to do a double take. Helen and Rachel. This had to be the Ely lease that Helen was referring to. The one which seemed to be a problem for some reason. Well, I certainly wasn't going to ask Piers if something had gone wrong, but it did make me all the more determined to find out what had happened. I didn't like this being another of Helen's little secrets with Jeff.

'Yes,' I said, 'I know them both. I'll tell them I met you tonight. I'm sorry, Piers, I should have mentioned the name of our firm when we first met.' I was kicking myself for this, because when we had introduced ourselves, I had added self-deprecatingly that we were 'just lawyers, I'm afraid', without saying where we worked.

*

I was in two minds about Lucy's performance once we had said our goodbyes to Piers. She had played him like a fiddle, which was to be commended. But I was also uncomfortably conscious that if anyone had been listening to the conversation, they would have assumed that she was the experienced lawyer and I was the bloody trainee.

I was still mulling over whether and how to make anything of this, when she hissed at me, 'What a sleezy tosser. I hate men like that.' I had never heard her speak like that before. Her carefully made-up face was expressionless but there was real distaste in her eyes. I couldn't avoid wondering uneasily what she might have said about me behind my back. There had been one or two occasions when, in order to try to make her feel at ease, I had had a go at engaging in laddish banter with her too.

I had supposed that Lucy had made up the bit about having spotted someone we needed to speak to. When she headed towards a loose group of people on the other side of the room, I was expecting her to hover for a while on the edge of the group until a break in conversation meant that she could insinuate herself amongst them. I really disliked doing this sort of thing, dreading to see the heart-sink expression on their faces when they realised they were being infiltrated by a lawyer on the make. So I was happy to trail behind her and let her risk being the one who got cold-shouldered. To my surprise, though, she ignored the group and went straight up to someone standing on their far side who had his back to us. Someone who suddenly looked very familiar to me when he became aware of her presence and turned to face her.

'It's Max, isn't it,' she said with a smile as she offered a hand.

'It is indeed.' Max shook her hand back and tilted his head to give her a quizzical smile. 'And, please forgive my shocking memory, you are …?' He was wearing the same kind of smart casual outfit as at our meeting on Friday, and had the same easy confidence of a man who can mix with everyone and knows how to adapt his manner accordingly. I had never knowingly met an Old Etonian, but he looked and spoke just how I imagined one would be.

'I'm Lucy Black, from Doveley's. I'm a trainee solicitor. We've not actually met before, but I'm working on one of your matters for my supervisor, Alan.'

'Hello again, Max,' I said, shaking his hand too. 'I hadn't seen your name on the guest list. What are you doing here?'

He gave me the look of a teacher who's just been asked by a parent what he does at school all day. 'The same as you, Alan,' he said. 'Demonstrating my smooth networking skills.'

Out of the corner of my eye I caught Lucy trying to stifle a smile.

'Of course,' I said. 'Lucy will be getting her draft of your terms of business to me by close of play tomorrow. I'll review them on Wednesday morning so you should have them in the course of the day, assuming nothing else urgent crops up. I am sure Lucy is doing a good job, so I can't imagine that I'll need to do much to them myself.'

Max waved a hand as if to say he wasn't fussed either way.

'Yours is such a fascinating business model, Max,' Lucy said. 'Alan has been explaining it all to me. Now's not the time, I know, but on another occasion I would love to hear more about how you operate.'

'I'd be delighted to tell you, Lucy,' he replied. 'But it's all very simple. I find out my clients' needs and then I fulfil them. I'm sure you are very good at doing the same.'

Lucy and Max shared a smile from which I felt excluded. Here we go again, I thought. But Max was young, good looking and rich, so what was the betting that Lucy wouldn't be calling him a 'sleezy tosser' afterwards. It reminded me a bit of how Jeff operated. He would come out with these cheesy chat up lines and have a secretary laughing. I would remember his lines and try them out on another occasion with someone else, and be met with an awkward silence.

I remembered Helen's e-mail to Tom, the firm's MLRO. Her concern about how Max was funding the purchase of his new office. The mention of how he had been pestering her to meet him for a coffee. I felt a flash of anger. It seemed never-ending. First Jeff, then Sam, now potentially Max. All of them after only one thing. Yet everyone who met these three men seemed only to think how wonderful they were.

'Max,' I said. 'I hope everything is going well with the purchase of your office. It should be quite a straightforward job for Helen. Normally she can do this sort of thing by e-mail and by phone. I wouldn't have thought she'd need to get you in for another meeting.'

This was perfectly true, even though I had my own reasons

for wanting to discourage a meeting. Helen and her team liked to refer to themselves as commercial property lawyers, but to my mind they were really only glorified conveyancers. Most of their time was spent organising routine searches, completing or replying to standard documentation, keeping their clients updated on each step of the sale or purchase or lease, exchanging contracts, and sorting out post-completion paperwork. All very process-driven and not involving much proper lawyering. The intellectual equivalent of colouring in, as far as I was concerned.

Max threw me an appraising look. 'A meeting doesn't have to be in the office, of course. Sometimes I find it more relaxing to meet people elsewhere. A chance to get to know them properly.'

I found myself clenching my fists by my sides. I wondered if Max had picked up on Friday that I hadn't liked the way he was salivating over Helen.

'Anyway, guys,' he went on. 'It's great to see you both here, but I need to catch up with some prospects before they go home. Your firm won't be very pleased if I'm not bringing in enough new work to pay your bills. Lucy, it was lovely to meet you for the first time, and I am very pleased to have you working on my terms of business. If you have any questions, please don't hesitate to contact me directly. I'm sure Alan won't mind, if it means you can do a more thorough job. Here's my card in case you need it. Just send me a WhatsApp message, any time day or night. I'll reply as soon as I can.'

With that Max smiled again and gently moved into the group nearest to us. I had to admire his technique. A smile here, a handshake there, and within seconds he was as much a part of the group as if he had been there all along.

*

I dropped Lucy off outside the house she shared in Cherry Hinton with Rachel and the two trainees from other firms. I wouldn't particularly have wanted to go in for a wind-down coffee and debrief, but all the same I noticed that she didn't invite me.

'Have a lovely rest of your evening, Alan,' she said as she was closing my car door. Whether that was meant sarcastically or not, I couldn't tell.

It was only when I was almost home that something suddenly occurred to me. How could Lucy have recognised Max across a crowded room if she had never before met him?

10

Tuesday

'What did Tom say?'

Even in normal circumstances, I would have wanted to know what Tom had said to Helen in his role as the firm's Money Laundering Reporting Officer (or MLRO). The Solicitors Regulation Authority had issued detailed anti-money laundering guidance for the legal profession, emphasising that the use by criminals of property transactions to launder dirty money was a major problem. Money from, say, the sale of drugs might be used to fund the purchase of a property. The property could later be sold and the purchase price, received from the buyer's respectable solicitors, would be free of any association with the drugs trade. The MLRO's job was to risk assess any proposed transactions that might involve money laundering and, if necessary, make a suspicious activity report to the National Crime Agency. Now that Helen had flagged her concerns to Tom, it was his responsibility to decide whether to take them further; and, potentially, his neck that was on the line if he got it wrong. But it was a difficult balancing act. The firm naturally wanted to comply with its legal requirements, but at the same time they wouldn't want to risk prejudicing their relationship with clients by making unnecessary reports, with all the delays to transactions that this could cause.

So that was the legal position. But I didn't mind admitting to myself that I had an additional reason to be interested in what Tom had said. I had seen the sort of person that Max was when it came to women. Sniffing around the receptionist last Friday. Doing the same with Lucy last night. And, worst of all, pestering Helen to meet up with him for a cosy coffee. I can't deny that I would have got a certain amount of satisfaction if Tom had felt it necessary to report Max and, even better, if Max had ended up having his collar felt by the police.

If I am honest, though, the issue with Tom was only a pretext for the meeting I had arranged with Helen for that morning. What I really wanted was to find out what was going on in her personal life. It had been bad enough when she was going out with Jeff. If she had now taken up with Sam, I wasn't sure how I was going to be able to cope. But I had to tread carefully. I didn't want another warning off from Jeff, and I certainly didn't want to fall foul of Sam just at the time when he was, supposedly, championing me for partnership.

My plan, therefore, was to ask about Tom first, to show a proper professional attitude, and then to probe Helen carefully on the personal stuff afterwards.

I had asked Hayley to book us a staff meeting room on the first floor. I was damned if I was going to have a long talk with Helen in a breakout space where we would be under the gaze of anyone who passed, most of whom would know something of our personal history. Ironically, Hayley had booked us the same room that I had used with Sam on Friday. As Helen and I took our seats, I wondered irrationally if she could still smell his presence.

'Tom phoned me straightaway,' she said. 'I knew he would. He's very conscientious. Or alternatively,' she smiled in that way I knew so well, 'very risk averse. He asked me the usual kind of questions and I could hear him tapping on his keyboard as he made a note of my answers. He then said that he didn't think it was anything for us to worry about, certainly not enough for him to have to report Max. But he did say there was no harm in me meeting Max outside the office if I wanted to. I had the impression, actually, that he wanted me to, without putting it in so many words. So I guess I'll have to have that coffee to keep

Max sweet, and maybe find out a bit more about why he is buying an office rather than renting one, and perhaps also where his money is coming from. Funnily enough, I think our two witches know something about Max. I told Rachel that I might get her to help me out on the purchase, and said I should have probably brought her to the meeting on Friday so she knew who Max was – and she said, with a bit of a knowing smile, that she and Lucy know who he is all right. It was a bit odd, but my report to Tom was confidential so I didn't say anything about it to Rachel.'

'It is odd,' I said, and I mentioned how Lucy had recognised Max at the networking event the night before. 'Speaking of Rachel,' I went on, 'what's the story on this Ely file? I met Piers last night on the Science Park, and he said that you and she did the new lease up in Ely for his company. Has something gone wrong and is that why you were asking Jeff for advice the other lunchtime? You do realise that he knows bugger all about property law, don't you? Bugger all about any law, in fact.'

For a moment I feared I had gone too far. Helen threw me a sharp look and took a deep breath as if she was about to have a go at me. Then, to my surprise, she gave me what I can only describe as a wistful smile.

'Look, Alan, if this had happened six months ago, you'd have been the first person I'd have come to. You're a bloody good lawyer and, yes, a better technical lawyer than Jeff. But, come on, the way things have been between us, I just didn't feel I could ask you for advice. Also, the client in question is someone who Jeff knows. In fact, it was Jeff who introduced them to me.'

I remembered how she had given me the same sort of smile just before she had broken the news, lying in bed together at my new flat, that she wanted to end our relationship. This had been followed by a long tearful explanation about how much my support had meant to her when her depression had been at its worst. How I hadn't done anything wrong. How she didn't want to upset me. But how she had realised that this type of relationship wasn't for her. 'So, as they say, it's not me, it's you,' I had replied coldly. The thing I had found hardest was seeing her take up with Jeff so soon after she had dumped me. Whatever our relationship had lacked, she was presumably discovering it with him. I would have found it easier if she had sunk back into depression - at least then I wouldn't have had to agonise so hard over what she found so wrong with me.

Helen was now telling me about the Ely file. My guess about it being to do with Piers's company's lease had been right. 'Rachel screwed up,' she said. 'She was supposed to be ordering the property searches. But she forgot to do a couple.'

'But Piers's company is leasing the premises, not buying them. Do you still need to do property searches?'

'We advised the company that they should, in the circumstances. Maybe not if they were only renting a room for a short period. But this was a long-term lease of the whole premises. The property searches would show if there were any potential problems that might, for example, prevent the company from using the premises as planned for the whole term of the lease. By the time I found out that Rachel had forgotten a couple of searches, the lease was signed and it was too late.'

'Did she report it?'

'No. I only found out by chance when I was closing the file last Thursday night before I went home. But I think she must have known she had forgotten.' And I remembered Rachel's face that night in The Drum when Helen had joined us. She had guessed something was up.

'So have you reported it?' I asked.

'Not yet. The thing is, in practice it almost certainly won't ever be an issue, for these particular searches in these circumstances. In fact, the chances must be close to zero. But that's not the point.'

'Insurance?'

'Yes.' It was a requirement of the firm's insurance policy that any negligence was reported to the insurers as soon as it came to light. Otherwise, the risk was that, if the negligence came to light later on and led to a claim from the client, the insurers wouldn't pay up. Rachel clearly had been negligent. She should therefore have reported her own mistake as soon as she became aware of it. Failing that, it was Helen's duty to do so.

'The thing is,' Helen went on, 'Rachel is on a fixed term contract until the end of the month, and all being well she will then almost certainly be given a permanent position. She's worked bloody hard and she deserves it. But something like this could tip the balance against her. And, poor girl, she's recently met someone at another firm in Cambridge, and they are planning to get a place together. The firm is normally tolerant of honest mistakes, but the timing of this for her is terrible. She would probably end up having to move to a firm outside Cambridge, as I can't imagine a mistake like this being hushed up if she moved locally.' I knew what Helen meant. All the property partners at the Cambridge firms knew each other, and a solicitor leaving one firm under a cloud would be likely to be faced with a row of closed doors at all the others in the city.

'What did Jeff say?' I asked.

Helen pulled a face. 'He said "Bury it". Say nothing, in other words, not even to Rachel. After all, if I hadn't checked over the property searches when closing the file, I would never have known. But, Alan, I've now let Rachel know that I know, and that's what makes it difficult.'

'What do you mean?'

'Well, if I bury it now, then I am complicit in any cover-up. And she knows that as well as I do. I trust her obviously, but I don't want to, well, give her that kind of power over me. What do you think I should do, Alan?'

What I really wanted to do was put my arms around her and give her a hug. Even when she was down, her face had that slightly cheeky look which I had always found devastatingly attractive. Instead, I said: 'I don't think you've got any choice, Helen. Tell her that it needs to be reported, but give her the chance to fess up herself. That way she does still have a chance. Just make it clear that, if she doesn't report it, you will have to do so.'

'Thank you,' she said. 'There's a big group of us going out for a drink and a meal tonight. Rachel is supposed to be coming as well. I'll tell her this afternoon. I couldn't face sitting opposite her all evening, gossiping about the usual stuff, knowing that come tomorrow I was going to have to put the boot in. Better to get it over with now. I'll let Jeff know too. I don't want him wondering all evening what's going on.'

So Jeff was out tonight with Helen, I thought. 'Is Sam also out with you tonight?'

She looked startled. 'Sam? No, any reason why he should be? I know he mentored me years ago, but I don't see much of him now, thank God.'

'Why "thank God"?'

She paused before going on. 'Well, I've got nothing against him personally. But I don't think he's been entirely fair to you. I think he's messing you around regarding partnership. And he wasn't very kind about you when he came to one of our Property team meetings last month.'

For God's sake, I thought. 'What do you mean "not very kind"?'

'We were planning a client football event which we were hosting jointly with your Commercial team. You know the sort of thing. Clients getting pissed in a marquee while a local amateur team plays a team of former semi-professional has-beens in the mud and the rain. No one paying the slightest attention to the game. And, well, someone asked Sam if you were coming along. He gave one of his smug smiles and said he thought you might have a prior engagement down at the tennis club. That's all. But I could see people sniggering to themselves and, to be honest, I felt a bit sorry for you. I know things haven't been great between us recently, but you work bloody hard for that man and for your team and you deserve better.'

That was quite a speech, and I was touched. It also made me feel bad about having spied on Helen the previous Saturday morning. But in for a penny, in for a pound. 'So Sam isn't top of the guest list for dinner parties at your house?' I tried to keep my voice light but even to me it sounded a bit strained.

Helen went very still for a moment. She looked at me as if trying to work out what I was getting at. 'That's a strange question,' she said. 'Why would I invite Sam to my house?'

How I would have loved to have had the courage to tell her why I was asking that question. But I couldn't humiliate myself by admitting that I had, in jealousy, driven past her house at 5 a.m. the previous Saturday morning to see who she was spending the night with. She had just told me that I deserved better treatment than what I was getting from Sam. I couldn't now say something which might result in her telling me that I actually deserved everything I got.

'I was only joking,' I said lamely. Then I went as far as I dared. 'Actually, I did think I saw his car a while back parked off Mill Road. I expect he was calling at one of the shops. He probably doesn't even know you live in that area though, does he?'

'If he ever knew, he's almost certainly forgotten,' she said firmly. 'I've never seen him near my house anyway, thankfully.'

11

Sitting at my desk after my meeting with Helen, I kept re-playing her words in my head to see if I could read anything significant into them. I was sure that something was going on with Sam. Why else would his car be parked outside her house so early on a Saturday morning? If there had been a work-related reason, Helen had had ample opportunity to say so. But if, God forbid, she was seeing Sam, it wasn't like her to lie so blatantly. She was normally such an honest person. She had been sorry about how I had reacted over her involvement with Jeff, but she had never denied it. Indeed, she had made sure that I had known before it became general knowledge within the firm. The only reason I could think of for her to lie was that she didn't want either Jeff or Julia to find out that she was carrying on with Sam. In which case she didn't trust me not to tell them. That I found quite hurtful. I hadn't betrayed any of her other confidences, the fantasies she had shared with me about her having sex at parties with other men and women. Something which had excited me too, but I had always been too scared to ask directly if she had ever wanted them to become more than just fantasies.

I struggled with my concentration for a long time after the meeting.

Even producing the final draft of my patent licence didn't improve matters. I normally enjoyed this stage, testing my wording against various 'what ifs' to make sure that all scenarios that might cause a problem to my client were covered off. But today, even though I was satisfied that the licence was bullet proof, it just felt like another meaningless task to be completed and then e-mailed out to the university's demanding in-house lawyer.

Rosemary must have noticed my mood because, shortly before lunch, she leant over and asked me quietly if anything was wrong.

'Things aren't great,' I said.

'Is it to do with your partnership application?' she whispered. Lucy and Hayley were both tapping away at their keyboards on the other side of the pod, but even so she knew I wouldn't want them to overhear her question.

'No, just something personal,' I replied. 'Something I'm not handling very well,' I added in a rare moment of honesty. I really liked Rosemary, and in different circumstances she was the sort of motherly person I could have confided in. I never sensed that she was laughing at me behind my back.

I had the feeling that she knew what I was talking about. For a moment she looked incredibly sorry for me. Hayley might well have mentioned the meeting room she had booked for me and Helen, and Rosemary knew of course something of our history. At first it looked like she was going to ask me another question. Then, as if she had thought better of it, she made a more general comment: 'They always say, don't they, not to bring your personal life into work. Easier said than done, though. I can't say I've always managed it.' She smiled sympathetically then turned back to her desk and continued with whatever piece of professional support work she was working on.

*

Sam was in the office today, and every time I turned in the direction of his pod, he seemed to have his eyes on me. No conceited smiles, and certainly no thumbs up. I pretended to myself that I hadn't found the right moment to try and find out from him why his car was parked outside Helen's house last Saturday morning. But the truth was that I was scared to ask the question: scared of the consequences for me, both personally and professionally. At one point Hayley asked me, with a slightly cheeky expression, if I had managed to catch up with Sam yet, on whatever it was I had wanted to speak to him about. She seemed to have guessed that I had an ulterior motive for asking about Sam, although I couldn't think how.

After lunch Lucy brought over to me a hard copy of the terms of business she had drafted for Max. It was what I needed. Some comfort work that would keep me occupied but not be too taxing. There were the inevitable couple of typos in Lucy's draft, and I took my usual satisfaction in circling these with my red pen. As I always told my trainees, there was no reason for them not to be as good at spotting typos as I was. Other than that, Lucy's drafting was good: the terms of business were written in plain English, which was what I liked, and they covered everything important. I made a few handwritten amendments to tighten up the drafting, then passed the document back to her over the low divider between our desks.

'Once you've made these amendments, Lucy, you can e-mail them over to Max for him to review. Ask him to let you have any comments in case we need to make any changes. Just remember to copy me in, please. You can also e-mail over the changes I have made to his data protection policy. Hayley will give you the correct version.' I now changed the subject while trying to keep my tone light. 'By the way, how come you recognised Max last night at the networking event? I didn't think you'd ever seen him before? I'd had a meeting with him only last Friday, and I didn't recognise him across that crowded room until he turned to face us.'

She looked slightly disconcerted by my question, which would have come out of the blue to her. 'I must have seen his photo somewhere,' she said. 'Perhaps on his company website or in his LinkedIn profile. I can't remember now, sorry.' She paused before continuing. 'By the way, Alan, I'm booked out to spend some time with Jeff tomorrow, on that corporate support task you kindly said I could help with. I'm really looking forward to it.

He was explaining to me this morning what I needed to do when you were in your meeting. He's really nice, isn't he?'

You little cow, I thought. Hayley and Rosemary were listening, and I noticed different reactions on their faces. Hayley seemed amused, albeit not in an unkind way, and was watching to see how I reacted. Rosemary however threw me a supportive glance, looking almost as if she was wincing on my behalf.

I can't remember if or how I replied to Lucy. I had had a lot of this from various people since I split up from Helen, and I had learnt to try not to let my feelings show. I did wonder how Helen would feel if she had heard Lucy singing the praises of her new boyfriend. Knowing her, though, she would probably just laugh it off or take it as a compliment.

For the rest of the afternoon, I immersed myself in the usual bustle of the firm on a busy weekday. The printers behind me and Rosemary clicked and whirred away incessantly. Fee earners tapped at their keyboards and secretaries occasionally scurried to and from the printers or the filing cabinets. The odd partner strutted around like a peacock in mating season. There was the regular ring of telephones, and then the subsequent raised voice of the person on the call trying to make themselves heard over the background noise.

At one point Rosemary made herself a coffee, and on her way back from the kitchen stopped for a word with Hayley and Lucy. They both welcomed her with a smile and made space for her to stand between them for a couple of minutes. I experienced a pang of jealousy and, irrationally, couldn't help but feel that Rosemary had been disloyal to me in some way.

All in all, I felt incredibly alone.

12

The news, when it came the next morning, almost made me pass out. Blood rushed to my head and I was overwhelmed with successive waves of dizziness, each wave stronger than the one before. Incongruously, it brought back a memory of being drunk on Old Rosie cider one night the previous summer, when I had made a bit of a fool of myself at a tennis club social.

The dizziness must have lasted less than a minute, but when it subsided, I feared momentarily that I had lost my sense of hearing. There was complete silence on the second floor. No solicitors typing. No secretaries chattering. No partners barking instructions. Lucy was doing her stint upstairs with Jeff's team, but Rosemary and Hayley were motionless in their chairs. Beyond them, the four people at the next pod were staring transfixed at their screens, as if they were watching a horror film on the television.

Suddenly a telephone rang. The firm's policy was for every phone to be answered within a maximum of four rings. However, on this occasion the phone was ignored. The sound of each ring reverberated around the floor, louder and more intrusive than seemed possible. I could imagine that people were remembering the last Remembrance Day, when a phone had rung during the two minutes' silence. Everyone except for Sam had let it ring, but he had picked up the phone and, instead of asking the caller to respect the occasion, had started loudly discussing a potential piece of intellectual property litigation.

Today no one wanted to be Sam, but neither did anyone want to have to explain the news to a random caller.

The call must have been for a solicitor, because after six rings it bounced to the phone of their secretary. There were six more rings before it bounced away to the receptionist downstairs. For a second or two there was silence again. Then, very slowly, I heard a low murmuring start to fill the floor. It reminded me of the noise of the incoming tide on a quiet day on a large flat beach, somewhere like Wells-next-the-Sea on the north Norfolk coast. I didn't immediately understand what was causing the noise, but then I looked around and saw countless pairs of heads now bent close together, whispering to each other in such a way that none of their words were individually recognisable as emanating from human beings.

Even if I had been so minded, my mouth was too dry for me to say anything to Rosemary. I read the e-mail for the third time, hoping in vain that it would say something different from the previous two:

Helen Eccles: FAO all staff

Dear Colleagues

It is with the greatest of sadness that I have to inform you of the sudden death, late last night, of Helen Eccles.

I know that this news will devastate many of you, as it has done me. Helen joined Doveley's as a trainee solicitor almost 8 years ago, and made friends in all the teams in which she worked.

Our sincere condolences go to Helen's family.

I will let you have further details when I can, including those relating to Helen's funeral arrangements.

Please let me know if the firm can offer you any support at this most difficult of times for us all.

Sam Snape

When the e-mail from Sam had landed in my in-box, I had assumed from its 'all staff' subject line that it was an announcement relating to Helen's career.

Not an announcement that she had been made a partner, because she had long made it clear that she had no interest in sacrificing her personal life for the perceived benefits of professional advancement. More likely, I had thought, an announcement that she was leaving the firm to become an in-house lawyer, at a company which was either an existing client of the firm or which the firm hoped to gain as a client in the future.

I had made this assumption with some confidence, because there were usually only three ways of leaving Doveley's. The first way was to jump ship for a rival firm of solicitors, in which case you were akin to the walking dead from the moment you gave notice. During your notice period you would be kept away from clients, given the grunt work that no one else wanted to do, beasted like a dog, and have the threat dangled over you that you might not get the reference that your new employer would insist upon.

The second way to leave was to give up law entirely. Here you would be pitied rather than despised. The unspoken belief would be that you couldn't hack the legal profession, not that you had found something better to do with your life. The latter would be unthinkable for your colleagues, as otherwise they may be forced to admit that their own lives were mostly being wasted.

The third way to leave, to go in-house, was the one which I had assumed Sam was announcing. In this case, your final months at the firm would be filled with lunches out with partners who would tell you what a fine chap or chapess you were and how much you would be missed. And how you must feel free to call Doveley's at any time in your new role if you had any legal issues you needed help with.

I am sure that most people receiving Sam's e-mail would have made the same assumption. So to then see the words 'sudden death' in the first line of the e-mail had completely knocked me, and them, for six.

In my first reading of the e-mail I had raced to the bottom, hoping with a complete lack of logic that it would end with an apology for the mistake at the top and congratulate Helen instead on her new job. I had then turned in my seat to look at Sam, in a desperate desire to see him give me a self-congratulatory smirk and a thumbs-up and to hear him say he had only been joking. But Sam's seat was empty. He had obviously sent the e-mail from the privacy of his office at home.

I was too shocked to cry, or even to wonder if I was going to cry.

Less than twenty-four hours earlier, Helen and I had been sitting opposite each other in a meeting room on the floor below, close enough for me to breathe in her favourite Paco Rabanne perfume that I knew so well. Now I was being informed, at the same time as every Jack and Jill in the firm, that I would never have that experience again. Informed, moreover, by a man I so actively disliked, someone who was possibly even the most recent usurper of my place in Helen's bed.

As I started to think rationally about what I had read, I don't deny dreading the pain that I knew I was going to feel, for a very long time.

Funnily enough, it didn't occur to me just then to wonder how Helen had died. Looking back on this later, I supposed this was because, whether it was a heart attack or a car accident, it wasn't going to make a difference. It wasn't going to bring her back.

13

'Poor Jeff.'

That was the last thing I wanted to hear. Hayley's voice was always louder than it needed to be, and she made no attempt now to quieten it out of consideration of my feelings.

'I felt so sorry for him,' Lucy was saying. 'I was sitting next to him upstairs when the e-mail from Sam came in. He'd been briefing me on the work I was going to do for him. He must have seen the subject line flash up on his screen out of the corner of his eye, because he then turned away to read the e-mail. The blood just drained from his face. He went absolutely white. I didn't know that could actually happen.'

'Did he say anything?' Hayley asked.

'He gestured me to read the e-mail on his computer. Then he said that we could pick up our work another time. I think he just needed to be alone. I can't believe that no one had thought to break the news to him privately beforehand. I know that he and Helen hadn't been together for long, but all the same ...'

Lucy had come back downstairs a short time after Sam had circulated his e-mail. She had looked slightly excited, a change from the inscrutable look that was often on her face.

'Does anyone know what happened?' Hayley was asking now.

'I don't,' Lucy said. 'She was OK last night when we all left. All right, a bit drunk, but then most of us were. She was walking home on her own, I assumed. She didn't leave with anyone. Certainly not with Jeff, because he was going on for another drink with a couple of the guys. But I'm not one hundred per cent sure of what her plans were, because I hardly spoke to her last night. I was hanging out with Rachel and a couple of trainees, further down the table. It was all a bit random, though. At one point I even saw Sam sitting in her chair. Apparently, he'd been there for a curry with his wife at around the same time, and he'd joined the table for a few minutes before they left.'

It sounded like half the firm had been out last night. Helen, Jeff, Lucy, Rachel, and countless others. And now it turned out that even bloody Sam had joined the party. I didn't know what the occasion was, whether it was someone's birthday or leaving do, or just a chance for everyone to let their hair down mid-week. In any event, I hadn't been invited. Not that there was anything unusual in that, especially since Helen and I had split up.

'So could she have had an accident on her way home?' This was Hayley again. 'Or was it illness: a heart attack or something?'

'I've no idea,' Lucy said. 'I'm not sure if anyone knows yet. But, apart from Jeff, I haven't spoken to anyone else who was out with us since the news came through. It's terrible, though. Helen was lovely. As you say, poor Jeff.'

Poor fucking Jeff, indeed, I thought. I hadn't been that impressed with Lucy's description of how he had reacted. Judging by how he had been flirting with Lucy the other day, I couldn't imagine he would have been that broken-hearted.

I had strained my ears to listen to every word of the conversation between Lucy and Hayley. Neither of them had given a second's thought to what effect Helen's death was having on me. Their insensitivity made me angry. But, irrational as it was, I was also angry with those people who had been out with Helen last night, and who had been lucky enough to share some of her last hours alive. As to Jeff, I was slightly ashamed to take some pleasure in the pain he was apparently feeling. That'll teach him, I couldn't help thinking. I'm not sure what lesson I expected him to take from this. I suppose, sub-consciously, I was thinking that Helen's death would be a deserved punishment for him having taken her from me. But, to be fair to myself, I suspect I was lashing out in my pain at anyone and everyone in range.

Around me, the floor was by now starting to return to something like its normal sound. Quieter than usual, and of course without any of the forced jollity that was never far from the surface. But people were starting to work again, and even Lucy and Hayley had turned back to their screens.

By my side, however, Rosemary looked shattered, and I remembered how warmly she had greeted Helen in the lift the other morning. Perhaps, I wondered, I could share some of my emotions with her at the right moment. I was sure she would understand how I was feeling.

*

The second floor was normally sparsely occupied at lunchtimes, but today I was the only person at my desk at 1 p.m. Everyone else seemed to have made arrangements to go out. I saw various little groups of twos, threes or fours form up and then go through the doors together. Clearly people wanted to discuss that morning's news. Someone I vaguely knew from the firm's Diversity and Inclusion Group came up to collect Rosemary. Sam had made an appearance, just before lunch, having a quiet word with Hayley before going over to his pod, but completely ignoring me. Tom now came down to meet him, the two partners then heading downstairs talking quietly to each other. No one had come over to ask me how I was feeling. And no one had invited me to join them for lunch, or even for a stroll on Parker's Piece.

I did what I often did when overwhelmed by my feelings. I focussed on work. I had e-mailed my patent licence to the university client's in-house lawyer the previous day. He had replied just before lunchtime, asking if a particular clause might risk being a breach of the laws relating to anti-competitive business practice. This kind of response really irritated me. If I had thought my clause might be a problem, I wouldn't have included it in the first place. The in-house lawyer had copied in various big-wigs at his university, and was clearly wanting to show that he had read the licence and understood some of the legal issues that it contained. He was probably also wanting to show that he could add value and not just be a post box between the university and its external lawyers. However, I played the game by the rules, copying the big-wigs into my reply and praising the lawyer for the 'good point' he had raised. I added a chunky paragraph, copied and pasted from an e-mail to another client, to justify why 'on this occasion' I was satisfied that my drafting was legally compliant. I wasn't going to waste time producing some long bespoke legal advice when the work was being done on a fixed price basis. I would have to either write off some of my time, or grovel to the client for an uplift on my original quotation. Neither option would please Sam if and when he heard about it.

14

The first sign that people had been talking about me was when Hayley came back from lunch, before either Lucy or Rosemary.

Normally she would have thrown me a cheery 'Hello, Alan', sometimes asking with a slightly mocking smile if I had had a good lunch hour. But today she sat down quietly and concentrated on her screen. I bent down to my own work, then looked up after a couple of minutes to ask her something, and saw her immediately drop her eyes. She must have been watching me for some reason. The same thing happened again shortly afterwards. Lucy was the next of our pod to return to her desk, and she also seemed to be avoiding making eye contact.

When shortly afterwards I went off to the kitchen to make myself a coffee, I had the uncomfortable feeling that I was being watched. A couple of keyboards fell silent as I passed; a couple of conversations were audibly paused. There was a young female solicitor from the Tax team in the kitchen already. As with most lawyers who choose tax as their specialism, there was something a bit different about her at the best of times. She was an attractive enough redhead, but always gave off the sexless impression of someone who would prefer to curl up in bed with a book rather than with a living, breathing, sweating person of the opposite, or even the same, sex. When she saw me, her eyes widened, her mouth opened slightly, and a flush of red appeared in the centre of both of her cheeks.

'I'm not going to eat you,' I said automatically. This was one of Jeff's lines, which invariably got a giggle and a flirty response from whichever lucky female he used it on. The tax solicitor just stared back at me though as if I had belched in her face. I edged past her to the kettle, and by the time I had filled it and switched it on she had left the kitchen. On my way back to my pod a few minutes later with my cafetiere, I noticed that she and the other three tax lawyers with whom she shared a pod were all watching my progress. Feeling rather self-conscious, I casually checked the flies of my trousers and wiped the back of my hand against my nostrils, in case there was something embarrassing about these two areas of my body that I wasn't aware of.

Rosemary had returned to her desk from lunch while I was in the kitchen. 'Alan,' she whispered. 'Can we have a word? Perhaps in an empty meeting room?'

Usually I got Hayley to book my meeting rooms, but now I did the necessary few clicks myself, finding it surprisingly easy given the fuss that secretaries often made of this task. I deliberately chose a different room on the first floor to the one in which I had met Helen yesterday. Two minutes later we were seated next to each other at the table. Both of us had, without saying anything to each other, pulled the old trainee trick of picking up a couple of random files to take with us, to make it look like we were having a work-related meeting. I wasn't sure what Rosemary wanted, but I had guessed it was to do with the news about Helen. Her plump little body looked slightly deflated in its practical dark suit.

'I was really sorry to hear about Helen, Alan,' she said. 'I know what she meant to you. I'm sorry for not saying more earlier, but you looked awful and I didn't want to intrude.'

'Thank you, Rosemary,' I said. 'I still can't quite believe it. Yesterday she was with me in the room next to this one, as close to me as you are now. And suddenly I find out that I'm never going to see her again. I don't even know what happened. No one has told me, and I don't want to have to ask in case it looks like I am being intrusive. Sometimes I can't do right for doing wrong. Do you know what happened?'

'I do now,' she said. 'I heard at lunch. That's why I wanted a word with you. Before anyone else says something.'

'What does it matter who tells me?'

Rosemary took a deep breath. 'Helen was killed in a fall from a multi-storey car park. I think the one you use. Late last night. No one saw it happen, but her body was found behind the car park by a couple of students who were taking a short cut home from the pub. They phoned the police, who in turn got hold of Sam via the firm's emergency out-of-hours number which would have been on Helen's business card.'

I was stunned. Something like that hadn't even occurred to me. I had expected Rosemary to tell me about a car accident, perhaps a hit-and-run, or something else on those lines. The thought of Helen's soft, supple body twisting in the dark as it fell to the ground with a crunching thud made me feel sick. A remembered image of people falling to their deaths from the Twin Towers in New York, after the terrorist attacks of 2001, came unbidden into my mind. 'That's awful,' I said. 'But how could it have happened? What was she doing up there? Do people think she … she killed herself?'

'No one knows for sure. The police are investigating. But you do know that she was out last night in town with a big group from the firm? Drinks at The Drum and then on for a curry.'

'Yes, I'd heard.' It seemed like everyone wanted to rub in the fact that I hadn't been invited on the night out.

'Well, at the curry house she was sitting next to a friend of mine. I've just had lunch with her as it happens. Apparently, Helen was saying early on that she was under a lot of pressure, that she wasn't sleeping properly, and so on. I understand she's had work worries, also that she has had personal issues in her past.'

This wasn't news to me, of course, but I decided not to interrupt.

'But Helen also left the table for a while towards the end of the meal. She'd just checked her phone so people guessed that she had probably had a message from someone. She must have been away for five or ten minutes, because Sam had time to come over and sit down in her chair for a bit. It seems he'd been there for a meal at the same time with his wife. When Helen came back, it looked like she had been crying. When someone asked her what was wrong, at first she didn't want to say anything. But then she started saying to everyone that you were still finding it hard to accept that she had moved on. That you didn't like her seeing Jeff. Even though she had split up with you quite a long time ago now.'

Not yet ten weeks ago, I thought irritably. I didn't care for how this made me sound like a jealous teenager. But I didn't see what relevance this had to me. So I simply said: 'And …?'

Rosemary paused for a few seconds, her eyes not meeting mine. This was becoming a bit of a habit with people, I thought. 'People have been talking about the message which Helen seems to have received,' she went on. 'It was obviously something which upset her. And it must have been sent by someone who wasn't at the meal.'

'Christ,' I said, as it dawned on me what Rosemary was getting at. 'They think it was me who messaged her on a night out?'

'Well, from what I've heard, Alan, it wouldn't be the first time. I suppose … well, some people are wondering if she left the table to speak to you on her phone, and then met up with you after the meal. She left as soon as the bill had been paid and headed off on her own. At about 9.30 p.m. They are wondering if perhaps you had a row with her after you met up, and if she might have ended up getting even more upset. And if, well, on top of everything else that was worrying her, it was enough to make her do what she seems to have done …'.

Bloody hell, I thought. So that's what it's all about. I upset Helen and I'm to blame for her jumping to her death.

15

I hid myself away at my desk for the rest of the afternoon.

Rosemary had told me everything she knew about Helen's death. It didn't take me long to find a report in the online edition of the local newspaper:

Woman dies after falling from Cambridge multi-storey car park.

A woman fell to her death from a Cambridge multi-storey car park late last night. Police and an ambulance were called, but the woman was pronounced dead at the scene. Her death is not being treated as suspicious.

A spokesperson for Cambridgeshire Constabulary issued the following statement: 'At 11.10 p.m. yesterday evening, officers were called to a multi-storey car park in Cambridge city centre after a woman fell from one of the upper levels. The woman, who is believed to be in her early 30s, was sadly confirmed dead at the scene. The death is not being treated as suspicious and the Coroner's Officer will be continuing enquiries.'

Although the newspaper wasn't saying so expressly, the implication was clearly that Helen was believed to have taken her own life.

If Rosemary was right, Helen had fallen from the multi-storey where I normally parked my Prius. She must have fallen sometime between me collecting my car last night, and parking it back there again this morning.

The report didn't say from which floor Helen had fallen. But

I had parked on all of the floors over the years, and as far as I could remember they were basically all the same. Each floor had a waist-high concrete wall running around the perimeter, with a motorway-style metal barrier a couple of feet in front of it. The main purpose of the wall and barrier was to stop cars accidentally driving off the floor, not to stop someone intent on suicide from jumping off to their death. However, the walls were high enough to make it virtually impossible to tumble over one by mistake, even if you were drunk or not looking where you were going.

I shuddered as I pictured Helen climbing over the wall she must have chosen. Had she thrown herself straight over head first, as if diving into a swimming pool? Or had she carefully lifted over first one leg, then the other, and remained seated a while on the top of the wall, facing outwards with her legs dangling down, before taking a deep breath and letting herself slide off into oblivion. If she had jumped from one of the top floors, at least twice the height of a house, she would have had enough time during the fall to tell herself that she was going to die and that there was nothing she could do to avoid it.

I kept running these images through my mind with a kind of fascinated horror. From nowhere I remembered a random fact I had once read about people who committed suicide by jumping from a height – that those who wore glasses invariably took them off before the final fall.

I thought back to that morning, when Helen's body must already have been found and removed by the time I parked my car. The multi-storey had been open as normal, and there had been no sign of anything untoward having happened the previous night.

I was interrupted by the ring of my desk phone.

'Alan, it's Jeff. Look, mate, I'm so sorry about what's happened, for your sake as well as for everyone else's. I know how much Helen meant to you. And believe me, I know you meant a lot to her as well. I didn't want to come downstairs to say this to you in person because, well, you know what this place is like. But I wanted to give you a call to check you were OK. I can't believe that Sam didn't break the news to you in person. Or to me, for that matter. Now's not the time, but perhaps in a bit we can meet and have a chat about things? I'll e-mail you my personal mobile number. Just text me whenever you want and we'll sort something out. And, of course, if there's anything I can do to help you in the meantime, just let me know. Cheers, mate, and I'm sorry again.'

I hadn't said a word during this monologue. I didn't want Jeff's faux-sympathy. He had taken my place in Helen's bed, and now he was pretending he was sorry for how I was feeling. I didn't care, either, for his comment about knowing that I had meant a lot to her. That was just a painful reminder about how they must have talked about me. And I certainly didn't want to meet up with him to 'have a chat about things'. Either he would be going on about how heartbroken he was, which would show him up for the hypocrite he was after the way he had been sniffing around Lucy. Or he would be putting on a brave face, asking how I was coping, which would be like rubbing salt into my wounds. It didn't make any difference to me what Helen and Jeff had said about how nothing had happened between them until after Helen and I had split up. As far as I was concerned, he had taken her from me. I wasn't therefore going to give him the satisfaction of sitting down with him to share our feelings about her with each other. If it hadn't been for him, Helen would probably still have been alive. I didn't know what had caused her to jump, but I was damned sure that she wouldn't have done so if she'd still been with me.

16

The rush hour traffic around Parker's Piece was as sluggardly as ever when, a couple of hours later, I left the office for the day. Cars were barely managing to overtake me as I took the fairly short walk to the multi-storey where I parked my car. The same multi-storey from which Helen had fallen less than twenty-four hours previously.

From the front of the multi-storey, you wouldn't have known there had been a sudden death in the vicinity so recently. Cars were entering and leaving as normal, like busy ants going to and from their nest, their drivers looking intently left and right as they made their move, in case of absent-minded pedestrians as well as other vehicles. In spite of the many streetlights and headlights, it would have been so easy to make a fatal mistake in the dark evening which had fallen upon Cambridge.

On a hunch, I swerved away from my pedestrian access to the multi-storey. I had never been around the back before, but I saw now a narrow passageway which ran between the side of the multi-storey and the building adjacent to it. I would have passed the entrance to this passageway hundreds of times over the years, but its presence had never really registered with me. Realising that this passageway must lead to the place where Helen had landed, I felt myself compelled to follow it. It didn't have any lighting of its own, but the lights from the floors of the multi-storey cast enough illumination into the passageway for me to see where I was heading. Not surprisingly, there was no one else in sight in the passageway. It turned left around the back of the building, and I felt my heart pumping in my chest as I turned the corner.

At first, I saw nothing out of the ordinary. The passageway stretched all the way along the back of the multi-storey, then forked both left and right at the far side. Presumably the left-hand fork led back to the main road, and the right hand one must lead to some other street entirely, as this was the short cut that the students who found Helen's body had apparently taken. Either a short cut, I thought, or a private place for a snog. Then, only ten metres or so in front of me, I saw a short strip of police barrier tape flapping slowly in the breeze. The other end had been tied to a drain pipe that ran down the outside of the building. This must have been where Helen fell. The police would have cordoned off this area of the passageway while they examined her body and carried out their other investigations. Although it would have rapidly become clear that she had fallen from the multi-storey, at first the police would have had to consider every possibility, such as her having been bludgeoned to death in the passageway by some random thug. After everywhere had been examined and photographed, Helen's body and the barrier tape would have been removed, but they must have forgotten about this one small strip. As I watched, the breeze eased and the tape hung limply alongside the drainpipe.

Feeling a strange mixture of horror and fascination, I edged closer to the tape and then to the area just beyond it. I wondered where exactly Helen's body had landed. There was enough lighting to see my surroundings and where the passageway led, but not to examine the floor of the passageway closely. I took my phone out of my jacket pocket and pressed the icon which switched on the torch light. Carefully I inspected the tarmac floor. There was no blood that I could see, but as I looked more closely, I noticed a circle of tarmac, about a foot in diameter, which was slightly lighter than its surroundings. It looked like the tarmac here had been cleaned very recently. I shuddered as I realised that this was probably the spot where Helen's blood had pooled as it ran out of her broken body, probably from her mouth or her nose. Very slowly I turned my head to look upwards, and I shivered at the sight of the sheer vertical multi-storey towering above me. I felt sick as I imagined her body tumbling through the air, arms flailing helplessly, and landing with a thud on the hard tarmac. I speculated about what had gone through her mind as she fell, and whether she had regretted her decision to jump on her way down.

It felt so weird to be on the scene of a recent sudden death just a short distance away from the mundanity of a Cambridge evening rush hour. I wondered if any of those people driving in and out of the multi-storey even knew of Helen's death, let alone were thinking about it as they went about their business. And even if they were, I doubted any of them knew or cared about me and how I was feeling.

As I turned back, I spotted a bunch of flowers lying on the ground, against the wall of the multi-storey. I could see no card attached to them, but they were fresh and could only have been left there today. I felt a flash of resentment at whoever had brought the flowers. They were obviously wanting to demonstrate how sorry they felt for Helen, but I wondered how well they really knew her and how much they really cared about her. I was honest enough, though, to recognise that part of my resentment was because it highlighted the fact that I had not got there first with an expression of sympathy. I started wondering whether a group of people at work had arranged to buy the flowers and, if so, who had chosen them and left them here. Whoever it was certainly hadn't asked me if I wanted to be involved.

The rush hour had started to thin by the time I had recovered sufficiently to collect my car from the first floor of the multi-storey. As I drove out of the exit and onto the main road, my eyes were drawn again to the entrance of the passageway in which Helen had died. I can't remember anything more about my journey home.

*

When I was back in my flat, I cooked a ham and cheese pizza in the oven and washed it down with a bottle of chilled Magner's cider. Then I sat in my usual chair in front of the television. Most evenings I would have been scrolling through my phone while watching some rubbish on television, but this evening I put on a YouTube recording of a James concert in Manchester. They were one of Helen's favourite bands, as I remembered her telling Max. I wanted to listen to some music which reminded me of her, while I thought about today's events.

It all seemed really unfair that I was getting some of the blame for Helen's suicide. Deep down, I wasn't proud of everything I had said to her since we had split up. But our last conversation, on the day she died, had shown that we remained on the same wave length. She still had feelings for me even though she had taken up with that oaf Jeff. She had valued me enough to ask me for advice regarding Rachel. I genuinely couldn't see how anything I had done could have contributed to her decision to throw herself to her death from the multi-storey.

What, then, had caused her to do such a terrible thing? She had a history of depression, but had never previously tried to kill herself as far as I was aware, and she was no longer sufficiently affected by her illness to be on any form of medication.

I wasn't going to be stupid enough to pretend that she had killed herself out of regret from dumping me.

One obvious source of any romantic grief was Jeff. He was a player, of course, and his relationship, if it could be called that, with Helen wasn't ever going to end in wedding bells. But from what Helen had said to me, she was well aware, and accepting, of this. He might have taken things further with Lucy already, and Helen might have found out about this. If so, then whatever she had previously said, she would have felt betrayed. But surely not enough to kill herself.

But I wasn't forgetting the thing with Sam. I couldn't think of any reason, other than the obvious one, for his car to be parked outside Helen's house so early on a Saturday morning. And if something was going on with Sam, then Helen was hardly going to be bothered if Jeff had chanced his arm with Lucy. But what if the thing with Sam was actually serious? What if Sam had been promising to leave his wife, Julia, for Helen, and had then had cold feet 'for the sake of the kids'? Might this have upset Helen sufficiently to make her do what she did? It was a more likely scenario than her getting upset over some shagging around that Jeff might have done. But the timings didn't make sense. It wasn't even ten weeks since Helen and I had split up. She surely couldn't have fallen in love with Sam, as well as getting involved with Jeff, in the short time after she had dumped me. And I knew Helen wouldn't have two-timed me with Sam. She had told me once, in a way that I felt sure was absolutely truthful, that she would never be unfaithful to me with another man.

What other things could have been bothering Helen?

There was the thing about Rachel having forgotten to do the property searches. Helen had been worrying whether to report her. But you wouldn't kill yourself because of that. And, even if Helen was going to be criticised for not having reported Rachel sooner, that was the kind of mistake that would get easily forgiven even at a reputable firm like ours.

And there were also her concerns over Max. But Helen had reported these to Tom, and even supposing she was now being put under pressure to investigate them further herself, that was a routine part of her job as an experienced property lawyer. A bit stressful, but ultimately not a big deal. If her suspicions were right and Max was doing something wrong, and the firm didn't report him, it was Tom's neck on the line as the MLRO, not Helen's.

I therefore started wondering if Helen had had any bad news away from work. I had never actually met any of her family, which was a slightly sore point with me, but I had heard enough about them to know that her family background was conventional. There was a mother and a father not far away, but if one of these had died then, well, it was very sad, but that's what tended to happen to parents as they grew older.

None of it really made sense.

Nevertheless, I determined to try to find out what had been worrying Helen so much that she appeared to have taken her own life. If someone such as Jeff or even Sam was to blame, then I wanted this to be recognised throughout the firm. They should get the public censure, not me, for what had happened. Jeff wouldn't be quite so popular, I surmised, if his acolytes found out that he had driven Helen to her death. And Sam wouldn't be wearing his self-satisfied smile, either at work or back at home with Julia, if he was known to have been the cause of her suicide.

It was also possible, of course, that a number of different worries had combined to overwhelm Helen. But that wouldn't make it any less important to identify them and apportion blame appropriately.

Deep within me, though, there was another feeling that I had to acknowledge. A feeling of relief that Helen would never again be able to do something to hurt me. I felt ashamed of this feeling, but I didn't attempt to pretend it wasn't there. I was deeply upset by today's news, but I also recognised that it would be the last big upset that Helen would ever cause me. I mulled over what people at work would think if they knew all that was running through my mind.

I had another bottle of Magner's, then decided to have an early night. Once in bed, with a warm electric blanket under me, I flicked through the library of my Kindle looking for something to take my mind off what had occurred today. I had a great fondness for true crime books, especially ones about famous murderers or miscarriages of justice. I had explained to Helen that I took a lawyer's professional interest in seeing how killers were, or were not, caught. There was some truth in this, but there was a greater truth in the fact that I simply enjoyed reading about the gory details of the crimes and, in the olden days, of the executions that often followed.

Tonight, I returned to one of my favourite recent purchases: an account of life in the condemned cell of an English prison in the days before the abolition of capital punishment. Prison officers spent weeks with the convicted murderer, playing board games with him and trying to engage him in ordinary conversation. But no one could ever forget that the morning was inexorably approaching when the murderer's neck would be judicially broken by the hangman's noose. I must, over the previous few weeks, have pored three or four times over the moving description of the last family visit allowed to the murderer, less than twenty-four hours before he was put to death. Reading about someone whose plight had been measurably worse than mine always made me feel better, and tonight after a little while I fell into a deep sleep.

17

Thursday

'Alan, there's a police officer downstairs to see you.'

Even at the best of times, Hayley was one of the loudest secretaries on the second floor. The sound of her working-class Cambridge accent was a feature of our daily life. But as she put down her phone and made her announcement, she seemed to be trying to be just that little bit louder. I eyed her closely over the divider between our desks, but she smiled back at me as if she had done no more than announce the arrival of the day's post.

'To see me?' I replied, rather superfluously.

'Yes, she's asked if you would be free to pop down for a few minutes. I forgot to tell you, but she called me first thing from the police station to see if you were in today. I said yes and, well, here she is. I hope you haven't been speeding again in your Prius, Alan?'

Rosemary and Lucy had both stopped typing when Hayley had first spoken, and now I was sure I heard a stifled giggle from Lucy. As casually as I could, I turned in my seat to see if anyone else had heard our exchange. Sam was watching me, as were the junior solicitor and two paralegals with whom he shared his pod. The paralegals had even turned right round in their chairs to get a better view, making no attempt to pretend that they weren't following events.

I saw no point in having a go at Hayley. It was usually a big mistake to fall out with support staff. 'Thank you, Hayley,' I said,

'I've no idea what she wants, but I can certainly spare her a few minutes.'

'She's in Room 1,' Hayley said. 'Reception thought you might want a bit of privacy. There are refreshments ordered in case she, er, detains you for longer than you are expecting.'

There was no doubt now that she was milking it. We both knew that the visit would be connected with Helen's death. I wasn't surprised to hear that reception had already hidden the police officer away in a meeting room. Doveley's didn't practise criminal law, but even so the firm wouldn't want a uniformed police officer hanging around and giving clients a guilty feeling.

I walked downstairs as casually as I could. The police officer got to her feet as I came into the meeting room.

'Hello, I'm P.C. Dawn Smith,' she said.

It really was true, I thought, what they said about police officers looking younger as you get older. She was in her mid-twenties at most, in what I assumed was standard police uniform. She had a pleasant rather than a pretty face, and longish blonde hair that was neatly fastened up at the back above her collar. Either she was wearing no make-up, or her make-up was so discreet as not to be noticeable.

I was never sure if you were supposed to shake hands with people like police officers when they were on duty. I tentatively proffered my hand, but when P.C. Smith made no matching movement with her own hand, I changed the direction of my hand movement and scratched the end of my nose instead. I noticed that she had short, unvarnished nails and wore no jewellery other than a fairly basic-looking watch and what looked like an engagement ring.

'Pleased to meet you,' I said, as we both sat down. 'My secretary said you wanted to see me?' I was going to let her state the purpose of the meeting. I didn't want to launch into stuff about Helen and then find out that P.C. Smith had, after all, called about a speeding offence.

'Yes, that's right. Thank you for sparing me the time. I'm sure you are very busy.' There was no ironic smile as she said this, so

I realised that it must be one of her standard warm-up lines. 'I am following up the sad death of Helen Eccles on Tuesday night. First of all, please accept my condolences for the loss of someone close to you. It must have been very upsetting news.'

I decided that now was not the time for a sarcastic response. 'Yes, it was,' I said. 'Helen was a lovely girl. I don't know what drove her to do what she did, but if I can help in any way it would be the least that I can do.'

On my way down to the meeting room, I had been rehearsing what I was going to say. If someone was going to have to be blamed for upsetting Helen, I wanted to make sure that the police looked in all the right places. That would mean them having to ask some difficult questions of Jeff, Sam and Rachel. Possibly also of Max, if only to teach him a lesson for the way he had been leching over Helen. But I didn't want it to look like I was dobbing someone else in as an act of petty revenge. I cringed at the thought of Sam finding out that I had been spying on Helen's house on the Saturday morning when he had been there. I also didn't particular want to rile Jeff, and have him dishing dirt on me back to the police. For this reason, I had been hoping that P.C. Smith would say something to show that we were on the same side, and offer me the chance to tell her, confidentially, what I knew or suspected.

I was therefore surprised when, after a brief explanation of Helen's death and what the police were doing, P.C. Smith started to ask me some very direct questions. 'I understand that you and Helen were in a relationship until relatively recently?' she asked.

'Yes. Until, er, nearly ten weeks ago.' I gave myself a mental kick. I was conscious that my reply might be misinterpreted as sounding slightly obsessive, as if the date of our break-up was written in big red letters above my bed. P.C. Smith made a brief scribble in the notebook on the table in front of her.

'And how did you feel when the relationship ended?'

'Like most people do, I suppose.' I wasn't sure where this was going, but I didn't much care for it all the same. 'How do you feel when one of your relationships ends?'

She ignored my question. 'So you were upset?'

'Well, I wasn't happy.'

'It was Helen's decision to end the relationship?'

'We talked about it in a civilised way. We are professionals. We work together. But, yes, she felt that it wasn't right for her at the moment.'

'And did you accept her decision?'

What a stupid question, I thought. I had planned for me and Helen to move in together, hopefully to subsequently get married. So what did P.C. Smith expect me to have said when Helen had dumped me? Something on the lines of 'I hope you will be happier with someone who is better looking and better in bed than me. Don't forget to invite me to the wedding.'?

'Of course,' I said. 'You can't force someone to stay in a relationship. I don't mind admitting that I hoped we would get back together in the future. But that was for Helen to decide.' I was quite pleased with my response. I was careful not to make it sound like I had thought that Helen was making a mistake.

'Did you try to persuade her to change her mind?'

'As I said before, we continued to spend time together in the office. We shared some clients, and we worked on some of the same files. So, yes, I also occasionally checked in with her as to how she was. To make sure she was happy with the decision she had made. But if you are asking whether I sat her down in a room like this one and begged her to take me back, of course not.'

'Do you think your attitude might have upset her?'

For God's sake, I said to myself. So is that what they think? That Helen might have jumped because of me putting her under pressure? Whatever else might have caused Helen to kill herself, I knew that it wasn't because I had been trying to get back with her. I was too annoyed even to take as some kind of back-handed compliment the fact that P.C. Smith seemed to think I might have had that sort of power over Helen.

'No,' I said. 'I don't. We'd been together a while, so of course there was upset on both sides. But nothing out of the ordinary. However,' and I paused for effect, 'you might be interested to know that Helen was already seeing somebody else at our firm when she died. Someone who has had a few girlfriends at the firm before, and whose love life doesn't always run particularly smoothly. You might want to talk to him about Helen's mood when she died.' I leant back in my chair feeling quite pleased with myself. I missed out on a lot of the firm's gossip, but I knew that Jeff had, as they say, broken a few hearts over the years at Doveley's. P.C. Smith was going to be very interested to hear all about him. Then, all I would have to do would be to find a natural way of bringing in Sam as well.

'That would be Mr Jeff Parker?'

'Yes.' I was surprised that she even knew his name.

'I've already spoken to him as it happens. He's been very helpful. But thank you anyway.'

Well, that explained a lot, I thought. Bloody Mr Nosey Parker clearly hadn't wasted any time in putting the boot in on me. I bet he'd loved speaking to P.C. Smith. A real chance to exert his laddish charm on her and to get her to see things from his perspective. I could see him now with that earnest and open expression on his podgy face that he put on so well. No doubt he'd been pouring his heart out to P.C. Smith, telling her how much he missed Helen and how much of a pain in the arse her former boyfriend had been. I bet he hadn't told her about his flirting, and maybe more, with Lucy before Helen died. About how keen he had been to invite Lucy to work with him upstairs in Corporate on one of their special projects. It wouldn't surprise me if Jeff was already on first name terms with the officer, and she with him. Perhaps the lecherous sod had already even asked her for a date. I wondered irritably if Jeff had already spoken to P.C. Smith when he had made his conciliatory phone call to me yesterday. He'd subsequently e-mailed me his personal mobile number, so I could certainly now think of a message I'd like to send him.

'When did you speak to Parker?' I asked.

'Initially yesterday. We had to ask him for details of Helen's next of kin. But we had a longer conversation today, in this room, before you came down.'

So it wasn't just me she had called to see at the office. I felt annoyance again at how Hayley had announced the visit from the police. She must have known that P.C. Smith was also seeing Jeff, and maybe others as well. Clearly, all that stuff about speeding tickets and P.C Smith possibly detaining me longer than I expected had just been her idea of a bit of fun. I clenched my fists in annoyance below the level of the table.

'Mr Parker was very understanding about your position,' P.C. Smith went on. 'He said that the aftermath of your break-up with Helen must have been difficult for you. He also told me about Helen's history of depression and about the other things that had been worrying her, including various pressures at work.'

I waited a moment to see if she was going to expand on 'the other things that had been worrying her at work'. She wasn't. The police no doubt felt that Jeff was the oracle of wisdom as far as Helen's life at Doveley's was concerned. Their only interest in me was whether I had contributed to whatever pressures had pushed Helen over the edge. Both metaphorically and literally, I couldn't help thinking, as an image of her twisting, falling body flashed into my mind.

'I'm sorry if I have had to ask some intrusive questions,' P.C. Smith went on. 'However, we need to get a complete picture of whatever might have had an influence on Helen's state of mind the night she died.'

'You mean whatever might have made her jump from the multi-storey?'

'If that's what she did, then yes.'

'You say "if"?'

'It's not my job to form a final view of what happened. It's the Coroner's. But yes, informally, that's the way everything is pointing. I am expecting to have it confirmed when I get the CCTV footage from the multi-storey. For completeness, though, I have to ask you when was the last time you spoke to her?'

'The day she died,' I replied. 'Here at the office. We had a meeting to discuss a client matter. She told me she was going out after work for a meal and a few drinks with friends. I wasn't going. Jeff Parker was, though.' I was sure she already knew that Jeff had been out on the Tuesday night. However, I wasn't averse from hinting that he might have done something to contribute to Helen's state of mind. Perhaps he had been flirting again with Lucy. Or perhaps he had even gone further than flirting and Helen had spotted them together …

'So you definitely didn't speak to Helen, or message her, after work on Tuesday?'

'No.'

'And you didn't see her either after work?'

'How do you mean?'

'I mean you weren't also out in Cambridge that night? You didn't happen to see her and try to have a word with her?'

For fuck's sake, I thought. Did they really think I was the sort of man who would follow Helen across Cambridge in the dark like a stalker? I didn't mention my Saturday morning swing by her house. I knew that would get misinterpreted.

'No,' I said.

'May I ask where you were that Tuesday evening? Just for the record.'

'At home. In my flat.'

P.C. Smith made a note of my answer, as she had done of all my others. I was expecting her to ask if I could prove I had been at home all evening. I hadn't seen anyone, but I had been browsing the Internet most of the time, looking at a mixture of tennis and true crime websites. I was sure there would be a record on my laptop of my evening's activities, showing the times at which I had visited the various websites. I was pretty sure also that the development had CCTV cameras all over the place, so if the police wanted to waste their time checking my whereabouts that evening, they were welcome to do so.

'There's one final thing,' she said. 'Would you have any objection if we borrowed your phone? Just until, say, Monday?'

'My phone?' I must have looked startled.

'Just so we can check there is nothing on it that might help us to understand Helen's state of mind. For example, any messages between the two of you that you might have thought were routine but which might have some significance with hindsight. It wouldn't be a full forensic examination, as that would take weeks if not months. Only a quick informal check of anything obvious. It's entirely voluntary, but Mr Parker has been very willing to cooperate in this respect.'

Only because he's got nothing to hide, I thought. Not that I had anything particular to hide, although it would be slightly embarrassing if they did a full search of my Internet browser history. I had inevitably stumbled across the odd pornographic website when carrying out research into one or other of my hobbies. Purely out of curiosity, I had sometimes clicked on links on these sites that had seemed especially bizarre. I wouldn't have wanted anyone to believe that I had an interest in some of the material that I had then unexpectedly been presented with.

'Your firm has no objection,' she went on, 'as long as we take steps to protect client confidentiality.'

That was an important point because, like most solicitors at Doveley's, I used the same phone for work and for my personal life. I had separate profiles and accounts for each, with different passwords and codes. Occasionally it could be annoying to get a reminder about work when sending a text to a tennis partner, but generally it made my life easier as I didn't have to remember to carry two phones around with me the whole time.

Realistically I had no choice but to agree to P.C. Smith's request. If I didn't, I was sure this would get back to the firm. They would then wonder what I had to hide. 'That's fine,' I said. 'I'll need a receipt, of course. I'll write down the password and code for my personal profile and account. I don't think you'll need access to my work profile and account, but if you do can I suggest you ask the IT team here at Doveley's in the first instance. They'll then need to get partner approval to give you access to anything work-related, as I'm sure you will appreciate.'

P.C. Smith nodded her agreement. We both knew that she

would only be interested in my personal account. Nowadays no one was foolish enough to use their work account to send any but the most innocuous of personal messages.

My main feeling at this point was relief that Helen had insisted we use a special app for the conduct of our relationship. An app which automatically caused all messages to self-destruct shortly after they were received, and which apparently left no record of the messages on the phone. She had said that she didn't trust the firm not to snoop on our personal messages. My own view had been that she liked the excitement of pretending we were doing something illicit. Either way, we had both used the app for messaging each other on private matters (and, OK, for sexting each other), while continuing to use ordinary texts or WhatsApps for day-to-day non-work stuff. The use of the app had always struck me as slightly odd though. It had felt like Helen had everything planned. I had certainly never heard of the app until she downloaded it for me, and she had been a bit vague about how she had found out about it. I had often speculated about whether she had done this before with someone else, and also whether she was subsequently doing this with Jeff, but I was too frightened – all right, and too jealous – to ever dare to ask the question.

Once I had handed over my phone, P.C. Smith was done with me. I didn't bother trying to find out who else, if anyone, she was asking to see. I would have sold my mother's virginity, to use a phrase favoured by one of Jeff's Corporate cronies, to know what exactly he had told P.C. Smith. But I most certainly wasn't going to ask her.

*

Walking up the stairs afterwards to the second floor, I congratulated myself on knowing that I could, if necessary, prove my whereabouts on the night of Helen's death. There was no way they could claim that, for example, I had had a row with her which had caused her to take her own life. Then I suddenly remembered the concept of triangulation, which meant that the police could probably check on my phone where I had been, or at least where my phone had been, at the time of her death. This meant that they wouldn't even need to examine my laptop or the development's CCTV. So that was perhaps why P.C. Smith hadn't pursued the point.

Shit, I suddenly thought. I had been carrying my phone on the Saturday morning when I had driven past Helen's house. If the police went back that far into my phone history, would they be able to work out exactly where I had been, or would they just know that I had been in the Mill Road area? If they discovered I had been spying on Helen at 5 a.m. on the Saturday morning, they might look more closely at our relationship and its aftermath. Which, at best, would be embarrassing. And, worse, if the truth got back to Sam, it might kill off any hopes I had of being made up to partner.

The meeting room had of course been air conditioned, but I was sweating as I swiped my way back onto the second floor. I had planned to swagger nonchalantly to my pod, to forestall any cheeky comments from Hayley. However, I now felt incredibly self-conscious as I walked to my desk. Sam and the others at his pod were watching me, as were most people on the floor. To give Hayley credit, she must have seen the state I was in, because she gave me a genuinely warm smile and a 'Hello, Alan' when she saw me. I wondered if she felt bad for having teased me earlier or, worse, if she thought I had been given a grilling by the police. Unlike most staff at the firm, she would, with her working-class Cambridge background, know just how hard a time the police could give people if they felt they deserved it.

Once at my desk, I was itching to do some Google searches, to find out how routine this meeting with P.C. Smith had been, and how closely the police could use triangulation to pin a phone user down to a specific location. However, I didn't dare to do so. For all I knew, the firm's IT team might be asked to hand over to the police a record of my Internet activity at work.

I noticed that none of Hayley, Lucy or Rachel asked me how

the meeting with P.C. Smith had gone. In their places, I would have been very curious to find out, so they clearly realised it was a sensitive subject with me. This didn't bode well for the coming days. I was grateful though for the sympathetic smile that Rosemary gave me when I looked in her direction.

After I had caught up with my e-mails, I took some solace in printing off and reviewing some proposed new website terms and conditions that a client had sent over. Boring stuff that I could do off the top of my head, but today I found it strangely comforting.

I kept an eye on Sam for the rest of the morning, but he didn't leave our floor the whole time. Clearly, he hadn't been called down to meet P.C. Smith. He came over at one point to commiserate with me over Helen's death, but it all felt very perfunctory.

I stayed late at the office that evening, only being able to relax once everyone else on the floor had gone home. I felt safe at my desk, in control of my work and confident about managing my clients' expectations effectively. I knew that, as soon as I left the office, my fears and insecurities regarding Helen's death would take over. I therefore wanted to delay that moment as long as possible.

18

'Hey, mate, I like your pussy magnet.'

It took me a few moments to realise that the little toe-rag was speaking to me. I had visited a client on the Babraham Research Campus first thing that morning, driving there straight from my flat. It was therefore around 10.30 a.m. when I arrived at my usual multi-storey. Normally I got there early enough to be able to park on the ground or first floor, but today I had to go up to the third floor. There were a lot of cars there already, but I took my usual pride in parking neatly in the centre of a free space without a lot of to-ing and fro-ing. I had made sure that the two cars on either side of me were clean, expensive-looking and well cared for. Owners of cars like that were, I believed, less likely to carelessly open a door onto my car when they returned to theirs.

As I headed towards the pedestrian stairway, I hadn't noticed the two teenage boys standing by a big black SUV in the next row. I had been too wrapped up in my own thoughts, still thinking about my meeting with P.C. Smith yesterday, and wondering what exactly she would be doing with my phone.

The boy who had called out to me was pointing to my Prius. 'I bet that makes you popular with the chicks,' he now said.

The two boys grinned at each other. I remembered it was half-term. They were probably waiting for a parent to meet them back at the family car after a couple of hours' early morning shopping in one of the city centre arcades. Both were dressed in the standard uniform of middle-class Cambridge kids trying to look cool: jeans, box-fresh trainers, and hoodies.

It wasn't the first time I had had to deal with some oik's prejudiced opinion about my choice of car. As if the only valid reason for choosing a particular make was to try to impress members of the opposite sex. The fact that my car was reliable, economical to run and environmentally friendly evidently carried no weight with them whatsoever.

I decided not to engage with the boys. A brief fantasy did run through my head of striding over to where they were standing, and banging their heads together until they begged for forgiveness. But, instead, I looked straight ahead in the direction of the stairway and walked on. Behind me I heard some sniggering and a half-whispered 'wanker'. Perhaps foolishly, I gave them the finger while simultaneously increasing my walking speed.

The door to the stairway had a glass panel in its upper half. Covered in grime but nevertheless still transparent. I let the door swing shut after me and then turned to look back through the glass. I was slightly concerned in case the boys decided to key my car once I was safely off the scene. I recalled with annoyance that I currently had no phone with which to dial 999 if I needed police assistance.

However, the two boys seemed to have lost interest in me already. As I watched, they wandered towards the nearest section of the concrete wall which ran round the perimeter of the floor. They stepped over the safety barrier and then, side by side, both leant over the wall and looked downwards. I assumed they were trying to catch sight of whichever parent was due to drive them home. After a few seconds, one of the boys stood up and stepped back behind the other. He bent down, gripped each of the other boy's lower legs with one of his hands, and jerked slightly upwards. The other boy turned around and they both burst out laughing.

I felt a shiver run down my spine. I put out my hand to steady myself against the wall. For a few seconds I stood there taking deep breaths.

I knew what I now had to do. But I could hardly go back onto the third floor - I didn't want to risk a confrontation with the boys. I therefore went up a flight of stairs and through the door onto the fourth floor. I took a second or two to get my bearings before walking with some trepidation towards a section of the perimeter wall in the far corner. There were concrete pillars about ten metres from the corner, effectively turning the area into a little alcove half-hidden from the rest of the floor. I stepped over the safety barrier and then looked over the wall. I was afraid of heights, so in any circumstances I would have hated doing this. But I felt I had no choice and, as I had expected, I found myself looking down at the spot where Helen had landed less than three days ago. To my amazement, the remnants of the bunch of flowers were still there, in the angle between footpath and wall.

Notwithstanding my fear, I was momentarily tempted by how easy it would be to climb over the wall and let myself fall. No more worries about work, or about what people thought of me. I could bring it all to a swift end. I wondered whether I would experience regret on the way down, and whether I would call out for help that I must know could never arrive in time. I wondered also whether I would experience pain when I landed, or whether death would be instantaneous.

But this was not what had made me shiver on the floor below, while watching the two boys indulge in their horseplay.

What had made me shiver was the memory of a book I had read only a few months earlier. It was about Joseph Smith, the so-called Brides in the Bath serial killer. Smith had been hanged in the early years of the last century for the murders of three women, in each case shortly after his marriage, bigamous or otherwise, to them. The women had all drowned in their baths, and initially it had been presumed that they had first had some kind of seizure. But the famous pathologist Bernard Spilsbury had demonstrated how the three women could actually have been murdered. Smith could have grabbed them by their feet when they were enjoying a bath, and suddenly pulled their legs up towards himself, causing their heads to slide under the water. The sudden flood of water into their noses and mouths could then have caused shock and a very quick loss of consciousness. It was reported that Spilsbury had practised on a volunteer before giving evidence in court, and had accidentally almost caused her death even though she had known what he was going to do.

Could something similar, but the other way round, have happened to Helen? Could someone have grabbed her by the lower legs while she was looking over the wall, and suddenly jerked her legs upwards so that she went over the parapet to her death before she realised what was being done to her?

The two boys had given me the idea, and when I had stood by the wall, I had realised how little effort would be required to propel a person over.

But who could have done that to Helen, and why? And, more importantly, how could they have managed it without Helen putting up resistance? First, Helen would already have had to be looking downwards over the wall. And second, whoever did it must have been someone she trusted, someone whom she would unhesitatingly allow to stand right behind her as she looked over the wall …

Most days, I used the time from when I parked my car until I arrived at the office to create a short checklist of the first tasks I was going to do as soon as I had logged on. Today, though, that habit was abandoned. I don't even remember how long I spent on the fourth floor. My only focus was on Helen. I was thinking about all the various people in her life, and I was asking myself which, if any, of them might have wanted to kill her.

It didn't occur to me who might be the obvious suspect should the police have the same idea as me.

19

Jeff and half a dozen others were finishing their lunch when I arrived at The Drum, just before 1 p.m., later the same day.

I had sent him a short e-mail as soon as I got into the office, thanking him for his conciliatory phone call on Wednesday afternoon and asking if he might be free for a catch up before the weekend. He had replied almost straightaway. He had a working lunch already scheduled at The Drum from 12 p.m. to 1 p.m., but suggested I meet him there at the end of the hour so that we could walk back to the office together.

I had spent some time before 1 p.m. killing time in town, thinking about what to say to Jeff. I had first walked diagonally across Parker's Piece from our office, feeling irrationally guilty as I passed a patrolling police officer and wondering if my phone was being examined by one of his colleagues at that very moment. It was too cold for any picnickers, but the paths that criss-crossed the common were busy with people walking briskly in one direction or the other. Some kids were playing a game of football on one patch of grass. Too young to be students, I thought they were probably local sixth-formers enjoying their half-term break. From Parker's Piece I walked down St Andrew's Street into the old city centre, then continued straight on as far as the bridge over the river. For a few minutes I leant on the bridge parapet and watched the punt operators chatting at their moorings outside Prezzo, while I ate a ham and mustard sandwich I had bought on the way. When I had first moved to Cambridge, I had loved walking around these streets, revelling in the juxtaposition of modern shops with centuries-old College buildings. Now, on my way back out of the centre towards The Drum, I barely noticed famous landmarks such as St John's College on my right and Sidney Sussex College on my left. It was only tourists who stopped to admire them and to cause a nuisance of themselves by taking group selfies on the pavement outside their entrances.

*

As I had expected, Jeff was at a window table at The Drum with a small group of solicitors from his Corporate team. What I hadn't expected was to see Lucy sitting alongside him. She was my trainee after all. I knew that she was providing support to Jeff's team on one of their projects, and that this would entail working with them independently of me. But, all the same, it rankled to see her smiling and chatting with the others as if she didn't have a care in the world. She didn't need to ask my permission to take part in this lunch, but all the same I felt it would have been courteous for her to mention it to me.

I nodded at Jeff to let him know I was there, and found myself a small table on the other side of the pub. While I waited for him to join me, I paid a couple of pounds to one of the bar staff for a coffee mug and poured myself an americano from the self-service machine.

After about another ten minutes, Jeff's table was done. I noticed that each of the people at the table, including Lucy, paid for their own meal. Jeff might have described it as a working lunch, but it wasn't being paid for by the firm. Effectively, therefore, it was a social event. I wasn't going to say anything to Jeff, but it did strike me as inappropriate so soon after Helen's death.

'Good to see you, mate,' Jeff said as he sat down opposite me, giving my hand a firm shake. 'I've been a bit worried about you, about how you've been coping.'

Sod off, I thought. 'As best I can,' I said. 'I still can't quite believe what happened. The hardest thing is seeing life go on as normal for everyone else, at least on the surface, while knowing that Helen will never be part of it.' I had decided to try not to rile Jeff. At least not until I had asked him what I wanted.

'Very true,' Jeff said. 'It's all incredibly sad. Everyone in my team is very upset. Some of them knew Helen well. We thought we'd get out of the office at lunchtime just for a change of scenery. I'm not sure how much it helped though. Either we didn't mention Helen, in which case we started feeling insensitive, or we did talk about her, and that reinforced how awful it all is.'

I didn't care for how he seemed to include Lucy as part of his team. 'I had a meeting yesterday with a police officer,' I said, changing the direction of our conversation. I wasn't going to get into a cock-measuring contest with him as to who was missing Helen the most. 'The officer told me you had been very helpful in giving them information about Helen's recent past.'

Jeff blinked. 'Ah, yes, you mean Dawn.' So he was on first name terms with her already, I thought. This leopard most certainly didn't change his spots. 'I think I was the first person at the firm she wanted to speak to,' he went on, 'once she heard that Helen and I had been seeing each other. I suppose she thought I would be best placed to know what state of mind Helen had been in when she, er, did what she did.'

'So you told the officer about me?' I wasn't going to bandy the officer's first name around with Jeff.

'Well, yes, obviously,' Jeff said. 'It's not that long ago that you stopped seeing Helen.'

Not yet ten weeks, I thought. But I didn't say that.

'But, don't worry,' Jeff went on, 'I explained that you seemed to have got over the worst of it. That you had found the break-up difficult and that you had probably said a few things you regretted. But that, by the time she died, you seemed to be a bit more accepting of things.'

This was the kind of thing I really hated about Jeff. He was making himself sound oh so bloody reasonable. As if he had done me a favour. And there wasn't really a decent response I could make. If I agreed that I had been more accepting, then it sounded like I was giving him and Helen my blessing. But if I didn't agree, then it just made me sound obsessive. It also wouldn't help back at the firm, where people seemed to be blaming me for Helen's state of mind when she died. However, this kind of thing was Jeff all over. He could be appropriately deferential to the partners at Doveley's without coming over as sycophantic. He could banter with the lads. He could provide a sympathetic shoulder for struggling trainees. He could remember the names of the secretaries' kids and boyfriends. And he could chat up any female between the ages of sixteen and sixty without coming over as being in the slightest bit sleezy. A man for all seasons, all right. And a real shit, to my mind.

It seemed as if Jeff was reading my mind. 'I couldn't deny what had happened, Alan. But I know that Helen wouldn't have wanted you to be blamed in any way. I've also explained that to a few people at work. Whatever caused her to take her life, it wasn't anything you had done. I'm certain of that.'

That's if she did take her own life, I thought. Though I wasn't going to say anything to Jeff about the other possibility which had occurred to me that morning in the car park.

'The police asked if they could borrow my phone,' I said. 'Did they ask you too?' I knew the answer to this already, but I wanted to see his reaction.

'Yes, but just for a routine check. Dawn wanted to see if there were any indications as to Helen's state of mind. I guess the police might need these for the inquest. Fortunately,' and he gave me the merest hint of a wink, 'there's nothing on it which would embarrass me.'

I bet there wasn't, I thought. On occasions I had heard him joke about pornography in the laddish way that almost all men do when there are no women around, but I would have bet a pound to a penny that there would be no trace of pornographic websites on his phone. Like many corporate lawyers, he wouldn't know his way around a lot of the provisions in the

Companies Act, but he was smart enough in his own cunning way.

'What was Helen's state of mind the last time you saw her?' I asked. 'That would have been shortly before she died,' I added pointedly.

'To be honest,' he replied, 'she was in a bit of a funny mood. We didn't sit together at the curry house. Nothing odd about that, she was with her mates and I was with mine. But she was definitely on edge. I know she was beating herself up about what to do about Rachel. Don't worry, she told me that she had explained all this to you. And she was a bit nervous about this new client called Max who had been on at her to meet up with him for a coffee away from the office. Apparently, he'd spotted her on her way to the meal on Tuesday and crossed the road for a quick word with her. But there was something else on her mind, I am sure. So that's why I felt I had to tell Dawn all about her medical history, or at least that part of it which she had shared with me.'

I was interested to note that Jeff had made no mention of Sam. Even though Sam had turned up at the curry house like the proverbial bad penny. Therefore, either Jeff knew nothing of this aspect of Helen's life, or it was something which he wasn't prepared to share with me. I did wonder if he knew more than he was letting on. In his position, I wasn't sure how happy I would have been with the seating situation in the restaurant. I wouldn't describe myself as overly possessive, but I wouldn't have wanted to spend the entire evening in a separate group from Helen if we had still been seeing each other. I would also have been unhappy about Sam coming over to sit in Helen's chair – I would have wondered what interaction might have taken place between them.

'Might Helen have been feeling in any way insecure with you?' I asked.

'How do you mean?'

'Well, I'm grown up enough to admit that she seemed to really like you. But you do have, how can I put this, a certain reputation where women are concerned. With me, she never had any doubts of my loyalty. But, well, I've seen the way that Lucy, for example, looks at you. And how, to some people, it might look like you have been encouraging her. For example, by inviting her to your working lunch today when actually she is my trainee. Could Helen have got the wrong end of the stick here and been upset?'

Jeff gave me a long hard look. I was pleased to see he was rattled. 'Alan, you just don't stop do you. You're like a kid picking a scab. Look, I'll be honest with you. More honest than you deserve, and more honest than you will probably want. Helen and I were seeing each other. But that's all. Nothing serious in other words. Frankly, she'd had her fill of that with you. We weren't joined at the hip. And we were both free to go out for a drink with other people if that's what we wanted.'

'Including with Lucy?' I asked.

His face flushed. 'Alan, if it wasn't for the sake of Helen's memory, I would do something I would probably regret. It always has to be about you, doesn't it? I don't actually think you give a toss about the effect of Helen's death on her friends and family. You are so wrapped up in your own misery that it wouldn't occur to you to stop and think about theirs. I'm going to leave it here, if you don't mind. But, genuinely, mate, do try to leave some of your bitterness behind.'

He got up, turned around, and walked straight out of The Drum. I didn't need telling that we weren't going to be walking back to the office companionably together.

Fortunately, there was no one left from Doveley's to witness the scene with Jeff. I don't think any of the rest of the lunchtime crowd had noticed anything amiss. If anyone random had been watching, they would have assumed that Jeff was rushing back to a meeting he had forgotten about.

I was going to be late back at the office, but for once this didn't worry me. Sam could glare at me from his pod all he liked, as far as I was concerned. I re-filled my mug and sipped the coffee down slowly, mulling over what Jeff and I had said to each other.

There was a ring of truth in what Jeff had said about the nature of his relationship with Helen. Certainly, Helen had never, to my regret, shown any signs of possessiveness or jealousy during her time with me. Sometimes I had wondered if she would really have cared if I had had a fling with someone else. My deepest fears, based on some of her fantasies, had been that she might be the one to have the fling. For Helen, therefore, to have fallen so passionately in love with Jeff in such a short time seemed unlikely. But even if she had done, she knew his reputation and wouldn't have been unrealistic enough to believe she could change him overnight. And, in any event, I had no evidence, first, that Jeff had started something with Lucy, and, second, that Helen had found out about it. In some ways it was a shame, because I would have loved Jeff to get the blame within the firm for causing Helen to kill herself.

Similarly with Jeff, he had a reputation at the firm of 'easy come, easy go' where women were concerned. It was difficult to imagine him in the grips of a jealous frenzy. If Helen had been unfaithful to him with Sam, I could envisage, even enjoy, his alpha male pride being upset. However, much as I couldn't stand the man, I struggled to see him as a potential murderer.

It was now nearly 2 p.m. Jeff would have long been back at his desk on the third floor. I wondered what he had been saying about me to his hangers-on about our meeting in The Drum.

I still hadn't reached a decision either on how I was going to approach Sam. I could hardly ask him directly what had he been doing in Helen's house at 5 a.m. on the Saturday morning before her death. I had a meeting scheduled with him for the following week, so although I didn't like to wait that long I could see that being the most natural opportunity to try to find something out. I also had to think about what I was going to try to find out, and how, regarding Rachel, Lucy and Max.

*

When I got back to the office, Lucy was hard at work at her desk.

She acknowledged my return with a slight nod. I was finding it difficult to concentrate on my work, but I saw that I had received an e-mail from the in-house lawyer at the university to say that the final draft of my patent licence had been approved. Now the licence only had to be signed. The signing procedure was well within the competence of the in-house lawyer, but as usual he wanted a bit of hand-holding. Rather than risk looking ignorant to his own people by asking 'What happens next?', he had cleverly framed his query in terms of asking about the 'most efficient' way of getting the licence signed 'given that the licensee is in a different jurisdiction'. I copied and pasted a standard reply from another e-mail I had sent recently to a different client, then asked the in-house lawyer to send me a copy of the licence once it was signed. My excuse was that I wanted a copy on my file 'for the record', but the reality was that I wanted to check that it had been signed correctly. All sorts of things could go wrong with signings, even with an in-house lawyer supposedly holding everyone's hands. I had lost count of the number of times that people had signed a contract in the wrong place, or got the wrong person at their organisation to sign, or put in the wrong date of signing.

Next, I had a quick look on the time recording system. As I had expected, I had spent more time on the licence than my fixed price quote had anticipated. I made a mental note to discuss this with Sam. Either the firm would have to write off some of my excess time, which would affect their profits as well as my own realisation rate. Or I would have to bite the bullet and see if I could agree a higher price for the work with the in-house lawyer. It would be Sam's decision, but I was pretty sure he would want me to have a go at getting the extra money. The in-house lawyer would undoubtedly then enjoy being arsey, as it would show his superiors that he was keeping a tight rein on their external lawyers' costs.

*

I left the office shortly after 5 p.m. I remembered that the previous Friday I had left early in order to go for drinks at The Drum. Tonight, I was leaving because there was an early evening session at the tennis club for hopeful men's team players. I was still irritated by the implication at last weekend's social session that I had been trying too hard, so I had decided to offer my services where my efforts might be better appreciated. It might have seemed strange for me to be thinking about tennis when Helen's body was lying in a mortuary somewhere, but I needed some kind of distraction from her death and from all the thoughts about its cause that were spinning around my head. One of the attractions of tennis for me was that, while I was on court, I was able to immerse myself in the game and forget about all the things that were worrying me elsewhere.

At the club, we were split up into groups of four, and played doubles on three courts, swapping opponents every half hour. I was clearly a bit better than a couple of those who already played for the lowest men's team, and certainly a lot fitter. At the end of the session, I made sure I mentioned to the organiser that I had been on the winning side for each of my four matches, and that some of the other older players seemed to be feeling the pace a bit. All in all, it was a good evening, and although I wasn't invited to go along to the nearby pub for a drink afterwards, I went back to my flat hoping that I would have some challenging tennis to play in the summer.

20

Monday

'Alan, there's a police officer downstairs to see you again.'

Hayley really was skating on thin ice this time. Lucy openly grinned, and when I turned to my left I was disconcerted to see a brief smile cross even Rosemary's face. I would have loved to be able to make a Jeff-style riposte that would have had the three women laughing with me, but instead I just felt my cheeks flush.

Hayley must have noticed my discomfort because she continued in a more kindly tone: 'I think it's the same officer who visited on Thursday. Reception say she's dropping something off for you, but that if you've got a couple of minutes to spare she can also update you on what you discussed last week.'

To be fair to Hayley, she must have been bored out of her mind when reception phoned her. She had spent all morning printing off and collating the month end draft bills for the whole of the Commercial team. These would be distributed to the fee earners in charge of each file, who would have to compare how much unbilled time there was on the file against their earlier estimate or quote to the client. They would then have to decide, in conjunction with Sam, how much time could be billed that month, how much should be written off as unbillable, and how much should be carried over for reviewing in a month's time. The last of these was often the lazy lawyer's option, deferring a difficult decision in the Micawberish hope that something would turn up.

I went down to the first floor as casually as I could. P.C. Smith had been put in the same meeting room as on Thursday.

'Sorry to trouble you again,' she said, as I came in and sat down. 'I wanted to bring your phone back as soon as we had finished with it. It must have been a real pain to be without it over the weekend. I couldn't survive without mine. We are very grateful to you for your cooperation.'

I eyed her carefully as she passed over the phone, to see if she had a hidden agenda. I was still worried that the police might have trawled back far enough in my phone records to know that I had been in the vicinity of Helen's house on the Saturday morning before she died. I had rehearsed a couple of possible excuses over the weekend in case they had, but I was uncomfortably aware that neither of them would present me in a favourable light. I was also slightly concerned that P.C. Smith might mention the pornographic websites that I knew would be in my phone history. I wasn't sure I had the confidence to say brazenly that there was nothing illegal in what I had viewed. But I also didn't really want to have to say that I had come across some of the sites by accident. I would sound like the man who went to A&E with his penis stuck in a vacuum cleaner hose, claiming that he had fallen on it accidentally while cleaning the house in the nude.

'I was pleased to be able to help,' I said eventually. 'All I want, all everyone wants, is to know what might have caused Helen to do what she did. Have you found out anything which might throw some light on this?'

'I can't tell you everything about her state of mind on the evening she died,' P.C. Smith said, 'as I'm sure you will appreciate. Some of it is confidential, at least for now. However, given your closeness to Helen, I can tell you that our officers have looked at the CCTV which covers the multi-storey. They discovered footage which shows her arriving, on foot, at the multi-storey shortly before she is believed to have fallen. The footage shows her walking up the pedestrian stairway, then going through the door onto the top floor. In all the footage she was on her own. At first, we thought she may have been going back to her car, but that can be ruled out because the car was found parked outside her house the following morning. Unfortunately, there is no footage showing how she spent her time on the top floor before she fell. However, everything that our officers have seen does seem to confirm our preliminary view that there was nothing suspicious about her death.'

I noticed that P.C. Smith was using the word 'fell' rather than 'jump', as if Helen might have lost her balance while admiring the view over the city from the top floor and accidentally tumbled over the wall.

'So there is definitely no footage showing Helen as she, er, fell?' I asked.

P.C. Smith must have seen many ghastly sights in her time, but she still threw me a slightly shocked look. I realised that I would have sounded incredibly ghoulish, almost as if I was asking whether there was a video clip I could borrow which showed Helen's body tumbling helplessly to the ground.

'I suppose I am just clutching at straws,' I went on quickly, 'hoping it might have been some kind of tragic accident. I would find that easier to accept. I can't begin to imagine how desperate someone must be to make a deliberate decision to jump from such a height.'

There, I had said the word 'jump', but the heavens didn't fall in. I wondered how P.C. Smith would have reacted if I had used the word 'push', and told her something of my suspicions. Not that I could do so, of course. I would have to tell her about seeing Sam's car parked outside Helen's house on that Saturday morning. And, whatever the police did with that information, I knew for sure that Sam would find out that it had originated from me. And that would signal the end of my career at Doveley's, and probably in the rest of Cambridge as well. The last thing I wanted was to have to move firms to another area of the country.

'That's OK, I quite understand. But, sadly, it isn't looking like it was an accident.'

'I can see that,' I said. 'What happens next, then?'

'We write our report,' she said. 'There's the usual paperwork. There will be an inquest in due course, of course. And I expect Helen's body will be released to the family very soon so they can make the necessary arrangements. I'm sure a lot of people will want to pay their final respects.'

For some reason I hadn't thought about Helen's funeral. I wondered where it would take place. Her parents lived in Cambridgeshire so presumably somewhere fairly local. I just hoped that Jeff wasn't insensitive enough to try to hog the limelight.

P.C. Smith tied up a few more loose ends. Then, slightly awkwardly, we thanked each other and I went back upstairs.

*

Hayley had dumped a pile of draft bills on my desk while I was away. Most months I delayed going through my bills as long as possible. But now they were ideal cover, allowing me to think things through while pretending to look busy.

Of course, there would have been CCTV to capture Helen's last walk. The natural conclusion, which the police had understandably come to, was that Helen had chosen the multi-storey as the best place to commit suicide. Jumping from the top floor would guarantee instant death. Not something you would do if you were only making a cry for help.

However, if Helen had been killed, there must be footage of the killer arriving at the multi-storey, whether on foot or by car. There was no way to get to the top floor other than by one of the few official entrances. This wasn't a film where a killer could slide down a rope from a helicopter which was hovering over the top of the multi-storey. Unfortunately, if Helen had been killed by a random stranger, it would be almost impossible to work out who was responsible from the CCTV footage of the entrance alone. Hundreds of people must have come and gone during the few hours before her death. A random killer could have been any of them.

Wasn't it much more likely, though, that any killer was someone who Helen already knew? Someone who she had arranged to meet up there, or possibly someone she had followed. There could, however unlikely it might seem, be all sorts of reasons why that person might want to kill her, and why she might put herself in a position where they could do so.

The obvious way to check this would be to see if anyone who Helen knew, personally or professionally, had appeared on the CCTV footage in the period shortly before she died. If they had, then they could be investigated further. But this would have to be done by someone who actually knew the people in Helen's life. The police could hardly do it themselves based on a list of names and mug shots. However, unless they had other evidence pointing to a possible murder, they weren't realistically going to ask someone to do this. It would all be massively time-consuming. And I wasn't going to volunteer, as I would then need to reveal why I had my suspicions.

Something else occurred to me. Any potential killer would have no way of knowing for sure whether Helen's push would have been captured by CCTV. Most people were aware nowadays that CCTVs were all over the place in the centre of cities. A multi-storey car park could be guaranteed to have CCTV cameras somewhere. No one with a modicum of intelligence would therefore plan to kill someone in such a spot. If Helen had been killed, it must have been done in a fit of anger or passion.

Either way, I resolved to investigate further. In spite of what Jeff claimed to have said to other people at the firm, I still felt that I was in some way being blamed for what happened to Helen. The only way I could dispel this was to find out what had really gone on. And then to make sure that whoever was responsible got their rightful share of the blame. If the person responsible turned out to be someone I didn't like, well I wasn't going to pretend that this wouldn't be a bonus.

21

Tuesday

I had spent much of the previous evening pondering over how to approach Rachel.

I didn't know if Helen's death was connected in any way with what had happened between her and Rachel regarding the Ely lease. Deep down, I thought it probably wasn't. But I didn't have the courage to tackle Jeff again so soon after he had flown off the handle in The Drum. And I was still putting off the time when I would have to ask Sam why his car had been parked outside Helen's house so early that morning. So by speaking to Rachel, I felt I was at least doing something useful.

Rachel worked, with all the other property lawyers, on the firm's fourth floor. This meant that most days, even most weeks, I never actually saw her in the office unless we both happened to be arriving or leaving at the same time. As a commercial lawyer, I was used to rubbing shoulders on a daily basis with the other specialist teams on the second floor, such as Employment, Pensions, Litigation, and Tax; and also with the Corporate team that ruled the roost on the third floor. This was because the advice we gave to clients would often require input from more than one of these teams. But property law was very much a specialism of its own, and occasions when property lawyers and commercial lawyers had to give advice together, such as when Helen and I had met Max, were relatively rare.

There was no obvious excuse, therefore, for me to go up to the fourth floor. Even when I had been going out with Helen, everyone's heads had turned in my direction on the occasions I had wandered up there to see how her day was going. After a while, Helen had asked me to stop coming up, saying that people were wondering if I was checking up on her.

In the old days I might have gone up and knocked on Rachel's office door and asked for a private word. However, now that we all worked open plan this wasn't possible, because she shared a pod with other fee earners who would be in earshot. I didn't know her well enough to ask her out for a coffee, and my cheeks flushed at the thought of what she would say to Lucy if I did.

In the end I had had a brainwave. Everyone at the firm had access to everyone else's electronic calendar. I had found this useful when I was going out with Helen, and even more so in the aftermath of our break-up. It had enabled me to find out when she was in the office, and who she was meeting when she was out. As soon as I got into the office, therefore, I dipped into Rachel's calendar to see what she was doing that day. She had an appointment marked as 'private' over lunch, which meant that I couldn't tell where she was going and with whom. But between 3 p.m. and 4 p.m. she was scheduled to see a client in one of the meeting rooms on the first floor. The room had also been booked by someone else for another meeting at 4 p.m., so I could be pretty sure that Rachel would finish her own meeting on time. Given her lack of seniority, I was slightly surprised that she was being trusted to meet a client on her own, but this could probably be explained by the fact that so much commercial property work was very routine and did not require a great deal of intellectual input.

I spent the day clearing my desk of everything urgent, and at around 3.30 p.m. I slipped downstairs to an empty client meeting room next but one to Rachel's. I was carrying a new file I had just opened. I had been asked to review a complicated proposed franchise agreement for a client who was wanting to branch out into new territories. It was the kind of wet-towel-round-the-head job for which some quiet time was essential, and the more conscientious fee earners such as myself often disappeared for an hour or so in these circumstances to an un-booked client meeting room where we could guarantee to be undisturbed. Even Hayley wouldn't have been able to find me.

As the meeting room doors were windowless, I left mine slightly ajar. Just before 4 p.m. I heard the door to Rachel's meeting room open. There was the sound of footsteps along the carpeted corridor. I peeped through the gap between my door and the frame, and saw Rachel, carrying what looked like a brand-new file, leading a portly middle-aged man, whom I assumed to be her client, towards the lift. As soon as the lift doors closed, I darted down the back stairs quickly enough to see Rachel and her client coming out of the lift on the ground floor.

Rachel shepherded the client out and gave his name badge back to the receptionist.

'Hello, Rachel,' I said as she headed back towards the lift. 'How are you?'

'Very well, thank you. I hope you are too, Alan.'

This wasn't starting well. Her second sentence was definitely a polite statement rather than a question. Fortunately, I had planted myself between her and the lift, and unless she wanted to swerve past me and tackle four flights of stairs she had to wait until the lift doors opened again.

'Yes, I'm fine, thank you,' I said. I took a deep breath. 'Er, I'm glad to have bumped into you, Rachel, because I was just wondering if everything had been sorted out on the Ely file?'

I'd always found it easier to imagine Rachel in a nightclub than in a law firm. Lucy, at least, looked like a lawyer, even if I could seldom read what was going on behind that expressionless, carefully made-up face. Rachel, on the other hand, invariably looked like she had slapped on her make-up, with her usual heavy mascara look, in a mad rush to get onto the dance floor. She always seemed happiest in a group, throwing flirtatious looks or touches to the men, and sharing conspiratorial smiles with the women. She now had a boyfriend, apparently, but I had noticed that this had hardly caused her to modify her behaviour. I had seen her socially a few times when I was going out with Helen, and it had irked me that she had never behaved towards me as I had seen her do with other men.

I was therefore quietly satisfied by her reaction to my question. The lift doors had opened, and if she had simply laughed and walked past me into the lift, I wouldn't have known what to do next. Instead, she went very still. Her eyes narrowed slightly, and I saw her blushed cheeks redden further.

'What do you mean, "sorted out"?' she asked.

'The problem that Helen mentioned to me.' She was silent. 'About the property searches?' I added lightly.

'I don't know what you're talking about, Alan, but let's go somewhere.'

It was easiest to go into the lift, and I pressed the button back up to the first floor. Neither of us spoke. I led the way from the lift to the meeting room I had just vacated. I noticed that I had forgotten to pick up my franchise agreement file when I had left the room a couple of minutes before. Rachel shut the door behind us and remained standing just inside the room, while I sat down at the table. I was doing what had to be done, but I confess that I wasn't finding it a wholly unpleasurable experience.

'Well, what's this all about, Alan?' she asked quietly, when she realised that I wasn't going to speak first. 'Are you saying there is a problem on one of Helen's files?' She paused, almost for dramatic effect. Then she nodded her head as if to indicate that she had suddenly understood something. 'Are you thinking that Helen made a mistake on a file, and that this might have had something to do with what she did? Oh dear, that would be terrible. Poor Helen.'

She was cool, all right, I had to give her that. In her position, I wouldn't have regained my composure so quickly. Poor Helen, indeed.

'Yes,' I said, 'Helen told me there was a problem on one of her files. The lease in Ely that you are doing for Piers's company. But she hadn't made a mistake. She said that you'd made the mistake. You'd forgotten to order the property searches that she'd asked you to do. Without them, Piers's company won't know for sure that they can use the property in the way they have planned. That's professional negligence.' I added the last sentence with relish.

'And Helen really told you this? I thought you two were hardly speaking. Hadn't she made it clear that she had moved on?'

You little bitch, I thought. I wasn't going to go easy on her now. I could just imagine her making these sorts of comments about me to Lucy, when they were back gossiping at home in their cosy house share.

'Helen asked me for advice,' I said. 'She knew that your mistake would have to be reported. But, being the sort of person she was – very kind - she was worried about the consequences for you. You being on a fixed term contract which is up for renewal.' I don't mind admitting that my final sentence was intended to give her a taste of her own medicine.

Credit where credit's due, though; Rachel had clearly been thinking fast.

'I think you must have misunderstood things, Alan,' she said. 'Yes, a mistake was made. And, yes, it was on the lease I was drafting for the property in Ely. But Helen was my supervisor and she told me that she would order the searches and check they were OK. When she realised that she had forgotten to do this, she was very upset. It wasn't like her to make a mistake like that. Do you think she was distracted by how she felt you had been behaving towards her?'

This wasn't going quite as I had expected.

'Helen was quite clear,' I said, 'that it was your mistake. Not hers.'

'I know it's difficult for you to accept, Alan, but it definitely wasn't my mistake. Helen and I discussed the searches, and I made a note in my notebook that she was going to order them and check them. I can show you my note if you like.'

She really was being very clever now. She wasn't going to produce a printed attendance note that proved her version of events, because the time when the document was created could be checked by our IT guys. And if it had only been created after Helen's death, she would be in big trouble. But if she was able to produce a hand-written note of her alleged conversation with Helen, no one would be able to prove that it hadn't been made before Helen's death. They might not necessarily believe her, but that would be another thing entirely.

'It does now all make sense,' Rachel went on. 'Helen looked awful when we all went out for that curry. She must have been worrying herself to death over it.' She paused, as we both realised the loaded significance of her last few words. 'I can't understand why she would try to blame me, though. That wasn't like her at all.'

I didn't know what to say. I knew Rachel was lying, and I was pretty sure she knew that I knew she was lying. But if it all came to light, the firm would have to decide whether to accuse a living employee of lying, with all the HR and publicity consequences that could have; or whether to accept that someone who was no longer around to face the music had made the mistake. The temptation to believe Rachel, or at least to pretend to believe Rachel, would be overwhelming. I really hadn't foreseen this. I had expected her to break down and beg me to keep quiet. Whether or not I would have done so, I hadn't decided. But I had been rather looking forward, for the sake of my investigation, to having that power over her.

Rachel was speaking again. 'I know how much Helen meant to you, Alan. It's up to you, of course, but you might not want all this to come out. It would be a shame if people ended up remembering Helen for the mistake she'd made, and for what she did to herself because she couldn't live with the consequences. Don't you think, for the sake of her memory, that it might be better to forget it all? From what Helen said to me, I don't think in practice it's likely to make any difference to Piers's company.'

Until now I had been hoping to keep Jeff out of it, so that it was just between me and Rachel. But in view of the line she was taking, I didn't think I had that option any more. 'It isn't just me who knows about this,' I said. 'Helen told Jeff Parker too. Piers was his client, and he had a right to know what had gone wrong first. You'll have to speak to Jeff.'

I was bottling it, but I knew that, for all his flaws, Jeff would make a better fist than me of dealing with Rachel. Strictly speaking I knew that I also ought to tell Sam, or a partner in the Property team, but there would then be no going back. Helen would be blamed for the mistake that had been made. And, if Sam had any responsibility for what had happened to her, it would then be all the harder to bring him to book. I could just see the smug smile on his face as he took the opportunity to blame Helen for something which he had, directly or indirectly, himself caused.

Rachel was looking icily calm. She had clearly decided on the path she was going to take, and was sticking with it. 'All right,' she said. 'I'll go and speak to him now, before he goes home. I'm sure he will agree with me, though.'

Part of me had to admire her. If I had been in Rachel's shoes, I don't mind admitting that I would have gone to pieces if confronted by someone such as myself. I worried enough about making mistakes at the best of times, and on the very few times when I had made one I had almost driven myself into the ground with self-blame. In Rachel's position, I couldn't have brazened it out, and I certainly couldn't have come up with a plausible way of blaming someone else, like Rachel had done.

*

I sat for a long time in the meeting room after Rachel had gone out, looking out over Parker's Piece. Outside it looked cold and wet, and there was the usual slight lull in the traffic before the onset of the Cambridge rush hour.

I had no doubt that Helen had been telling the truth about whose mistake it was. She had been worrying over the consequences for Rachel if the facts became known, but it was inconceivable that she would have killed herself over this.

If Helen had still been alive, it was also inconceivable that Rachel would have dared say that Helen had agreed to order the searches. Helen would have skinned her alive. So, clearly, Rachel benefited from Helen's death. But was it possible that she had killed Helen in a fit of panic? Might she have begged Helen to keep quiet, and then done this terrible thing when Helen had refused to do so? The two women were about the same size and strength, so if Helen had been tricked into looking over the parapet on the top floor of the multi-storey, it was physically possible that Rachel could have sent her tumbling to her death.

However, it was difficult to see how Helen and Rachel could have ended up on the top floor of the multi-storey in the first place. Helen's car had been found the following morning outside her house near Mill Road. It wasn't therefore possible that she had been returning to pick up her car from the multi-storey, and that she been followed there by Rachel. In any event, Helen lived only a couple of minutes' drive away from the multi-storey, so it would have made no sense for her to park there.

The other possibility was that Rachel's car had been parked in the multi-storey, and that she had offered to drop Helen off at home on her own way back to Cherry Hinton. But this had its own improbabilities. Rachel had a reputation as a heavy drinker on firm nights out, so it was much more likely that she had come back into the city centre after work by public transport, or possibly by taxi. She might have decided to have a night off drinking, but in that case wouldn't it have been natural for her to have given her housemate Lucy a lift into town and then home again afterwards? If an unusually sober Rachel had offered Helen a lift home, where on earth had Lucy been?

All in all, it seemed unlikely that Rachel had killed Helen, even though she was probably secretly relieved that she was dead. However, it wouldn't be possible to rule Rachel out completely, without knowing more about her movements on the night that Helen died. I would have to try to find out, perhaps from Lucy or perhaps even from Jeff, what Rachel had done after the two women had left the restaurant. Also, whether she had been drinking, and whether she had agreed with Lucy that the two women would go home separately.

But I would also have to think about who else might have had the motive to kill Helen.

22

Wednesday

I had been itching all night to find out what Rachel had said to Jeff, and what Jeff's reaction had been. I doubted very much that either of them would bother to tell me. I decided, though, to give it a few hours before asking one of them directly. To tell the truth, I was a little scared of what they might say, and what I might have to do next.

In the meantime, I tried to catch up during the morning with some of the work which I had neglected in the aftermath of Helen's death. It was strange how life in the firm had more or less returned to normal. Helen had been one of the most popular lawyers at Doveley's, but most of the time people on my floor were now carrying on as if nothing had happened to her. I hadn't been expecting an organised collective wailing every morning, but I had thought that a few more people would stop for an occasional word with me, to say they were sorry for my loss and to ask how I was coping. I did wonder if I was still being blamed in some quarters for Helen's decision to kill herself. However, it was hardly something which I could ask people about.

Rosemary was my closest ally, but that morning she was tapping away busily on her latest legal update for the second floor's fee earners. She had been an intellectual property specialist in the days when she practised as a solicitor. Now that she was a professional support lawyer, her ambit had broadened so that she provided assistance both to the general Commercial team and to some of the various smaller teams which worked closely with us, including Tax, Employment and Pensions. Once a month she would devote an entire week to producing a legal update. She would then circulate it with a cheery accompanying message, knowing that most recipients would only scan the contents page for anything directly relevant to their current matters before deleting the rest of it unread. Soul-destroying work for anyone reasonably intelligent or conscientious, but most of the time she didn't let it get her down.

Around 11 a.m. Lucy forwarded an e-mail she had received from Max. A couple of seconds later she raised her voice over the divider between our desks. 'Alan,' she said, 'Max has sent me his comments on the draft terms of business. He seems basically happy with them. Have you got time to have a quick look at what he says? I can then make any amendments that you think are necessary.'

I was already reading the e-mail as she spoke. As with many clients, the main point of his comments was to show that he had read what we had drafted for him, and was intelligent enough to understand it. There was nothing which meant that we would have to make any substantive changes.

'It all looks pretty straightforward,' I said. 'Pop round and we'll run through his comments. Then you can reply to him today.'

Lucy walked round the pod, wheeling her chair with her. As she squeezed herself into the gap between me and Rosemary, I got a whiff of a fresh floral perfume. Nothing like the Paco Rabanne perfume which Helen used to wear, but it reminded me that for all her equanimity in the office she was also a young, sexually active woman. I wondered savagely whether Jeff had yet had a closer smell of her than me.

'Reply to his numbered points in the same order,' I said, as we peered together at Max's e-mail on my screen. 'Put your comments in red underneath each of his. Most times you can just say "Yes" or "No" without needing to amend the terms of business. You will need to make some minor amendments to take account of his points 6 and 7 though. On point 8, you will need to include a brief explanation of how the limitation of liability clause works. Once you've drafted your e-mail and made the amendments, wave them in front of me and then you can send the terms of business back to Max for final sign-off. You should have time before your appraisal.' Something occurred to me as I had a final read of Max's e-mail. 'He doesn't mention Helen,' I said. 'Does he know what's happened to her?'

'I guess not,' she said. 'It's the first contact I've had with him since the networking event. And that was before Helen died of course. Jeff told me that Max had bumped into her in the street the night she died, but he wouldn't have known what was going to happen a few hours later.' She paused before going on. 'He might have read about the accident in the newspapers, but as far as I can remember they didn't name Helen. That means he'd have no reason to suppose it was her. I know that Helen was dealing with his office purchase, but Rachel hasn't mentioned his name to me so I guess they've not yet had to break the news to him upstairs in Property. Do you want me to say anything when I e-mail him?'

I thought quickly. I wanted to know how things had been left between Helen and Max. He hadn't liked her questions about the source of his money to fund the office purchase. He probably knew what she suspected. She had been asked by Tom to try to get some more information out of him. And he had been pestering her to meet him away from the office. This might have been because he wanted to reassure her about the source of his money, but I guessed it was more because he had had designs on her. I hadn't forgotten how he had eyed her during that first meeting which Helen and I had had with him. He would have been all over her given the chance, pawing her body with those neatly manicured hands of his. Coincidentally, he had also bumped into Helen on the evening of her death. For all I knew, he might have engineered that encounter. Or he might have made an arrangement to see her later that same evening. I would love to know what had been said. Now I had a natural opportunity to try to find out.

'Leave it with me, Lucy,' I said. 'I'll call him.'

*

The only number I had for Max was his mobile. I hated calling people's mobiles, because I knew how I reacted when my own mobile rang. Calls to my desk phone were to be expected, but whenever my mobile rang, I assumed it was some kind of crisis and always felt my heart accelerate.

'Yes?' Max answered before the second ring.

'Max, it's Alan Gadd from Doveley's. I hope now's a good time to call?'

'How can I help you, Alan?' Not answering my question. No doubt he was waiting to see what I wanted.

'Er, Lucy is going to send you a slightly amended version of your terms of business, taking account of your very helpful comments. Hopefully the terms of business can then go live. However, something has happened at the firm which I thought I ought to inform you about.' I was horribly aware that it must sound as if I was saying 'I've got some good news, and some bad news'.

'Go on.'

'It's Helen Eccles. The solicitor dealing with your office purchase. I'm sorry to have to tell you that she has very sadly died.' Christ, I thought, I was sounding like a BBC newsreader announcing a death in a pandemic. It wasn't as if Helen might otherwise be thought to have died 'very happily'.

There was a silence. Then just the one word. 'When?'

'Er, last week. She had a tragic accident. It's been a terrible shock for everyone.'

'That's awful news, Alan. I'm very sorry to hear it. Please pass on my condolences to those closest to her.'

I wondered how many times Max had said similar phrases before. They all sounded very practised. I recalled how his eyes had followed the line of Helen's buttocks under her skirt as he had followed her to the lift at our meeting. I wondered if he was

142

remembering this now himself.

'Forgive me if it sounds insensitive, Alan,' he went on. 'But it's important that we crack on with the office purchase. Business is booming, and I want to be able to move into the new office as soon as possible. May I ask who has taken over responsibility for the purchase?'

The truth was that I didn't have a clue. I had been so eager to call Max that I hadn't thought to find out beforehand the answer to this most obvious question. 'I'll ask Rachel, Helen's assistant in the Property team, to let you know,' I said. 'But don't worry, Max, your business is our priority. The purchase will be in safe hands.' Christ, I thought, I was now a walking talking advertisement for the firm. Sam would be pleased. I could imagine him giving me one of his thumbs up for that. I knew what I still had to ask Max, but I prevaricated: 'While we are on the phone, Max, can I check that you have been able to hire your new employee successfully, and that there was no attempt to enforce the restrictive covenant?'

'All was fine.'

'Good, good,' I said, taking a deep breath and deciding I had to go for it. 'There's just one other thing, Max. Helen mentioned that you had been suggesting another meeting with her. One that would be more informal than last time. May I ask if you had managed to catch up with each other before she died?' I couldn't help but notice that my final three words were redundant. Max could hardly have caught up with Helen after she'd died.

'No, unfortunately we didn't manage it,' Max said. 'I did bump into her in town one evening. She was on her way to a curry house with, I think, a group of people from your office. So we basically just exchanged a "hello" and went our separate ways.' He paused. 'That must have been quite soon before her death?'

'She died later the same night,' I said carefully. I hadn't mentioned the cause of Helen's death, and with a flush of excitement I wondered if Max was going to reveal some inside knowledge of how she had died which would show that he must have been on the scene.

'How sad,' he said. 'If only I'd known, I'd have … well you understand. Such a shame. You said it was an accident. Something to do with a car?'

'She fell from a multi-storey car park in the town centre.' I then remained silent. I wondered if he was going to speculate about the reason for her fall.

'Poor girl,' was all that he said. He was now the one choosing to remain silent. He clearly wasn't going to ask about the circumstances surrounding Helen's fall. However, the words I had used would, for most people, suggest suicide. Now was the moment when I wanted to ask him where he had been later that night, at around the time that Helen fell. However, my nerve failed me. I could just see him asking me angrily if I was suggesting that he knew more about her death than he was letting on. I had already faced Jeff's anger over my questioning. It would be ten times worse to have that from a client. Especially a client who seemed to be valued so highly by the firm's partnership.

After coming off the call, I wondered whether Max and Helen could have ended up together on the top floor of the multi-storey. Even if they had bumped into each other again after Helen's curry, Helen would hardly have wanted a lift home from Max when she lived just a few minutes' walk away. And if she had wanted one, they would surely have walked up to his car together; whereas, according to P.C. Dawn Smith, Helen had been seen on CCTV walking up the stairway to the top floor on her own. And why else would Helen have gone up there willingly to meet Max? He had been wanting to ask her out for a coffee. She had been tasked by Tom to find out more about Max's source of funds. But in neither case would they have ordinarily met up in a multi-storey car park late at night. That was the natural meeting place of criminals and spies; not a solicitor and her client.

I sent Rachel an e-mail asking her to confirm to Max who was now dealing with the office purchase.

A little later I cast a quick eye over Lucy's amendments to Max's terms of business, and said she could send them out to him.

From time to time, I noticed that Sam kept looking over in my direction. I had questions to ask him relating to why he had parked his car overnight outside Helen's house the weekend before she died, when he was supposed to have been out of Cambridge at a conference. However, I had persuaded myself that the best time to do this was during the meeting I had scheduled with him later in the week. I was trying to pretend to myself that this would give me more time to work out a clever line of questioning. But the truth was that I was dreading having to raise the issue at all.

I dictated instructions for a couple of letters of engagement to new clients, and e-mailed the recording to Hayley. She would then use my instructions to produce versions of the firm's standard letter of engagement, together with all relevant attachments, covering everything from the cost and time frame of my work to which partner the client should complain to if they were unhappy. Needless to say, Sam was the named partner for nearly all of my matters. Hayley would be in her element here, and I wouldn't need to see the letters again until they were presented to me for signature.

With this out of the way, I started thinking about how best to find out from Jeff what Rachel had told him about the Ely file.

23

After Jeff's rudeness in The Drum, I wasn't going to ask him for another meeting. I flushed around the collar at the thought of what he would be likely to say.

However, I clearly had to speak to him in person. The firm's electronic file management system would contain a complete record of e-mails, attendance notes and other documents on the Ely file. But there was no way that Jeff and Rachel would have formally documented any discussion they might have had about the omission to order property searches. They would, at least in the first instance, have discussed it informally, like I had done with Rachel.

After lunch I therefore checked Jeff's electronic diary to make sure that he was not in a meeting. Then I walked up the stairs to the third floor which was where he and the rest of the Corporate team strutted their stuff. Their floor was always a bit noisier than ours. In my experience, corporate lawyers liked to think of themselves as deal makers who didn't have to bother too much about the black letter technicalities of the law. When in their home territory, they were fond of loud conversations, both on the phone and with each other, like kings of the jungle demonstrating their prowess to potential rivals. Even their secretaries had bought into the act: most of them were just a little bit louder, a little bit more demonstrative, than those on other floors. Like attracted like, I supposed. I had often thought that Hayley would have been better suited to life on the third floor, but perhaps she enjoyed being the loud fish in a quieter pond on the second floor.

Jeff was at the pod which he shared with, inevitably, three women: his current trainee solicitor, who was coming towards the end of her six-month seat; his secretary, who was rumoured to have had a long unrequited crush on him; and a recently qualified solicitor who had been recruited from one of the most prestigious firms in the City of London, one of the so-called 'Magic Circle', and who would no doubt start popping babies out as soon as she had got a few years under her belt at Doveley's. Jeff was on the phone to what sounded like a client who was selling their business, leaning back in his chair as he discussed a disclosure letter he had apparently been drafting. To complete the stereotype, I thought, all he needed to do was to pop his polished black Oxford shoes on the desk.

'You must double-check, Dave, that there isn't anything else you need to disclose,' he said, pointing me to an empty chair at the pod next to his own. 'Remember that you are being asked, as an individual, to sign up to a load of warranties in the sale agreement about the state of your business. The disclosure letter is your chance to disclose matters which, if not disclosed, would be a breach of the warranties ...'

On and on he went. All bog-standard advice which he could have read out from a law school text book. None of the finesse that my advice often contained; it was what you expected from corporate lawyers like Jeff. I was honest enough to admit to myself that my views about Jeff, and by association his breed, were coloured by his involvement with Helen; and also by how he had philandered his way through many of the firm's women before her. However, my basic opinion of corporate lawyers as rough diamonds, at best, had been firmly held since my time as a first-year trainee in the equivalent team at my old firm in the North. I had prided myself on my careful handling of document filings at Companies House, only to find out that the experienced lawyers in the team were laughing at me behind my back for enjoying what they saw as 'grunt work'.

Finally, Jeff brought his conversation with Dave to a close.

'Alan,' he said, swivelling in his chair to face me, 'what can I do you for?'

Ha bloody ha, I thought. Self-consciously, I looked to see if the three women at his pod were paying attention to us. The way in which they were all very carefully concentrating on their screens told me that they were. No doubt Jeff had regaled them many times with tales about him, me and Helen.

'Can we have a quick word in private, Jeff, please?' I asked.

Jeff rolled his eyes but got up and led me to the nearest empty room, next to the third-floor kitchen. It was more of a cubby hole than a meeting room, filled almost entirely by a small square table surrounded by four chairs. There was a speaker phone in the centre of the table. I assumed the room was for use when a call with a client needed to be put on loud speaker for everyone involved in the deal to hear. Corporate had a reputation for over-manning their deals. If a client was paying £10 million to buy a business, they weren't going to quibble over whether the lawyers' bill was £10,000 or £15,000. Corporate lawyers therefore usually had little difficulty in reaching their billing targets. This was another sore point with me. I seldom had the luxury of being able to bill all of the time I recorded on a matter, which inevitably affected my realisation rates and therefore the profitability of my work for the firm. What particularly rankled was when, if I was providing support for a corporate deal, they only allocated me a small chunk of their fat fee, knowing that I would struggle to complete my task on budget.

'Fire away,' Jeff said. He had shut the door but neither of us had sat down.

'It's about Helen's Ely file,' I said. 'Did Rachel come and speak to you about it?'

'She did.'

'And?'

'And what?'

'What did she say?'

'She told me that Helen had made a mistake. That Helen hadn't ordered all of the property searches.'

'Did you believe her?'

'No, of course not. I knew she was lying.'

'So what did you do?'

'Nothing.'

I must have looked surprised. Jeff sighed. 'Alan,' he went on, 'Helen had already told me the whole story. About how she discovered that Rachel had screwed up. At the time she told me, she hadn't said anything about her discovery to Rachel. The chances of the mistake ever actually mattering were remote. Rightly or wrongly, I told her to bury it. But she was getting really worked up over it. That impeccable moral streak of hers, no doubt. She confronted Rachel. She later killed herself. God knows why. Rachel saw the opportunity, and decided to blame the mistake on Helen. Nasty piece of work that she is. And dead people can't tell tales.'

I was shocked, not so much by what Jeff had said, but by the matter-of-fact way in which he had said it. I had spent hours agonising over this issue, and here was Jeff summing it up as if it was a problem question in a law school examination. I felt a surge of anger at what seemed to be disloyalty to Helen's memory. Rachel was besmirching Helen's reputation when Helen wasn't around to defend herself. And Jeff was apparently going to let her get away with it.

'You can't just do nothing,' I said. 'It's not right.'

'What I actually said to Rachel was that, if there was a mistake, she needed to report it. So the ball's in her court. I'm not a property lawyer, so I'm not going to second guess what was, and what wasn't, needed.'

'But you must know she isn't going to say anything?'

Jeff shrugged. 'If she does say something, Helen gets the blame. She's not even been buried yet. Is that what you want? Be realistic, Alan, it's a technical mistake which will almost certainly never come to light. Better just to leave it 'as is'. Let people remember Helen for the sort of person she was.'

That last comment reminded me just how much I disliked the man. Jeff had been seeing Helen, at least as far as I knew, for barely two months before she died. I'd been going out with her for nearly six times as long. And the little shit was telling me how Helen ought to be remembered. If I'd had the courage, I would have thrown a punch at him. I had no doubt that, while he was genuinely sorry for her death, it hadn't affected him the way it had done me. I had seen him leering over Lucy while Helen was alive, and I was sure he hadn't stopped doing so after her death. Had he yet made a move on Lucy, and, if so, how had she responded? I even wondered if – God forbid – he was also considering making a move on Rachel. He had described her as a nasty piece of work, but his knowledge of the Ely file meant that he had a degree of power over her; and I wouldn't put it past him to mis-use that power.

How I wished that Helen could have heard him say that it was better to leave things 'as is'. If she had known the sort of person he really was, I wondered if she would have been so keen to jump into his bed. I would have loved to be able to go back in time to when Helen was alive, and play her a recording of Jeff's comment. I could imagine her saying how sorry she was for having misjudged him, and for having rejected me for him. Perhaps she would even have begged me to take her back. I would have been prepared to be magnanimous, I thought.

I wasn't going to say any of this to Jeff, though. At least, not at this stage. And I certainly wasn't going to tell him what I had worked out about how Helen might have died. All right, it seemed incredibly unlikely that Rachel could have killed her, but Jeff would still laugh in my face if I even hinted at it. I needed to do more investigating myself before I could think of telling anyone about my suspicions.

24

After I had finished with Jeff, I had scuttled back down the stairs to the second floor.

I had decided that I had to tackle Lucy. The main thing I wanted to know was whether Jeff had been carrying on with her, at the same time as he had officially been going out with Helen. If he had been, and if Helen had found out about it, it might have contributed to her state of mind on the night she died. But even if he had only got involved with her after Helen's death, it would certainly knock the halo off his head if this became common knowledge. It would be the same if it turned out that he was sniffing around Rachel, although I would have to be careful here because Lucy and Rachel were friends and house mates. I remembered Lucy's 'Poor Jeff' comment on the day Helen died. There wouldn't be many more 'Poor Jeffs' heard around the firm if the true nature of the man was revealed.

I was also interested to find out how Lucy had recognised Max at the networking meeting even though she hadn't apparently met him before. She had said that she had probably seen a photo of him somewhere, but surely that wouldn't be enough for her to recognise him at a distance across a crowded room? Not that I was sure of the significance of this. I didn't see any obvious way in which it could be relevant to Helen's death. However, there was certainly a possible link between Max and Helen's death, and anything which suggested he might be more closely connected to the firm than he had let on ought to be looked into.

Fortunately, I had the perfect excuse to probe Lucy. She

was coming towards the end of her six-month seat in the Commercial team as my trainee. Her next seat, as Jeff had recently made the point of reminding me, was in the Corporate team. That afternoon, I was due to do her end of seat appraisal. The feedback I gave would contribute in due course to the firm's decision on whether or not to offer her a permanent job on qualification. That put me in a position of some power over her, which I confess I was looking forward to. I had had the uncomfortable feeling recently that she was not always appreciative of the hard work I had put in as her supervisor. As was customary with trainees, we had scheduled the appraisal for the end of the working day; the idea being that if it went badly, the supervisor and trainee wouldn't then have to spend the rest of the day looking awkwardly at each other.

Lucy and I had already completed and swapped copies of the paperwork that each of us had to prepare in advance of the appraisal. This covered mostly factual stuff: details of the type of work she had done, people she had worked for, feedback she had had from clients, and so on. The purpose of the face-to-face meeting was to discuss her experiences more generally, and for me then to give my formal assessment of her performance.

We were booked into a staff meeting room on the first floor. As we left the second floor together, Hayley stage-whispered a cheery 'Good luck, Lucy, give him hell'. Lucy was always immaculately dressed and made-up, but I had the impression that she had made a special effort today. Once we were downstairs, I decided to begin with the formal appraisal rather than with what I now thought of as my investigation. With hindsight, that was a mistake.

'Well, Lucy,' I said, after we had gone through the initial paperwork, 'be honest. What have you enjoyed about your seat in Commercial?'

Unusually, her smile lit up her whole face. 'Having you as my supervisor, Alan,' she replied. 'I've learnt such a lot in such a short time. You've given me interesting, challenging and varied work. And even though I know how busy you are, you have always made time to explain things to me. I have never felt out of my depth.'

I felt proud to hear this. I just wished that Sam was in the room as well. One of the points I had emphasized in my case for partnership was my enthusiasm for training up juniors. I didn't believe in the 'sink or swim' policy that other teams, notoriously Corporate, seemed to go by.

'I've mentioned to Sam a few times,' she went on, 'how much I have enjoyed working with you, and how good you are at bringing people on. I think he was really impressed.'

I hadn't always received quite such positive feedback from trainees. One young woman, scared no doubt that I was going to review her unfavourably, had once mentioned to Sam that I had an 'obsessive' interest in her romantic life. The truth had simply been that she often lacked the concentration needed for the cutting-edge type of work I did, and I had been trying to discover the reason why.

I made a careful note of Lucy's comments about me in the relevant box on the appraisal form. Next, I turned to the page where I had to add my own feedback. In days gone by, I had been able to write as much or as little as I wanted here. Naturally, if I had warmed to my trainee, I would have gone to a great deal of trouble to recommend them to the firm; whereas if I hadn't, I would have only provided a bullet point summary of what they had done wrong. However, times had changed, and in the perceived interests of equality and non-discrimination we were now expected to provide much more standardised feedback. In particular, we had to mark trainees on a scale of 1 to 5 in respect of a whole range of skills and qualities, including communication, dependability, team work, self-reliance and eagerness to learn. This had, needless to say, been imposed on us by HR. The same time-wasters who insisted that, when interviewing potential new recruits, we had to ask them all the same initial questions: including gems such as, 'Can you give us an example of when you learnt from a mistake?'.

In all fairness to myself, I had been intending to give Lucy generally good marks anyway. However, I felt that she deserved a little more credit for having recognised the contribution I had made to the success of her seat. I therefore gave her mostly '5s' (outstanding) with a few '4s' (very good) to show that I had carefully weighed up each of her skills and qualities. I added a few helpful comments in the small box at the end, on the lines of 'Lucy will perform even better once she has had more experience of XYZ'.

The appraisal had taken around three quarters of an hour. We both signed the completed form and I left it with Lucy to give to HR.

Now it was time to move on to what for me was the main purpose of the meeting. Rather than jump straight in, I decided to test the waters inch by inch.

'Once you've gone upstairs to Corporate, Lucy,' I said, 'things will be very different. You won't get the same kind of support as you've had from me. They have a reputation for dumping all their crap on trainees.' I thought a bit of slang would go down well, to show her that although I was her supervisor I could still relate to her experiences as a trainee. 'I guess you will be a bit apprehensive?'

'Not at all,' she said, 'I'm actually looking forward to it. They always seem so busy up there. And their trainees tell me there's a real team spirit. Everyone feels they've achieved something special when they get a deal over the line. Whereas in Commercial it's often very theoretical. I know it's important legally, but the Commercial team's clients don't always appreciate what we do, in the way they would if we were helping them buy or sell a business.'

I felt as if a leg from my chair had fallen off. That sounded like the kind of thing Jeff would say. I could imagine him holding forth on these lines in The Drum, surrounded by his cheerleaders.

'A lot depends on who your supervisor is, of course,' I said quietly. 'Have you heard yet?'

'Not officially. But the word in the corridors is that it will be

Jeff. I really hope so. He's such a nice guy.'

I had hoped that she had a bit more nous than that. Even if she had been fluttering her eye lashes at him, she must in her heart know the sort of man he was. 'Jeff can certainly make himself sound charming,' I said. 'But, for your own sake, be careful not to take everything he says at face value.'

'What do you mean?' she asked. It sounded horribly like she was pretending to be puzzled.

'Remember, I've been at the firm a lot longer than you,' I replied. 'I've also worked alongside him when he was a trainee in Commercial. Don't quote me on this, but he can take advantage of people's good nature. He has a reputation for taking up with people when he thinks there is something in it for him, then moving on to something or someone else when it suits him. He's a long way from being the kind of person I would trust most in the world, basically.'

I had gone further than I intended, but my resentment at everything Jeff had done to destroy my happiness had taken a grip of me. Why couldn't other people see what he was like?

'That's not my experience of him, Alan,' she said. 'I've always found him very genuine. He's been fantastic to work with on that corporate support job I've been doing.'

'Believe me, Lucy,' I snapped. 'I've seen another side of him. And it's not very pleasant.'

'Do you mean over what happened with Helen? Yes, he told me about that.'

'What do you mean "told you"?'

'Well, he explained that you were finding it difficult to accept her decision to end her relationship with you. That you spent your time belittling her or belittling him. That you just couldn't let it go. I'm sure he must be exaggerating though.'

Lucy made her little speech with a look of innocence on her face, as if she was saying she had heard that I had lost a game of tennis the night before. Her eyes were looking straight into mine and I thought I saw a flash of amusement in them.

'When did he say this?' I asked.

'The last time we went out for a drink,' she said.

The last time, I thought. So she's been out with him for a drink more than once. Funny how she'd not mentioned it to me at the time. I'd not been out for a drink with Lucy the whole time she had been my trainee. I remembered that evening in The Drum when, to impress Sam, I had tried to socialise with other members of the firm. Lucy had, by her body language, made it clear that she had no wish to invite me into her drinking circle.

'This drink,' I asked, 'was it before Helen died, or after?'

For the first time she hesitated. 'Er, before, I think.'

'And who else was there?'

'It was just me and Jeff.'

'Did Helen know?'

'I have no idea. Look, Alan, it wasn't actually that serious between Helen and Jeff, you know. I think Helen just wanted a bit of a laugh after splitting up with you. I had the feeling from Jeff that she hadn't exactly had a huge amount of fun with you.'

I found it hard to believe what I was hearing. Again, Lucy stared into my eyes, her face expressionless. But this time there was no missing the definite glint of enjoyment in her eyes. She was bloody well enjoying this, I realised. God, how everyone in the office must have had fun gossiping about me. I eyed the appraisal form lying on the table next to her. How I wished I could take it back and start the appraisal again from scratch. But I knew, as would she, that this was impossible. One thing did start to make sense, though. To do with Sam Snape's car being parked overnight outside Helen's house the weekend before she died. If Helen had just been after a bit of fun, then maybe she had sought some of that with Sam as well as with Jeff. And maybe Jeff had been having his fun with Lucy at the same time. My mind whirled round in a maelstrom of black thoughts. I decided to try to shoot the messenger.

'And might Jeff have been having some fun too?' I suggested. 'Maybe with someone else up in Property? I had heard a whisper that he and Rachel were quite friendly. I know Rachel has a new boyfriend, but that sort of thing doesn't seem to matter these days at this place.'

Even to my own ears my voice sounded hoarse, as if I had a cold. Lucy gave me a strange look, as if she had suddenly seen something distasteful in front of her. We had both been sitting with our hands resting on the table in front of us, but now she pulled her hands back and placed them in her lap.

I realised I was on the verge of losing my temper. I decided to change tack. 'About Max,' I said. 'I've been thinking about that time you recognised him at the marketing event on the Science Park. You must have seen him somewhere else before. Where was it?'

There was a long silence. I had read books in which characters were described as having a range of expressions cross their face. I had always thought of this as sloppy writing, recounting something which was physically impossible. Now, though, I saw Lucy's face show puzzlement, understanding, irritation and then a hint of amusement, in that order.

'Now you mention it,' she said, 'I've seen him at our house in Cherry Hinton a couple of times. He's been delivering something to one of my house mates. One of the trainees from the place round the corner.' She meant from one of our rival firms in Cambridge. 'She knows Max quite well apparently. She told me he was moonlighting from his day job. I don't know exactly what he was delivering, but it was obviously expensive and, let's say, it gave my house mate a great deal of pleasure.'

It was clear to me what Lucy was hinting at. And if she was right, all sorts of things regarding Max dropped into place. Helen had wondered how he could be making enough money from his concierge business to buy an office in the heart of Cambridge. She had also wondered why, even if could afford it, he would want to buy rather than continue to rent. However, if Max was dealing in drugs on the side, he would have ample funds. And he might well want to use the purchase of an office as an opportunity to launder his drug profits. It was a horrible thought, but a concierge business and a drugs-dealing business would complement each other perfectly. Max would be rubbing shoulders with the cream of Cambridge society, some of whom would take the opportunity to put business his way on both fronts.

'Did Helen know this about Max?' I asked.

'I never said anything to her,' she replied. 'But Rachel knew about it of course. And it wouldn't surprise me if she had mentioned it to Little Miss Perfect.'

Interesting. In spite of her faux-sophisticated manner throughout the meeting, Lucy couldn't resist getting in a dig at Helen at last. Perhaps, after all, Lucy was jealous of Helen's relationship with Jeff. Perhaps, hard though it was to imagine, Jeff had even rejected Lucy's advances. Though surely that wouldn't be a sufficient motive for Lucy to do anything to harm Helen.

I was much more interested in what Lucy had said about Max. If Max was a drug dealer, and if Helen had cottoned onto this, then might that have been a reason for Max to silence her?

If so, I was going to have to be very careful how I handled things. I didn't want to put myself in any personal danger.

25

Thursday

My mind was still in turmoil the day after my meeting with Lucy. I had no doubt that she would have popped the completed appraisal form in the internal post to HR, then gone back to her cosy house share in Cherry Hinton and regaled Rachel with how she had pulled the wool over my eyes. To tell the truth, though, I was past caring that I had been duped into marking her too highly. I just wanted to know the whole story about Jeff and his various romantic entanglements.

I knew I had to do something quickly. The following day, Friday, I had another meeting scheduled with Sam, to discuss the updates I had made to my partnership business case. I had kept putting off the time when I would try to find out why he had parked his car overnight outside Helen's house; but I couldn't put it off any longer. I now also had to decide whether to tell him of my suspicions about Max. Professionally, I probably had a duty to tell him. However, I didn't want to be the messenger who ended up getting shot.

Before I met Sam, therefore, I had to try to get as much more information as I could out of Jeff. I couldn't face going up to the third floor on spec again. I started sweating at the thought of Jeff's colleagues seeing me arrive and speculating amongst themselves as to what I wanted now. But I also didn't want to send him an e-mail or text. I could hardly spell out what I wanted to ask him, and if instead I vaguely suggested another meeting, he would be quite likely to ignore me.

After mulling things over for a while during the morning, I had an idea. I checked via Jeff's electronic calendar that he wasn't in a meeting. Then I nipped downstairs to an empty client meeting room. There was a phone on the table which wouldn't identify me as the caller. I rang his direct number.

'Jeff here.' Typical of the man. As if he was the only Jeff who counted. None of this 'Good morning, Jeff Parker speaking' telephone protocol that we were instructed to instil into trainees.

'Hello, Jeff, it's Alan. I'm, er, phoning from a meeting room. Look, I'm sorry, but can you spare me another couple of minutes? It's about Helen. It's important.'

I could hear the background whirring of a printer in the silence that followed. Then, the slightly weary response: 'Alan, mate, let's have a drink after work. Not The Drum. The pub on Helen's road. 5.30 p.m. I'll see you there.'

*

It was a miracle that I was able to focus on work for the rest of the day. I did some preparation for my meeting with Sam on Friday. I passed some new work onto Lucy that had just come in from an established client. The client had undergone a corporate re-structuring and now, for tax reasons, wanted all of its registered intellectual property assets - a mixture of patents, trade marks and designs - transferred into a new specialist holding company. It was all pretty straightforward, but I still made a point of deliberately giving Lucy minimal instructions. I felt she deserved no less after what she had done in her appraisal. I chatted a bit with Rosemary, which I think surprised her as normally I only conversed about work matters during core office hours. She seemed glad of a break from something that she was, for some reason, working on for the firm's Diversity and Inclusion Group. And I made a point of asking Hayley a few questions about her young son, wishing only that I had been able to remember his name before she had to gently remind me. I had overheard Jeff say once that he kept details on his phone of the secretaries' children, including their names, ages and hobbies, for precisely this type of situation, and I could now see the sense of it.

Funnily enough, I had never been to the pub which Jeff had suggested, even though it was two minutes' walk from Helen's house. It would have seemed odd to me to traipse over to the Mill Road area to see Helen, and then not to spend the time in her house. I had also always been slightly worried that we might be joined by some random person who Helen knew locally, and who might take over the conversation. On the rare occasions that we had gone out for a drink, it had normally been either in the city centre or somewhere close to where I lived. I walked in the direction of the pub on my own, uncomfortably aware that this was the route that Helen would have taken many hundreds of times before me. The evening Cambridge rush hour was at its busiest, and the quickest people around were those on bicycles or the newer electric scooters. Some of the Mill Road shops were already closing for the day, but I still saw a fair share of bearded woke bros coming out of various food outlets proudly carrying their vegetarian, vegan or ethnic delights. It wasn't just the cold that made me shiver when I walked past Helen's front door. I hadn't been so close to her house since the Saturday morning when I had seen Sam's car. The windows of her house were dark, and I wondered who was collecting the post and dealing with the other practicalities of an unoccupied property.

I was at the pub before Jeff, at around 5.15 p.m. If it had been situated in an inner-city part of somewhere like Manchester, it would have been a classic 'old man's pub'. But this was Cambridge, and even in the Mill Road area you weren't going to find many pubs used exclusively by pensioners reminiscing about the good old days. There was a traditional sign on the outside brick wall of the pub announcing the supply of good ales and hot food, and the presence of a beer garden; but there was also a blackboard on the pavement outside the front door on which the weekend's special activities, centring around live music, were being promoted in multi-coloured chalk.

Once inside, I got myself a pint of Carlsberg, sat down at a table for two in a discreet corner from where I could see the door, and scrawled through the day's news on my phone while I waited for Jeff. He arrived dead on 5.30 p.m., bought himself a pint of lager as well, and plonked himself down opposite me. No small talk, he waited for me to begin.

'Look, Jeff,' I said, staring down at my hands which were gripping the edge of the table. 'I'll be honest. I was really upset when I split up with Helen. When she started going out with you, I was jealous as hell. Part of me was hoping that you and she wouldn't last, for obvious reasons. But, I suppose, another part of me was hoping that you might be serious about each other. That way I could try to persuade myself that the rejection wasn't so personal, that she was wanting something a bit different from me rather than just wanting to get away from me period. If you had split up with her, and then she had decided not come back to me, but instead to take up with someone else, well ... well I don't think I could have coped with that. It would have felt like she wanted anyone but me. Since she died, I have heard a few things. And ... and I just don't know what was going on in her life. How serious you two were. Whether there was anyone else. Either for you, or for her ...' To my horror, my voice started to break and I felt tears in the corners of my eyes.

I was half-expecting Jeff to start laughing at me. If it had been the other way round, I would probably have taken some pleasure in seeing him break down. Instead, there was a long silence. There were only a handful of other people in the pub and I could hear the sound of a pint being poured at the bar. Eventually I raised my eyes to meet Jeff's. He was looking straight back at me, and I was surprised to see a kind of wistful smile on his face. For a moment he looked just like any other youngish, not completely self-assured, guy in a pub, not the Svengali of my imagination.

'You've been talking to Lucy, I suppose?'

'Yes. How did you know that?'

He took a big gulp of his lager, then seemed to come to

some sort of decision. 'It's not difficult. Though Lucy's got an agenda of her own, of course. Look, I'll tell you how things were between me and Helen. I'd liked her for a long time. But nothing happened between us until after the two of you had split up. Once we started seeing each other, I was really keen. Much keener than I usually am, to be honest. It sounds silly, but I was never quite sure why she broke up with you. OK, you and I are chalk and cheese, but she'd known that from the start and you two were together for, what, about a year?' I nodded. Now wasn't the time to say exactly how many months, weeks and days we had been together. 'At first,' he went on, 'I thought she was just as keen on me. But very quickly I started to feel that she saw me more as a friend. She talked to me about the Ely file obviously, but there was other stuff, personal stuff, that you wouldn't normally share with a boyfriend. That was something new for me, to tell you the truth. I'm not used to being friend-zoned by women.'

It was my turn to take a big gulp of my Carlsberg. There was a question I was itching to ask, but I didn't have the courage. How I wished I was one of those men that could ask a question about sex in a bantering way, so that I could get information without looking like I was taking it too seriously. There was no need, though, as it seemed like Jeff was reading my mind:

'I tried to sound her out as to the reasons why,' he went on slowly. 'I even asked her if there was anything wrong in the bedroom department. But she said not.'

His honesty surprised me. In terms of both asking Helen, and telling me. I had spent ages during my time with Helen trying to second guess what she had done sexually with previous boyfriends. I had never dared to ask, for fear of a comparison that I wouldn't want to hear. So I had skirted around the subject, dropping hints about things she told me in her fantasies such as whether she wanted, or had ever wanted, to put them into practice. I would probably have rather died than ask her directly if there was, to use Jeff's words, 'anything wrong in the bedroom department'. The fact that Jeff had felt he had to ask, though, did make me feel slightly better. I remembered all the sweat-inducing thoughts I'd had about him and Helen thrashing around together in bed every night, her telling him how good it was and how she had never had experiences like that with me. And now, the idea of him disappointing her sexually, and especially of him being aware of having disappointed her sexually, made me feel magnanimous.

'Well, I suppose we all occasionally have thoughts like that,' I said.

'And so,' he went on, as if I hadn't spoken, 'I tried, like a teenager, to make her jealous. I knew Lucy had taken a shine to me. She was obviously angling for a seat in Corporate, but there was more to it than that. I chatted her up a bit in the office, therefore, knowing that she would tell Rachel, and that Rachel would probably drop a few hints to Helen. I took her out for a drink a couple of times after work, telling Helen that she had asked to pick my brains about her next steps as a trainee. I had a bit of a snog with her after our last drink. I didn't tell Helen that last bit of course, but it would have been pretty clear to her that something was going on.'

You really are a shit, I thought, immediately banishing all gratitude for his honesty with me. Not only had Jeff taken up with my girlfriend; it turned out now that he had also been snogging my fucking trainee. The trainee who supposedly already had a long-time boyfriend. The trainee who had only the previous day been making eyes at me in her appraisal and telling me what a great boss I had been, before then turning the tables and making critical comments about how I had handled the break-up with Helen. I could imagine easily enough what Lucy would have said to HR if I'd grabbed her and asked her for a snog in the meeting room. My feet wouldn't have touched the ground on my way out of Doveley's with my P45. I clenched my fists under the table. What was coming next, I thought, a joke about Jeff popping round to give my mother a good seeing-to while my father was at work?

'Wasn't she upset?' was all I said though.

'No.' Jeff didn't seem to be aware of the effect his words were having on me. He was looking in my direction, but not as far as I could tell at me. 'That's the strange thing, Alan. She made a jokey remark about Lucy trying to get on the right side of her future boss. With any other woman, even with some of the cool girls, there would have been a bit of an edge in her remark. Some wariness, even if not jealousy. But Helen genuinely didn't seem concerned. In fact, and it's not something I wanted to admit even to myself, I wondered whether she was even encouraging me with Lucy. Whether, in other words, she was hoping that I might break things off with her, rather than her having to do so with me. And that's something I will never now know the answer to.'

Jeff drained his pint. I didn't ask him if he'd like another. He got up and offered me a handshake. I accepted automatically. Apart from when we had first been introduced, more than six years ago, I didn't think I had ever shaken Jeff's hand; and now I had done so twice in a week. He pushed his chair back under the table and walked out of the pub without another word.

I stayed a while to finish my pint. I hadn't told Jeff about me having seen Sam Snape's car outside Helen's house that Saturday morning before she died. I wasn't trying to spare his feelings. Part of me would have loved to see him digest this information on top of everything else. It might really have rubbed his nose in the fact that he wasn't the bee's knees to women, and that Helen might have been obtaining her sexual satisfaction elsewhere. But now hadn't been the right time. I could always tell him about this on another occasion. First, I wanted to try to find out more from Sam myself.

26

Friday

With hindsight, it might have seemed odd that I'd had so little contact with Sam since Helen's death. All right, he'd come over to our pod after he had broken the news, to express platitudes about what a loss it was. And most days we had continued to nod our usual good mornings and good nights to each other, occasionally even exchanging a 'How are you?' and a 'Fine, thank you' when our paths crossed in the second-floor kitchen. But until today, we hadn't had a proper face-to-face conversation since our last meeting, before Helen died, to discuss my partnership business case.

However, to tell the truth, this wasn't that much different from how we had previously led our daily lives in the office. Work-wise I was mostly self-supporting – in fact I liked to think that I was a better technical lawyer than Sam. And, socially, well it hardly needs spelling out that we weren't best buddies. Our most common way of communicating was by e-mail, and these were usually terse and to the point.

The purpose of today's meeting was to discuss the feedback that Sam had apparently had from other partners on my updated business case. I had to second guess what this feedback was going to be about, so there was a limit to the preparation I could do. In fact, I had been half-expecting the meeting to be cancelled, and had come in that morning wondering if Sam would have the courtesy to tell me this himself, or if he would delegate the task to Hayley.

'Has Sam said anything about our meeting?' I eventually asked Hayley.

'Such as?' There was the customary cheery mockery in her response. As if she knew what was on my mind, but was waiting for me to come out with it.

'Er, he's not had to reschedule it or anything?'

'Not to my knowledge. Do you want me to ask him?'

Given that Sam was sitting less than twenty metres away, I wasn't going to say 'yes' to that. Instead, I tried, fairly successfully, to submerse myself in my work for the rest of the morning. At a few minutes before 2 p.m., I made a point of gathering my notebook, my partnership application file and a pen, then half-turned in my seat to make sure that Sam was doing something similar. Fortunately, he was.

We did our usual walk together down the stairs to the staff meeting room. Sam said that Helen's funeral was taking place on Wednesday the following week, at a church in St Ives. I asked if he was going, and he said that he'd been invited to deliver a eulogy on behalf of the firm, as the partner who had originally recruited Helen and who had then mentored her as a trainee. He expressed regret that he hadn't managed to see a huge amount of her recently. He wished he had done more than just nod a hello to her when he'd seen her in the curry house the night she died. However, his wife Julia had apparently bumped into her from time to time at the smart city centre gym they both went to. I wasn't quite sure of the relevance of that last bit.

Once we'd settled down in the meeting room, Sam read out some of the comments he said he'd received from other partners on my partnership business case. All unnamed, needless to say. The gist was that they wanted more evidence of my commitment to bringing in new clients.

'Here's what one very senior partner says,' said Sam ruefully. ' "Alan is very adroit technically, but has he got what it takes to persuade a FTSE CEO to instruct us rather than one of our rivals in Cambridge? I'm not yet convinced. What has he been doing differently since we saw the first version of the business plan? What *marketing events has he been to? What new contacts has he made and followed up on? What new business has he brought in*?" All very constructive stuff, Alan, as I'm sure you will appreciate. Now, to help me argue your case, how should I respond to that?'

The truth, of course, was that I had been too busy dealing with the aftermath of Helen's death to do anything 'differently'. I wondered what Sam would say if I replied that I had been trying to find out who had been shagging Helen before she died; and speculating about whether that person might even have killed her. I wondered what Sam's law firm partners would think if they knew what I knew about his whereabouts on the Saturday morning before Helen died. And, indeed, what Julia would think.

But now was not the time. 'Well, Sam,' I said, 'I went to that marketing event with Lucy which you recommended. The one on the Science Park, last Monday. It was well worth our time. I made some good contacts and had some promising conversations.'

'Who did you meet? Anyone interesting?'

We both knew that by 'interesting' he meant anyone who might be persuaded to give work to the firm. I mentioned the various people we'd had brief conversations with early on, and then Piers.

'So how have you followed these people up, Alan?'

The only truthful answer was that I had done sod all. I had more sense, though, than to admit to this. At the same time, I didn't dare to claim anything that could be disproved. It would have been stupid to say, for example, that I had left the follow-ups to Lucy. Oh, how she would have loved to tell Sam, with a look of regret on her face, that Alan was remembering things incorrectly, and that in fact Alan hadn't asked her to do any kind of follow-up at all.

'I'm planning to go to next month's event as well,' I lied. 'The people I met last time were fairly junior. I am therefore going to contact them the week before the next event, to see if they are going again and to suggest that they may want to bring a colleague if they have any legal issues they want to discuss with me. That way, I am hoping they might bring someone more senior who is looking for a legal freebie. I can give them some free advice as a loss-leader and then, er, reel them in.'

I was pleased with my fishing analogy; it was the kind of sporting talk that the partnership loved. I could see that Sam was momentarily stumped. He had probably been expecting me to fess up to having done no follow-up planning. He could then have pulled a face and shaken his head and said that unfortunately he would have to feed back to the anonymous partner that I hadn't yet done things sufficiently differently. He therefore tried a different tack:

'What about Piers, Alan? It's always easier to get more work from existing clients of the firm, than from people who aren't yet clients. What cross-selling strategies did you use with him?'

I felt I was now on a roll. 'I had a long hard think about that, Sam. I didn't want to look too pushy, given that he's only just given us his first instruction. I therefore thought it would be better to find out a bit more about the lease we have just done for his company on the new facility in Ely. Next time I see him, I can then talk sensibly about the legal issues surrounding the lease, before going on to suggest other ways in which we may be able to help him. I'm keen to get my hands on their patent licensing work, but he wasn't going to give me that on the basis of one quick chat at a networking event. Therefore, I discussed the Ely lease with Helen before her death, and subsequently also with Rachel and Jeff. I'm now bang up to speed on all the legal issues. I can look forward with confidence to seeing Piers again at next month's event. I have some ideas on the patent licensing front that I can tease him with.'

Quite a speech, I thought. Sam's eyes narrowed. He probably suspected I was bullshitting, but because most partners bullshitted about business development this was hardly something he could pick me up on. I did wonder if I had offered a hostage to fortune in saying that I had discussed the Ely lease with Helen, Jeff and Rachel. If the missed property searches ever came to light, it would be harder for me then to disclaim all knowledge of them. I felt, though, that this was a risk worth taking.

The bigger risks were still to come. I had to use this meeting as an opportunity to get more information out of Sam. In the first place, about Max. Had Sam picked up any information about Max, either from Helen or from someone else?

'I almost forgot to mention it,' I said, 'but Lucy and I also bumped into Max Blake at the networking event. You'll remember that he runs an upmarket concierge business. Helen had been asked to act for him on his purchase of a new office, and I have been drafting his new terms of business as well as giving him advice on a couple of other things. Anyway, you've probably had the heads-up from Tom already, but Helen saw a red flag about a possible money laundering issue. She couldn't understand why Max was buying an office outright in the centre of Cambridge rather than renting one, and she wasn't sure where he was getting his money from either. She reported it to Tom as the firm's MLRO. I believe Tom was going to look into it further, but he also wanted Helen to try to get a bit more information out of Max. I don't know whether she managed to do so before, er, ...'

Sam produced one of his classic smirks. One side of his fleshy lips turned upwards, but he didn't expose his teeth and the expression didn't reach his eyes. 'I know all about this, Alan. It's nothing for you to worry about. Of course, Helen did absolutely the right thing in seeking guidance from Tom. But Max is hardly some Eastern European chancer with a suitcase full of banknotes sprinkled with cocaine.' His lip lifted further, while I decided not to comment on the mixing of his national stereotypes. 'We've known the family for years,' he went on, 'and we are their trusted professional advisers. The father is a source of substantial fee income for the firm. Of course, that doesn't mean that we should ignore our professional responsibilities. Tom gave full consideration to what Helen told him. But he was satisfied that there was no need to take it further. I know that we are always telling trainees to be more commercial, but sometimes we also have to remember that we are mere lawyers. We aren't always best placed to know whether a business decision is a good one or a bad one. And sometimes we can perhaps be a bit too risk adverse. Even me.'

'Do you know if Helen met up with Max again? Tom seemed to be encouraging her to.'

'Just leave it with Tom, Alan. Remember, you aren't a partner, er, just yet.'

It was remarkable how Sam was able to maintain his self-satisfied smile while he was talking. However, his eyes, behind his black-rimmed glasses, were cold and hard. I decided that now was not the time to mention what Lucy had told me about Max's evening deliveries to her housemate and her suspicions of his drug dealing. If Lucy decided to pass on this information herself … well I was sure that Jeff would enjoy covering her back once she was sitting cosily alongside him in the Corporate team. I had bigger fish to fry.

'Yes, of course, Sam,' I said. 'I'm really grateful to Tom for clearing this up.' Sam was already tidying up the paperwork in front of him and getting ready to stand up. I had no time to waste. 'While I have your ear, Sam,' I went on, 'can I ask how happy you are with your Land Cruiser? I've got a Prius, as you know. But I've been thinking of upgrading to a Land Cruiser – although one that's not quite so plush as yours, obviously.' I forced out a chuckle before going on. 'Would you recommend a Land Cruiser? To tell you the truth, I'd completely forgotten that you drove one until I saw yours the weekend before last in the Mill Road area.'

Although it had come out in more of a rush than I had planned, I had thought through carefully the line I was going to take. I hadn't said that I'd seen his car actually parked somewhere, in case he realised straightaway that I must have seen it parked outside Helen's house. That really would be putting my head in a noose, at least professionally. But I'd also not wanted to say that I'd seen him driving the car in the Mill Road area on the Saturday, just in case it had been left parked at

Helen's all weekend – in which case he would know I was lying. I had hoped that my vagueness would cover all possibilities.

I had been expecting some sort of guilty or evasive reply, to which I had prepared a few follow-ups. Instead, Sam simply looked slightly puzzled. 'Do you mean the weekend before Helen died?' he asked.

'Er, yes, I think it probably was. It might have been the Saturday come to think of it.'

'You must have been mistaken then. That weekend I was away at a conference from Friday, straight after work, until Sunday evening. It must have been some other weekend you saw me. Or perhaps you just mistook someone else's car for mine. Anyway, in reply to your question, yes I would definitely recommend the Land Cruiser if that's really the kind of thing you are looking for. It does seem a slightly odd choice, though, for a man in your position. Unless,' he gave me a fresh smirk, this time with a hint of genuine amusement behind it, 'you have a couple of sprogs you haven't told any of us about.'

I threw him a forced smile. I wasn't expecting a response like this, and I had no follow-up ready. It had definitely been the weekend before Helen died that I had seen the car. And it had definitely been his car. I had recognised the personalised number plate. However, unless I was prepared to call Sam a liar, I could hardly tell him this. For the umpteenth time, I wished I had been bold enough to hang around Helen's house on that Saturday morning until Sam had come out. I could maybe then have taken a photograph of the two of them together on the doorstep, possibly even sharing a final kiss. How I would have loved to be able to put such a photograph on the table between us and watch the expression on his face. Or, better still, to send it anonymously to Julia so that I could sit back and enjoy the fallout.

Speaking of Julia, I wondered whether Sam had also told her that he was at a conference all that weekend. Of course, he would have done. He would have had the perfect excuse then to be away from home for two nights. Two nights of sex with Helen, in the soft sweet-smelling bed next to the radiator which I knew so well. The thought of him naked with her, enjoying the feel and taste of her body, made me feel sick. I pictured her doing the kind of things with him that she had used to do with me, as well as perhaps other things that I had never dared asked for. How I would have liked to punch him in the face in that meeting room, and then to kick him hard, where it most hurts, when he went to ground.

Instead, though, I thanked him for his time, and said I would let him know if I won some new business from the contacts I had made at the networking event. I got the usual self-satisfied smile in return. All in all, it hadn't been the best of meetings.

27

The weekend

I'd got through another week at the office. I now had a weekend on my own, back in my flat on the new development.

On Friday night I was too tired to think things through. I cooked myself a fillet steak, done medium rare, with oven chips, onion rings and peas. I washed it down with a bottle of Californian Zinfandel, one of a mixed case of Zinfandels which I had treated myself to before Christmas from a local independent wine merchant. Rather than watch my usual Sky News, I flicked through a variety of trashy dating shows until I chanced upon a female contestant who I found particularly attractive. Unfortunately, she ended up being paired with some oaf who had more muscles than brains. However, it passed the time, and after going to bed I had a surprisingly good night's sleep.

The following morning, I was scheduled to play in a team match at my tennis club. It was the first time I had been selected for the team, and I was looking forward to showing what I could do. Normally the team was picked at least a full week in advance of a match. I had therefore been a bit surprised only to be asked on the Thursday evening to play. However, when I arrived at the club, I soon discovered that one of the regular players had had to pull out on the Thursday morning with a leg injury. I got the impression that various other people had been asked to play before me, but had been unable to turn out at such short notice.

'We're very grateful to you for filling in on this occasion, Alan,' the team captain said.

I couldn't help noticing the 'on this occasion'.

Most of the other players had brought wives or girlfriends to watch them play, but I had come on my own. I found myself wishing that Helen had been there to cheer me on. While my team mates chatted in small groups before the matches started, I used my skipping rope to limber up in front of the club house. We were playing doubles, and I was paired with a middle-aged man, running to a paunch, who was accompanied by his wife and two children. He seemed to be taking a very relaxed approach to the match, joking with our opponents as we hit balls with them in the warm up, whereas I was very nervous and trying to focus on practising my shots.

I have always found it frustrating when others don't pull their weight in team sports. In my early days at Doveley's, I had sometimes turned out for their mixed five-a-side football team, which played matches against other local firms of solicitors, accountants and other professionals. But I used to get irritated by my team mates' preference to treat it as more of a social occasion than a competitive challenge. The captain would rotate players so that everyone, including the weakest female, got an equal amount of time on the pitch, even though this would often cost us the match.

Today I felt that my team mate wasn't really trying his hardest. All right, he hit the ball cleanly and with some real power, but I didn't get the impression that he was chasing every ball down the same way as me. Twice I ended up on the ground when desperately trying to pick up a shot before the second bounce. My team mate, however, gave up on a couple of balls which I thought he could have reached, calling out 'good shot' to our opponents before the ball had even gone dead. Sometimes this kind of thing wouldn't make a difference, but this morning we were up against two strong players who had a very good understanding of where to position themselves on court and who clearly played together regularly. I tried, probably not very successfully, not to let my frustration with my partner show too much. At times, I felt he was keener on cutting the right sort of figure to his family and the other spectators, than on winning the match.

Nevertheless, I still managed to make sure that we reached six games all, which meant a tie break. The controversy started when, on our opponents' first service point, I hit a passing shot down the line on my forehand return. It shot past the opponent who was standing opposite me at the net, and clipped the outside of the sideline a couple of feet from their baseline. I let out a cry of celebration and gave a vigorous fist pump.

'Just out,' said the opponent at the net.

'No, that was in,' I said straightaway. 'It clipped the line. I had a perfect view.'

'I'm afraid not,' said the opponent.

I turned to my team mate. 'You saw it, didn't you? It was in. Absolutely no doubt about it.'

My team mate seemed embarrassed for some reason. 'I didn't have a clear sight, Alan,' he said quietly. 'In any event, it's their call, as the bounce was on their side of the net.'

It was too important a point to let go though. 'That was in, wasn't it?' I called out to the spectators who were sitting at tables behind the fence at the far end of the court. From their position they would have had a perfect view of where the ball landed. I had expected to be backed up, as they were supporters of our team, but there was only an embarrassed silence.

'Come on,' I said to our opponents, 'that ball was definitely in.'

To my amazement, my team mate then said quietly to our opponents, 'The ball was out, good call guys, your point.'

I couldn't believe it. A few seconds earlier he had said that he didn't have a clear sight of the shot. Now he was saying that the ball had been out. I gave him a glare.

'Alan,' he said, 'it's our opponents' call and so it's their point. Let's just play the match.'

I was inwardly furious. I don't know whether our opponents were cheating, or whether their keenness to win had genuinely caused them to believe that the shot was out. Either way, though, they were wrong, and I felt let down that my team mate wasn't backing me up.

We lost the rest of the tie break very easily. I hit a couple of savage top spin forehands that went flying out, and my team mate seemed to have lost all enthusiasm for the contest, flapping at and missing a number of easy volleys. Neither of our opponents looked me in the eye when we shook hands, and my team mate walked off court with them rather than with me.

In the end, the loss of our match made no difference to the overall team result. Our team won by three matches to two. Both teams shared tea and sandwiches in the club house afterwards, where I tried to buttonhole our team captain about the bad call, hoping that he would say something in my favour to the opposing team captain. I was quite put out, therefore, when he said:

'That wasn't the right thing to do, Alan. It's fine to ask politely if a call was in or out, but once the call's been made you have to accept it. You certainly don't try to involve the spectators. I've just had the embarrassment of having to apologise to my opposite number for what happened. Please don't ever do that again.'

Although he stopped there, I could hear in my head the further unspoken words 'If you are ever selected again, that is.'

The injustice rankled all the way home. I take my tennis seriously and I always battle hard; but I am also scrupulously honest when it comes to line calls, and I couldn't understand why my captain wasn't supporting me.

28

That afternoon I tried to forget about the tennis and turned my mind to my investigation into Helen's death. I took out a pad of notepaper and began to put my thoughts into some kind of order. I deliberately didn't use my laptop. Perhaps I was being overly cautious, but I didn't want a record of what I wrote to be embedded on my hard drive. After what had happened with my phone, I wouldn't put it past the police to ask to examine my laptop at some point in the future.

It was obvious that Helen's death wasn't an accident. She had either jumped, or been deliberately pushed.

If she'd jumped, she must have had an overwhelming reason to do so. In spite of what they say about suicide being a cowardly act, it surely takes some guts to climb onto the parapet of a multi-storey car park and throw yourself off. You wouldn't do it because you were worried about whether to report a junior's mistake at work. And you wouldn't do it as a cry for help, hoping to be rescued; no one was going to survive a fall like Helen's.

If it was suicide, I could therefore rule out anything to do with the Ely file. Jeff and I were both convinced that Rachel was lying about the mistake over the missed property searches being Helen's. But even if Rachel was right, Helen was experienced enough to know that these things have a habit of panning out OK in the end. She might have worried herself sick, but not enough to kill herself. Even when she had been at the lowest point in her depressive illness, the previous summer, Helen had never got that wound up over work. She was conscientious, but she knew there was more to life than Doveley's.

I didn't know everything that was going on in her life, but the only other likely reason for suicide was some kind of relationship worry.

I was realistic enough to know that she wouldn't have killed herself over me.

What about Jeff? From what he said, Helen was fairly relaxed about him going out for a drink with Lucy, and hadn't exactly seemed that much into him in the end anyway. But could Jeff be lying? Could Helen have got wind of his snog with Lucy and been broken-hearted by his betrayal? Part of me would have loved that to have happened. If it had, then once other people at the firm learnt the truth, and I would make sure they did, he would never be able to look anyone at Doveley's in the eye again. The pleasure I would get from this would almost be worth the pain of knowing that Helen had fallen so strongly for him after all. However, looking at it objectively, it did seem unlikely. I was aware that women often like to feel they can change a man's ways, but Jeff's reputation as a player was well established and Helen had always had her head screwed on properly.

So was there anyone else? The obvious suspect was Sam Snape. Now, what if Helen had had a thing with him, and he had refused to leave his wife for her? That would certainly explain Helen's relative indifference about Jeff's antics – assuming Jeff was to be believed, of course. But, again, Helen was a down-to-earth pragmatic type. I couldn't see her taking such a drastic course of action over a clichéd married-man-and-other-woman scenario. If he had been stringing her along, she was much more likely to march down to the second floor and give him a good slap in front of everyone else.

However, if Helen hadn't jumped, she must have been pushed. I had already decided that, if it was a push, it must have been something done on the spur of the moment, in an act of passion or anger. No one of even moderate intelligence would plan in advance to kill someone that way. The risk of being recorded by some hidden CCTV camera would be too great. I didn't think a push would need any particular strength, if Helen was in the right position and had been taken unawares. But she would only have let someone get that close to her, on the edge of a deadly drop, if she knew and trusted them. So who could that have been?

Jeff might in theory have had a motive, if he was wanting to play the field and Helen had refused to accept this. But, despise him as I did, I just didn't find this remotely plausible. He'd jump into bed with half the women in the firm, given the chance, but he was more the type to break someone's heart than to break their bones. He would know that, if he was in prison for murder, it would be a very long time before he got his leg over again.

What about Lucy? OK, she'd snogged Jeff and might have wanted more. He might even have used Helen as an excuse not to take it further with her. But Lucy was a smart, modern girl who, I suspected, played the field herself and knew what the score was. I could envisage her pulling the hair of a love rival in the ladies' toilets on a drunken team night out, but no way could I see her deliberately doing something to kill Helen.

How about Rachel? Now, her motive was more plausible. She would have been terrified about not having her contract renewed, if her mistake on the Ely file had come to light. She had her new boyfriend in Cambridge to think about as well as her job. She wouldn't have known, on the night Helen died, that Helen had already discussed her mistake with Jeff and me. Could she therefore have killed Helen in a panicked attempt to cover the mistake up, if Helen had made it clear that she was going to have to report it to the partnership? She was certainly ruthless enough; look at how quickly she had turned things round in her conversation with me to point the finger of blame at Helen. But, once again, how and why would the two of them have ended up on the top floor of the multi-storey car park? Neither was giving the other a lift. They worked in the same building, at the same pod, so even if they were wanting a private conversation why on earth would they have it at a high-up outside location in the cold and dark? It didn't make sense. Besides, Helen was a very kind-hearted person. I was sure she would have tried to reassure Rachel that, if a mistake had been made, it wasn't necessarily the end of the line for her at Doveley's. The firm was ruthless enough when it had to be, but it wasn't always easy to attract bright young lawyers to a city where house prices rivalled those in London but where law firm salaries lagged behind those in the capital. Doveley's was therefore often tolerant of a first mistake if the culprit made a clean breast of things. It was generally only repeat offenders, or first offenders who didn't fess up, who left the firm overnight without even the courtesy of an exit interview with HR. Rachel was therefore an unlikely candidate, but I still had to find out about her movements on the night of Helen's death.

That brought me on to Max. Now, he certainly might have had a motive. Helen suspected he was laundering money, and if what Lucy said was correct then the source of his dirty money might have been drugs. He had been rattled by Helen's questions about why he was buying an office rather than renting one, and where the money to fund the purchase was coming from. He may, or may not, have guessed that Helen would have a professional obligation to report her suspicions. On its own, clearly that wouldn't be sufficient reason for him to silence her. The risks would be too great. But what if, contrary to what he had said, he had met up with Helen again for a coffee? And what if Helen had let slip what she had been told by Lucy, regarding Max's late-night deliveries to Lucy and Rachel's house share in Cherry Hinton? If Max was dealing in drugs, then for all he knew Helen had been told exactly what he had been delivering. In that case, Max would definitely have had a motive for murder. Drug dealers, after all, weren't known for their scrupulousness where human life was concerned. Max, therefore, was very definitely in the frame, and I would need to look further into what he had been up to. I would have to take great care though. I would be no match for him in a fist fight and, in any event, he would probably have access to a weapon such as a gun or a knife. He would also have any number of associates in the Cambridge underworld who could do something nasty to me on his behalf.

Finally, there was Sam. What if he had been having an affair with Helen, and she had threatened to tell his wife? That wasn't really the Helen I remembered, but who knows what someone can do if their heart is being broken. From Sam's perspective, it would have been a threat to his whole conceited existence. Divorces for law firm partners could be ruinously expensive, everyone knew that. Especially where children and private education were involved. There would also be the potential embarrassment for Sam of having his dirty laundry washed in public. Possibly even of a scene at work if Julia had turned up at reception to call her philandering husband out. So Sam certainly might have had a motive to shut Helen up permanently.

My conclusion, therefore, was that the two most likely suspects were Max and Sam. Though I wouldn't rule out any of Jeff, Lucy or Rachel completely. If I'd had a choice, then of the two main suspects I would have preferred the culprit to be Sam. I didn't care for Max: he was smarmy, and had clearly fancied Helen from the off. But exposing him would have been my duty, not anything personal. With Sam, however, it was different. I had had to put up with his conceited smiles and patronising ways for far too long. To bring him down would be a pleasure. Not as much of a pleasure as it would be to pin the blame on Jeff, but I wasn't going to let my personal feelings about him cloud my judgment.

*

It was only in the middle of the Saturday night that another possibility occurred to me. I had had a dream in which Jeff, Max and Sam had together carried me up to the top floor of the multi-storey and thrown me off the top. I had fought for my life, screaming at them that it was unfair to pick on me and that they should pick on someone else instead; but to no avail. I had woken up, sweating, before I had hit the ground. I hadn't been able to get back to sleep, and I had started imagining the night of Helen's death, trying to picture the moment when Max, or Sam, or someone else had heaved her over the parapet. An image came into my mind of Helen leaning over the parapet, head out of sight and buttocks tight under her skirt. I started to remember some of the sexual fantasies that she had shared with me, fantasies in which she had had sex with people she had never met before and would never meet again. Fantasies which had aroused me, but which had also made me feel incredibly insecure. Could Helen, I now wondered, have arranged to meet some random man from a hook-up website at the top of the multi-storey, with a view to having sex with him up there? Could the risk of being caught in flagrante, whether by another user of the car park or by CCTV, have been the attraction? Could the stranger have bent her forwards over the parapet and then, while she was at her most vulnerable with her knickers round her ankles, heaved her over? The thought made me feel sick, but I also felt a horrible fascination. At times, in bed with Helen, I had had glimpses of a person I felt I had never really known. Someone who was wanting something which I could not give. Was it possible that she had decided to turn a fantasy into reality, and that the reality had gone horribly wrong?

I woke up the next morning feeling slightly ashamed of my night-time thoughts. Even if Helen had wanted anonymous sex at the top of the multi-storey, it was inconceivable that her chosen partner would deliberately kill her. That really was the stuff of second-rate fiction. But, I now wondered, could she have fallen by accident in the course of such a sexual encounter? I had a book in my true crime collection about the death of a nurse in Saudi Arabia in the 1970s. Her body and that of another man had been found in the street below an apartment in which they had been present at a party. The official investigation, disputed by the family, had concluded that the couple had fallen from the balcony while drunk, possibly after or during a sexual encounter. But in my case, surely any evidence of sexual activity at around the time of Helen's death would have been picked up in her post mortem? As would any absence of knickers or other clothing. I wasn't going to make a fool of myself by asking P.C. Smith, but I was as certain as I could be that this was a red herring.

*

It was with some relief that I spent much of Sunday planning how I would take my investigation forward. I felt safer once I was back with my familiar suspects. I had to be careful though. I didn't want to risk my physical safety in the case of Max; and I didn't want to risk my job and my partnership prospects, such as they were, in the case of Sam. In the end, though, I had worked out what I had to do next.

But first I had to get through Helen's funeral the following week.

29

Wednesday

It was often the small things that I ended up worrying about the most.

My first worry that day was that I might be late for the funeral. It was taking place at 12 p.m. at a small church in the centre of St Ives, the market town about 15 miles from Cambridge. The e-mail which had been sent around the firm didn't give directions to the church, nor did it say where it was possible to park. I had set off in good time for the service, but I got confused by the town's one-way system, and then the first two car parks I tried were full.

I hadn't wanted to face anyone at the office that morning, so I had sent an e-mail to Hayley first thing saying that I was working from home until I left for the funeral. I was a bit put out when she simply replied 'OK'. I had hoped she might at least express some concern for how I must be feeling. I had been mostly out of the office on Monday and Tuesday, visiting clients, so I wasn't sure how many other people from the firm would be going to the funeral. Sam would be there, of course, as he was giving a eulogy, and Jeff would undoubtedly put in an appearance as the grieving boyfriend; but it was a big ask to expect other busy lawyers to take a half day out of the office, time which they would have to make up afterwards one way or another.

When at last I found somewhere to park in St Ives, I discovered that I couldn't pay for my parking ticket by phone.

I rarely carried coins, so I had to buy something with a ten-pound note from a nearby newsagent to get enough coins for a two-hour stay. Then I had to use Google Maps on my phone to get me to the church. It was one of the warmest days of the year so far, and a lot of people were wandering around the town centre slowly and, to my mind, aimlessly. It was approaching the time of the service, and I had to gently encourage a few elderly individuals to move out of my way in order not to risk being late.

My next worry was where to sit when I arrived at the church. Around half the seats were already filled, and there was no indication of where I should go. I looked around for a familiar face, but I seemed to have been the first from the firm to arrive. I didn't want to hang around looking indecisive, so I chose a random seat at the end of the third row back from the front. To avoid feeling too self-conscious, I studied the Order of Service which had been placed on each of the chairs. There was a photograph of Helen on the front - not one I had ever seen before although it looked fairly recent. She was sitting on a sofa in a room I didn't recognise, with a glass of red wine in her hand – her hair was as tousled as ever and she had a relaxed, warm smile on her face. The service was evidently going to be very traditional, including 'The Lord's Prayer', 'Jerusalem', and 'Abide with Me'. How much of that would have been Helen's choice, and how much her family's, I didn't know. Sam was down to deliver one of the eulogies. Although this wasn't a surprise, I still felt a stab of irritation at the sight of his name. I wouldn't have felt up to delivering a eulogy myself, but it would have been nice to have been asked.

After a couple of minutes, I turned round to find out if Sam had arrived yet. I was taken aback to see the back two rows now mostly filled with what must have been a couple of dozen people from Doveley's. Sam was there, his wavy brown hair as carefully arranged as ever. He was flanked by Jeff and Rachel, both of them looking very thoughtful and solemn. Next to Rachel were some of the solicitors and secretaries from the Property team. The rest were a mixture of Helen's personal friends and people from other teams with whom she had worked closely during her time at the firm. To my astonishment, I saw Rosemary at one end of the back row. She looked as if she had been crying. I remembered the surprise I had felt at seeing her and Helen exchange a warm greeting in the lift shortly before Helen's death. I had never had them down as being particularly close – certainly, Rosemary's name had only ever come up in passing between me and Helen. I felt a bit miffed that Rosemary hadn't contacted me to say that she was coming to the funeral. She should have guessed that I would have appreciated a bit of support.

I was uncomfortably aware that the people from the firm would have seen me sitting on my own near the front. Yet for some reason none of them had come and sat next to me. They must all have come into the church at around the same time, presumably having travelled together from the office in a convoy of four or five cars. Some of them saw me looking at them and gave me a nod. I returned the nods one by one until I realised that I was at risk of looking, as I told myself angrily, like a bloody nodding dog. As I turned back to face the front, I counted the number of empty seats in my vicinity, trying to work out if there would have been space for all of the people from Doveley's to come and sit around me if they had wanted to do so.

Fortunately for my equanimity, an elderly couple sat down next to me at that moment. They looked like typical respectable provincials, and normally I wouldn't have been likely to get into conversation with them. But I found it comforting now to engage them in the usual kind of small talk for situations such as this. I hoped the Doveley's crowd would think that I knew the couple and had arranged to meet them at the service.

I was, however, still relieved when the service started and everyone's focus turned to Helen. I experienced that strange mixture of emotions which I find is common at funerals. Sadness at the death of someone whose life has been cut short, coupled with a slightly guilty relief at still being alive oneself. Of course, I had been deeply shocked by Helen's death, and I still missed her; but I was realistic enough to know that, had she not died, I would no longer have been a significant part of her life. I didn't therefore feel the kind of distress which I can imagine I would have felt if the two of us had still been together.

I enjoyed belting out 'Jerusalem' with the rest of the congregation – it made me feel as if we were all part of the same community. And, like everyone else, I bowed my head and tried to keep my mind on track as the minister led us through the various prayers, poems, quotations and readings.

The first eulogy was given by Helen's father, a grey-haired man probably in his early sixties. In normal circumstances he could have been described as sprightly, but today he moved slowly across the church floor and looked haunted. I had never met him, or indeed any of Helen's family before, but she had often spoken fondly of him, describing herself as having been a 'daddy's girl' when younger. He broke down a couple of times as he talked about Helen's early life and what she had wanted to do when she grew up. On the second occasion, he said that he would have given anything to have had Helen burying him, rather than have been the one burying her. It was all very moving but also, if I am honest, slightly embarrassing. I stared hard at my Order of Service silently wishing he would pull himself together.

I had been dreading Sam's eulogy. I knew he had been her first supervisor at the firm when she was a trainee; but she had never spoken of him as a friend, or indeed with any particular affection, so I was still a bit annoyed that he had been chosen to speak. People who didn't know anything about her time at the firm would get the impression that he had had a more important part in her professional life than was actually the case. Of course, I wasn't going to say this to the elderly couple sitting next to me, but I wished they were aware of the truth.

I will give Sam his credit. He looked the part as he stood up during the singing of the second hymn and walked slowly and solemnly to the front. As he passed my row, he turned his head in my direction and lifted one side of his lips in what I supposed was a gesture of recognition. To me, though, it looked like a triumphal smile. I wondered irritably if he was going to give me one of his thumbs-ups as well.

'I am here,' he began, when the singing died away, 'to pay tribute to someone who had many dear friends at her place of work. Everyone at Doveley's who knew Helen would have wanted to speak of the affection she inspired. I feel very humble, as the partner who originally brought her to the firm and who subsequently mentored her as a trainee, to have been invited to speak on her behalf ...'

Christ, I thought, typical bloody Sam. In a matter of a few seconds, he has advertised the name of the firm, let people know that he was clever enough to have recruited Helen, and underlined his own status as a partner.

Sam went on to talk about Helen's time as a trainee at the firm. How she had impressed both colleagues and clients in each of the teams in which she had worked. How she had been offered a job on qualification in each of these teams. How she had done so well in the Property team since choosing them. How she had become a trusted adviser to many of the firm's clients. How she had devoted so much time to mentoring the trainees and more junior solicitors in her team. How she always found time to keep up with her many friends around the firm even when no longer working closely with them. And so on.

To be fair, I wouldn't have disagreed with any of this.

'Of course,' Sam went on, 'not everything in Helen's personal life was yet complete. She would have loved to have settled down with someone with whom she could spend the rest of the life, but one of the sadnesses of what happened is that she had not yet managed to do so ...'

I felt my cheeks burn. The cheeky sod, I thought. The implication was that I hadn't been the right person for Helen. What on earth gave Sam the right to stand up there in front of everyone and pontificate about Helen's love life. Especially when he might, secretly, have been a part of it. Of course, I wasn't going to interrupt the service to say something, but it wasn't fair of Sam to suggest that I was the reason why Helen and I hadn't settled down together. It had been her decision, and I had respected that, but people should know that if I had had my way Helen and I would have been together now. The only consolation I had was to hope that Jeff was also pissed off by what Sam had said. I was tempted to turn around to see the expression on his face, but I didn't dare to do so in case everyone from Doveley's was looking at me. I spent the next five minutes staring at the floor between my feet while Sam wittered on about what a wonderful person Helen had been.

'I hadn't, sadly, seen much of Helen in the period immediately before her death,' he concluded. 'And that will be a source of regret for me for a long time. How I wish I had been able to spend a few minutes with her on the night she died, when our paths crossed briefly in the Cambridge restaurant where she was surrounded by some of her closest friends. However, the memory of her professionalism, her sense of fun, and her consideration and kindness towards others will remain with me. I shall always feel privileged for having known her. Thank you.'

And that just about did it for me. Sam was claiming not to have seen much of Helen before she jumped, or was pushed. How I wished I had the courage to stand up and call him a liar to his face, in front of everyone in the church. He'd been with her, in her house, the Saturday morning before she died. Almost certainly all of the previous night as well. I'd seen the evidence with my own eyes. Now here he was, with that customary smug smile on his face, saying that 'sadly' he hadn't seen much of her before she died. I bet he'd seen one hell of a lot of her body that night, I told myself furiously. I could picture him now, pawing at her with those fleshy hands of his. How his wife would love to know where he'd been and what he'd been doing, I thought. In fact, how everyone in the church, indeed everyone at Doveley's, would love to know it. And even if they didn't want to know it, they ought to know it, if only to wipe that self-congratulatory smile off his face. I wondered if the police had asked him where he had been that Saturday morning, and if he had lied to them. But then I realised that, unless they had been planning to interview everyone at Doveley's, they would have had no reason to ask anything of Sam. I started to think about how I could get the police to take an interest in him. I was absolutely livid at his hypocrisy.

I turned to watch as Sam left the pulpit and walked back to his place at the end of the back row. I saw Jeff lean over and shake his hand, and mouth a 'Well done'. This really was becoming more than I could take. Did that fool Jeff really have no idea what Sam had been up to with Helen? Or did he just not care? Perhaps if Jeff was busy snogging Lucy, he was happy enough to share Helen with whoever else wanted a go. They were all shits, I thought. I was the only one who had been prepared to devote myself to Helen, and look at all the thanks I had had.

'Abide With Me' is one of my favourite hymns, and I had been looking forward to singing it with gusto at the end of the service. But now, because of how I was feeling, I only went through the motions, just mouthing the words so as not to draw attention to my annoyance. The service finished with a standard Blessing, Dismissal and Recessional, and soon I found myself in the queue to shake hands with Helen's parents outside the entrance to the church.

'I'm Alan Gadd,' I said to her father as I held out my hand, 'a friend of Helen's.' I had expected some kind of recognition. Perhaps a comment about how pleased he was to meet me at last, and how he hoped we could catch up further at the reception so I could tell him more about my time with his daughter. Instead, he returned my grip with a perfunctory, 'Pleased to meet you, and thank you for coming,' and already he was looking over my shoulder and preparing to shake hands with the person behind me. I couldn't help but wonder if Helen had ever actually mentioned me to her parents. There was so much I didn't understand about what had gone on between us, let alone what had gone on in her private life after we had split up.

I went to the toilet in the hall round the back of the church, expecting on my return to find the Doveley's crowd together somewhere at the front. But there was no sign of any of them, and the rest of the congregation was already dispersing fast. The wake was taking place at a local hotel on the outskirts of St Ives, so I headed off to the car park and once again braved the one-way system. It took me longer than I had expected to get to the hotel, and then I had to struggle to find a space in its cramped car park. When I entered the reception room to which I was directed, I spotted everyone from the firm sitting around two large circular tables at the far end, eating sandwiches and with a mixture of alcoholic and soft drinks in front of them.

Sam was holding court at one table, Jeff at the other. I put some ham sandwiches on a plate, grabbed a glass of orange juice, and made my way over to the tables. No one seemed to notice my arrival. There were no empty chairs, and those that were taken were evenly spaced out around the tables so that there was no obvious place in which I could fit an extra chair for myself. Momentarily, I thought of the pub scene from Ricky Gervais's 'The Office', where David Brent moves a disabled worker in a wheelchair out of the way so he can make room for himself at the table. In the end I managed to squeeze a chair into a gap on Jeff's table between Rachel and a secretary in the Property team, but other than a half-smile and an empty gesture of trying to make space for me without actually moving their chairs, neither of them really acknowledged my arrival.

In the next half hour, I don't think I actually uttered a single complete sentence. I nodded a lot, smiled where I thought it appropriate, and added a lot of 'yesses' and 'noes' to other people's conversations. It transpired that Rachel had spent the night of Helen's death at the house of her new boyfriend, who had picked her up at the curry house straight after the meal. It looked like she could definitely be ruled out as Helen's killer. I desperately wanted to go back to the office, where I wouldn't have to pretend to socialise, but I had the usual worry about everyone starting to talk about me as soon as I left. Eventually, the crew from Property announced that they had to get back to the office for a team meeting. I took advantage of this opportunity to leave at the same time.

Jeff came round the table to shake my hand as I got up. This was now the third time I'd had to shake the little shit's hand in recent weeks. 'Good to see you today, Alan,' he said. 'It can't have been easy for you. I didn't come over before because I guessed you would want some quiet time to think about Helen. I didn't want to intrude.'

That was typical Jeff, always coming out with the right words for the occasion. He made it look so simple. I hadn't tried to put myself in his position that day, but I supposed it couldn't have been too easy for him. He had, after all, been the closest thing to an official boyfriend that Helen had had at the time she had died. People must have wondered, therefore, if her state of mind had been affected by anything he had done. I just wished that some of them would say so openly, rather than keep coming out with all this 'Poor Jeff' crap. If they had liked Helen as much as they were claiming, surely they should be asking some searching questions of him.

Not for the first time recently, I ruminated over the unfairness of much of life as I headed back to Cambridge on my own.

30

The following Monday and Tuesday

With Helen's funeral out of the way, life at Doveley's for most people seemed to return completely to normal.

Lucy had finished her work on the intellectual property transfers, and had done a very satisfactory job. I had only had to make a few minor corrections to her documentation before it could be filed with the relevant authorities. I'll admit to having been slightly surprised. As she had already had her end of seat review, she would have had little to lose by being less than conscientious. It was too late for me to mark her down. I didn't like to give Jeff credit for anything, but I did wonder if he had had a word with her and asked her to pull her weight until she moved up into his team. Perhaps the slimy sod was feeling guilty about something, I thought.

Meanwhile, I was busy producing a suite of new template contracts for use by one of my big institutional clients. The idea was to save them having to use their external lawyers every time they had to draw up a new contract with their suppliers and service users. They wanted something which their administrative people could fill in themselves, without exposing them to any unnecessary legal risk. I was therefore enjoying being unusually creative, drafting the templates with lots of helpful user notes and alternative clauses for different scenarios. It required concentration, but wasn't particularly taxing work, for which I was grateful in my present mood. The best thing was that I had agreed a chunky round-figure price for the entire job. This meant that I didn't have to bother too much about recording every six-minute unit of time accurately. If the job took longer than I had quoted for, that would be my (or, more accurately, the firm's) loss. If, however, I could do it in less time than my quote had anticipated, I would still be able to bill the full amount, which would be bound to please Sam.

Sam, of course, was seldom out of my thoughts. And seldom out of my sight either, as he seemed to spend most of his time after the funeral at his desk, rather than in the mysterious marketing meetings and on the client-care visits that normally took up so much of his time. I did wonder if he had something on his mind. He clearly wasn't broken-hearted over the death of Helen. I doubted he was the type ever to be broken-hearted over anything. But if he'd been carrying on with Helen, it was possible that his wife, Julia, had suspected something. And if he'd done more than carrying on, if he had actually killed Helen, he might be worried that the police could still uncover something, in spite of Helen's death being provisionally categorised as a suicide. In any event, I knew that I had to speak to Julia. She may not herself know the truth about what Sam had been up to, but she might have enough information to enable me to work out the truth. The difficulty I had was in finding a reason to contact her, without raising her or Sam's suspicions as to my motives. I had never spoken to her before, so I could hardly just pick up the phone and ask her if she was having a nice day and by the way did she know where Sam had been on the Saturday morning before Helen died. Finally, I had an idea. I dialled an internal number, which was irritatingly familiar to me, on my desk phone.

'Jeff,' I said, when my nemesis answered, 'what was the name of that gym in town that Helen used to go to?' I had no interest in gyms so I had never bothered to find out its name from Helen. But Jeff worked out from time to time, and I had heard him once comparing the merits of Cambridge's various gyms with some of his Corporate acolytes.

'God knows,' he said, to my initial disappointment, 'but I can find out. One of the secretaries up here goes to the same place. Why do you want to know?'

I was prepared for this. Of course, I wasn't going to give the real reason, namely that according to Sam it was also the gym which Julia went to. 'I hurt my shoulder at tennis,' I said. 'The physio says I need to do some weights to build up its strength. Helen always said that her gym was a great place to work out, so I thought I would give it a go.'

'I'll get back to you,' he said.

And that was that. Five minutes later Jeff had called back with the name and address of the gym. Feeling slightly pleased at my ingenuity, I looked at their website. It was the sort of the place where I could just imagine someone like Sam's wife would want to go. Lots of pages on the website devoted to beauty therapists, massages, sauna and steam rooms, and spa treatments; there was also a café which boasted a named chef, and even a resident hair dresser. You had to make a lot of determined clicks before you got down to the stuff about state-of-the-art gym equipment for cardiovascular workouts. A cynic would think that they weren't serious about attracting hardened gym users.

I sauntered as casually as I could around to Hayley's desk the next time Lucy and Rosemary were both away from our pod.

'Hayley,' I said, 'I was at my new gym this morning before work. Apparently, it's the same one that Sam's wife uses, and I thought I saw her there on one of the machines. I was surprised to see her there so early. Does she usually go there the same time that Sam comes to work?'

'It wouldn't have been Julia,' Hayley replied. If she was surprised at me making small talk, she didn't show it. 'She goes most days during the week, but never before ten o'clock.' She lowered her voice theatrically, 'Sam's always grumbling about her enjoying herself for two hours and then going into the café at twelve when they start serving lunch. She only works part-time as a GP and doesn't actually do any surgeries until the afternoon.'

If Hayley hadn't been able to give me the information I

needed, I had been trying to think of another way to get it from Sam. But now I was able to formulate a plan.

*

The next morning, I came in early and then told Hayley at around 11.15 a.m. that I was taking an early lunch. Relying on what I'd seen on trashy American detective television series, I didn't go into any kind of explanation in case this invited further questions. But Hayley didn't show any interest – she was already reaching over to answer her phone before I had finished speaking.

It took me about fifteen minutes to walk to the gym. I had booked a free two-hour trial pass the night before. I arrived sporting my tennis rucksack into which I had stuffed a towel, my swimming trunks and goggles, and a toiletries bag. I was hoping not to have to use them, but I wasn't sure how closely I would be watched as a potential new member and had thought I'd better be prepared to put in some kind of performance. However, once they had scanned my pass, the two young women at reception went back to talking about their personal Facebook pages and seemed to forget about me entirely. I went into the men's changing rooms, to make it look like I was checking them out, then walked up the stairs to the swimming pool viewing gallery. The pool was almost empty, just one solitary masochist ploughing her way up and down. It was presumably too early for the lunchtime lane swimming enthusiasts. Still no one was paying me any attention, so I went back downstairs and into the café. It was one of those places where the menu choices were written on blackboards, to make it look like they were all carefully chosen for that day. From the way in which some of the writing was smudged, however, I suspected that not much of the menu changed from day to day. I ordered a large americano coffee and a BLT sandwich which looked light on bacon and heavy on tomato and lettuce, and settled down in a chair at a corner table from where I could watch the entrance.

I had been slightly worried that I wouldn't recognise Julia, but the night before I had found a nice close-up photograph of her on her GP practice's website. I therefore knew it was her straightaway when she walked into the café with three other women just after 12 p.m. They were all about the same age, late thirties or early forties, slim, and stylishly but casually dressed. In fact, they could almost have been sisters even though they all had differently coloured or styled hair. Julia had brown, slightly damp-looking hair which fell loosely to her shoulders on either side of her face. I couldn't help but notice that she looked very fit and athletic under her loose clothing. Although the four women were hardly deep in conversation with each other, they projected an aura of exclusivity around themselves which was as effective as a 'Keep Away' sign as they placed their orders and sat down at a free table. But I had no intention of trying to strike up a conversation at this point; I didn't even want to draw any attention to myself. I therefore continued to munch my sandwich and drink my coffee while avoiding any eye contact with them, then I wandered off to the separate lounge area which was between the café and the reception. I settled down in a comfy chair and fiddled with my phone, not bothering to ask for the code for the gym's Internet connection.

I didn't have too long to wait before Julia left the café. I had decided only to approach her if the moment looked right. There would be plenty of other opportunities if it didn't. Fortune favoured me, though, because whilst the four women came out of the café together, Julia then waved the other three a cheery goodbye and disappeared into the adjacent ladies' toilets on her own. When she emerged a few minutes later and headed towards the gym exit, I was already walking from the lounge area in the same direction.

'It's Julia, isn't it? Sam Snape's wife?' I said, in what I hoped was a tone of pleased surprise, as our paths merged just past the reception desk. Close-up, I could tell that her practice's website photograph must have been air-brushed – she was very attractive in a MILF way, but there were definite wrinkles on her forehead, around her mouth, and especially on her neck. I always looked at women's necks; I found it a fail-safe indication of their true age.

'Yes, it is.' She smiled, in a slightly cautious way. She wouldn't have recognised me, and wasn't yet sure if I was someone by whom she would want to be approached or not. She probably thought I was one of her patients about to ask her to inspect my haemorrhoids, I thought.

'I work with your husband. I've seen you occasionally at firm socials. I hadn't realised you were a member here.'

To my dismay, it looked like she was already deciding that I wasn't the sort of person she would want to spend any time with. She gave me a tight smile and her eyes turned towards the exit door, clearly ready to leave as soon as she had completed the least possible pleasantries she could get away with.

'I'm Alan Gadd,' I went on, slightly desperately.

She went very still. Her eyes searched my face. She had a strange, slightly curious expression. Christ, I thought, has Sam really been bad-mouthing me that much? Has he been telling Julia after each of our partnership business case meetings that he is running out of excuses not to recommend me for being made up? Although the content of my meetings with Sam was supposed to be confidential, no one for a second seriously expected the participants not to discuss what was said with their nearest and dearest.

'Of course,' she said eventually. 'You were a, er, friend of Helen's, weren't you?'

That threw me. I hadn't expected her first reaction on hearing my name to think of the connection with Helen. Straightaway, though, I realised that Sam must have talked about Helen's death with Julia. Inevitably he would have mentioned my romantic past with her. And if Julia had bumped into Helen from time to time at the gym, it wouldn't be that surprising if Julia had taken some extra interest in what had happened to her. I went cold at the thought that Helen might even have discussed me in the ladies' changing room with Julia. Surely, I hoped, they hadn't had a girly gossip and giggle about my perceived inadequacies.

'Er, yes,' I said. 'It was terrible what happened to her. Sam gave a very moving eulogy at her funeral.'

There was more than a hint of cynicism in the half-smile that Julia gave me. 'Yes,' she said, 'he's very good at that sort of thing is my Sam.'

I had still been half-expecting her to make her excuses and leave as soon as she decently could. But, instead, she continued to look at me. 'Study' was actually the word that came to mind. I felt a bit like an animal in a zoo. Perhaps, I wondered, this was how she looked at her patients in the surgery. But I'd been very lucky so far because Julia had been the first to bring up the subject of Helen. I had assumed that I would have to, and that was what I had expected to be the most difficult part of our encounter. I decided to take full advantage.

'Sam must have been very upset too,' I said. 'He'd known her since she started at the firm. I hadn't realised, though, that they had stayed close even after they no longer worked with each other.'

Julia gave me another cynical half-smile. Perhaps that was her equivalent of Sam's smirk, I thought. 'I don't think they were that close, to be honest,' she said. 'Sam hardly mentioned her normally.'

I bet he didn't, I thought. He certainly wouldn't have told Julia that he'd been at Helen's house on the Saturday morning, and probably also for the whole of the Friday night, before she died. However, I didn't dare tell Julia straight out when and where I had seen Sam's car. She would be bound to relay this back to him and it would look like I was making mischief. That would be the end of any partnership prospects I had left. I decided to adopt the same kind of vague approach that I had tried with Sam.

'Sam probably didn't even know where she lived,' I said. 'I don't have a clue where most people in my team live. It's funny, though, because I'd dropped something off at Helen's house the Saturday morning before she died. It's just off Mill Road. And I thought I'd seen Sam's car nearby. But when I mentioned it to him in passing, it turned out that he'd been away at a conference all that weekend, so it couldn't have been his car after all.'

I wasn't quite sure how I was going to follow this up if Julia just said nothing. But she gave me a sharp look; this time without the hint of a half-smile.

'You dropped something off at Helen's house on the Saturday morning?' she said. 'What time?'

'Er, very early. I was playing an away match for my tennis club,' I lied, 'so I had to call before I set off for the tennis.'

'Did you see Helen?'

'No, I just put my, er, thing through the letter box.' Christ, I thought, that makes me sound like a flasher. If Julia pressed the point, I quickly decided that I could say it was a work file which Helen had urgently needed to see.

'And where did you think you saw Sam's car?'

This was difficult, just as it had been with Sam. If I said I'd seen Sam's car parked outside Helen's house, Julia was obviously going to confront Sam with this. And that was me then in big trouble. It was easy enough to misidentify a car which went past you at speed. It was much harder to do so if you walked past it when it was parked – especially when, like Sam's car, it had a personalised number plate. I therefore had to reflect in my answer what Sam had said to me, and hope that was enough to get Julia thinking without it looking like I was accusing Sam of something.

'Well, as it turns out, I was mistaken,' I said. 'Sam hadn't been in Cambridge that weekend. I must have mixed his car up with someone else's, or got the weekend wrong.'

My God, I thought, I was making a complete mess of this. First, I all but say that I've seen Sam's car somewhere I shouldn't. Then I say that I was mistaken and I didn't see it at all. She's going to think me a fool, and ask Sam what he is doing employing a fool like me. And Sam is either going to think me a fool as well or, worse, he's going to suspect what I'm up to. I was really beginning to wish that I had never taken that early lunch.

'So was the car parked, or moving?' Julia asked.

'As I said, it wasn't Sam's car after all,' I replied desperately. 'But it was, er, parked.' I could hardly pretend that I didn't know.

Julia gave me a very searching look. 'So when you saw this parked car, which you thought was Sam's, were you driving your own car or were you on foot near Helen's house?'

This was getting worse. She was turning into a jealous wife. I could imagine Sam's reaction if that night she challenged him about my sighting of the car. How I wished I had had the guts on that Saturday morning to spy on Helen's house until Sam had come out. Then I wouldn't have had to get involved in all these games.

'I can't really remember,' I said weakly. 'But I think it may have been while I was walking back from Helen's house towards my own car. But I know now that I got it wrong.'

Julia seemed to come to a decision. 'Yes,' she said, 'you must have made a mistake. An easy one to make. Sam was right, he was at a conference all weekend. It can't have been his car you saw.'

There was nothing really left to say. We exchanged a polite 'nice to meet you' and left the gym together, Julia walking to her red sports car and me heading back to the office on foot. As I walked, I tried to analyse our conversation. At first, when I said that I thought I'd seen Sam's car near Helen's house, Julia had reacted quite violently, as if she had had suspicions about Sam which had now been confirmed. But then, once I had conveyed what Sam had said to me about having been away at a conference, she had immediately accepted that as evidence that I had been mistaken. The only reason I could think of was that she had indeed had suspicions about Sam, but was scared to have her suspicions confirmed for all that would entail. She would probably feel that she would have to confront him, have to decide whether to leave him or try a reconciliation, and so on. I could see how, if the option was open to her, she might prefer to go along with the story that I had made a mistake. That way, she could continue to turn a blind eye to what he was up to, without having to confront the reality of what a shit he really was.

Because the one thing I knew for certain was that I hadn't made a mistake about seeing Sam's car early that Saturday morning before Helen died. It had definitely been Sam's car, and it can't have been a coincidence that it was parked right outside Helen's house. I wasn't going to let this go, even if for now I wasn't sure how to take it forward.

31

Back at the office from the gym, Max's name stared up at me again from my to-do list.

Most solicitors now used one of their computer functions to list their daily tasks. I did this too of course for my longer-term workload, but each morning I also liked to write out by hand a list of things I was planning to do that day. Sometimes, if I was feeling stressed, I would include in the list a few tiny jobs that I knew could be done in a few minutes. I could then have the satisfaction of crossing them off very early in the working day, and this would make the rest of the day's tasks look more manageable. It gave me great pride at the end of a day to look at my list of tasks and see a neat line through each of them. The only downside to my approach was that once a task was on my daily list, I found it almost impossible to go home until it was crossed off. No doubt this was one reason why I normally worked such long hours.

With Max, however, I had broken my own rule. At the start of each of the days since Helen's funeral, I had added his name to my to-do list, and then gone home at the end of the day without having done anything about it. I tried to rationalise this to myself by saying that I was still working out the best way to get information out of him. But, deep down, I knew that I was just scared of tackling him out of the blue.

I had tried scripting a possible telephone conversation, with arrows pointing towards different follow-ups depending on what answers he gave to my initial questions. But nothing quite seemed to work. If I had been scheduled to meet Max for work purposes, I would have found it easier to bring up the circumstances of Helen's death, but the thought of cold calling him as part of my unofficial investigation made me break out in a sweat.

Rosemary had been very pleasant to me since Helen's funeral, and I saw her looking at me in a kindly way a few times while I procrastinated, as if she was minded to say something. However, the thought of her hearing my end of an awkward conversation with Max had made me even more reluctant to phone him. Now that I had met Julia, though, and got not much further forward, I realised that I was running out of excuses. After a final bit of thought, I took my mobile out of the inside pocket of my jacket on the back of my chair:

Hi Max (I WhatsApp-ed)

It's Alan Gadd here. Just checking that the terms of business and revised data protection policy are doing their job? Any questions, just give me a call. No charge for a bit of follow up advice!

Btw, Lucy mentioned she's seen you delivering something to one of her housemates in Cherry Hinton a couple of times. Small world! I hadn't realised you had a second string to your bow. Do let me know if I can help with any legal issues here too.

All the best,
Alan

I wasn't bowled over by my creativity, but it was the best I could come up with. I pressed 'send', then put the mobile face up on my desk. Within seconds there were the two grey ticks to show that my message had been delivered, and almost immediately afterwards the ticks turned blue, showing that Max had read the message. I kept staring at the screen, waiting to see if Max's status would indicate that he was typing a reply.

'Are you OK, Alan?' It was Rosemary.

'Er, yes, thank you,' I said. 'Just seeing if I get a reply to a message.'

She gave me an amused look. 'It's normally only my teenagers who actually watch their screens while they wait for a reply. And then only if it's someone they are romantically interested in.'

'It's a client, as it happens,' I said. 'Max Blake.'

'You must be worried, then, about something. I've never known you message a client before, let alone be desperately hanging on for their reply.' She paused. 'Anything you want to tell me?'

I looked hard at her, expecting to see some hint of teasing on her face. But no, Rosemary looked her usual kindly and motherly self. I had always tried to resist opening up to her, as I didn't want to reveal any weaknesses in the office. And I knew that I couldn't tell her exactly what I was up to. But the thought of going back to my flat straight after work for yet another evening on my own in front of the television, pondering what to do next about Sam and Max, filled me with dread. There would be no harm, I decided, in having a general conversation with Rosemary about how I was feeling. And it might make me feel a little bit better.

'I guess you've got to get home straight after work for your kids?' I asked. 'Otherwise, I was thinking that maybe we could have had a quick drink. But not to worry, maybe some other time?' As always, I found it incredibly difficult just to ask a woman out for a drink, preferring to frame it in such a way that she could say no without making it look like a rejection. I was therefore surprised by her immediate reply:

'A drink after work would be lovely. Where do you want to go?'

I thought quickly. No way did I want to go to The Drum with Rosemary, and have people from the firm wondering what we were doing together. 'There's a pub I was in the other night,' I said. 'Not the most modern of places, but you can always get a place to sit after work. How about there?'

'I'll look forward to it. Shall we leave at five? Or is that a bit early for you?' There was a definite roguish element to her accompanying smile.

'That's fine. If I haven't finished my work, I can, er, always pop back in before going home.' Typically, I was already giving myself and Rosemary an excuse to cut our drink short. If I thought she was looking bored, I could always say I had some urgent client business to finish off.

With The Drum ruled out, I had chosen the first pub that had come to mind – the one on Helen's road where I'd had my drink with Jeff almost two weeks ago. I was fairly sure that no one else from the firm would be there straight after work. Jeff had almost certainly chosen it for that reason for his drink with me – it didn't strike me as his kind of local.

*

Rosemary and I left the office together at 5 p.m. sharp, surrounded by the usual flood of secretaries. Stupidly, I felt guilty for leaving so early. Sam raised an eyebrow as we went, and Hayley did a double take and said something about how nice it was to see me leaving before her for once. I searched her face for an element of sarcasm, but to be fair to her she seemed absolutely sincere. Fortunately, I don't think either of them realised that I was leaving with Rosemary, as opposed to just leaving at the same time as her.

As we walked along the busy Mill Road pavement towards the pub, I desperately tried to remember something about Rosemary's children. I knew she had two teenagers called Alex and Charlie, who seemed to share their time between her and her ex-husband. I knew that one was a boy and one was a girl. I also knew that Alex played in a football team and that Charlie was very musical. But, ridiculous though it must sound, I realised that I didn't know which of them was the boy and which was the girl. Rosemary, of course, had never talked directly to me about them. Everything I knew I had picked up from overheard conversations between her and Hayley, or occasionally between her and Lucy. I decided not to risk making an obvious faux pas, and managed to steer our conversation onto more inconsequential subjects until we reached the pub.

'Well, Alan, what's bothering you then?' Rosemary asked, after I had bought her a dry white wine and myself a pint of Carlsberg, and we had settled down at a table. The same table, ironically, that I had sat at with Jeff. I decided not to share that bit of information with her.

'Um, it's difficult,' I said. 'But, basically, I can't come to terms with what Helen did. It just doesn't seem the kind of thing she would have done. You were at her funeral. You saw the state her father was in. I can't believe she would have been prepared to inflict that kind of suffering on him.'

'When people are that upset, or unhappy, sometimes sadly they can't think beyond the moment,' she said. 'I'm sure that if Helen had known before she died what her own funeral would be like, how many people would be there and how upset they would be, she would never have done what she did. But, unfortunately, whatever her reasons, we have to assume that she just wasn't in a fit state to think all this through. I agree, though, that she didn't seem the sort of person to have taken her own life. I can't say I knew her well, but she came to me for advice on a couple of occasions last year, and she seemed very level-minded. Not the kind of person to do something drastic in a bad moment. But perhaps it just shows that none of us know each other as well as we think we do. Was there anything in particular, though, that you thought she was worried or upset about?'

My first thoughts weren't about Rosemary's question. They were about what she had said immediately before that: about Helen having come to her for advice. Having come to her for advice last year when Helen and I were together. Having done so on more than one occasion too. This was all news to me. I'd had no idea that Rosemary was more than a passing work acquaintance to Helen; let alone someone to whom she would go for advice behind her boyfriend's back. And what on earth could Helen have been asking Rosemary for advice about anyway?

It could hardly be work, as Rosemary's role as a professional support lawyer didn't extend to property law. And, surely, she couldn't have been asking for advice about our relationship? Christ, that was a toe-curling thought, given that Rosemary's desk was next to mine. I did remember, though, that occasion, on the Monday morning after I had seen Sam's car outside Helen's house, when Rosemary had given Helen a warm smile as the two women met in the lift. I should have paid more attention to that at the time. There must have been some kind of connection between the two of them that Helen had never wanted to share with me.

However, I wasn't going to dwell on this in front of Rosemary. 'There were a few things worrying her,' I said. 'Someone who reports to her in Property had messed up on a file, and she was stressing over whether she ought to dob the person in. I've been there too, and yes it worries you to death because you don't want to be responsible for someone else getting into trouble.' I paused, realising that my choice of words hadn't been the most appropriate. 'But you don't kill yourself over it,' I concluded. 'Helen also thought that a client may be using his business to launder dirty money. However, she'd told Tom, the compliance partner, so it wasn't really her responsibility anymore.' I didn't dare say anything at this stage about whether Max might have silenced her to stop her reporting him for drug dealing. 'And she'd had some relationship problems,' I went on, 'but those I know about couldn't realistically have led to what happened.' I paused again, then decided to test the waters regarding Sam. 'I did wonder, though, and please keep this to yourself, whether she might have got involved with Sam Snape. He's married, of course, so that might have made things complicated. He doesn't strike me as her type but, then, he is a partner of course.' We'd all seen it many times. Middle-aged men, nothing special about them in looks or personality, but able to attract all sorts of unlikely women because they wore the badge of partnership. This was something that had always irritated me.

To my surprise, Rosemary burst out laughing.

'Helen definitely didn't have a thing for Sam. She really didn't like him at all. Yes, I know he was the partner who recruited her, but it was never more than a purely professional relationship. On her side at least. Among other things, I don't think she cared for how he treated you. Judging by Sam's keenness to give the eulogy at her funeral, though, I do wonder if there was more to it on his side. I know his wife, Julia, as it happens, and well, without wanting to tell tales out of school, I wouldn't be that surprised if he was looking elsewhere.'

Her last sentence surprised me. Cambridge was a small city, and I could easily imagine how Rosemary's and Julia's paths had crossed socially. But it sounded like Rosemary had some inside information about Julia's marriage. However, I was more interested in what Rosemary had said about Helen not caring for how Sam treated me. I had complained to Helen many times about Sam, but although she had always made sympathetic noises, I had sometimes wondered whether she really understood how badly he could behave.

All in all, I was feeling quite moved by Rosemary's kindness. I was also enjoying the camaraderie of our chat. There were only a few other customers in the pub, and none of them looked like professional office workers. I liked the feeling of superiority that this gave me – I even wondered if this pub might become my private local. I looked again at Rosemary's round face smiling across the table at me, and decided that in spite of her undoubted mousiness she was not unattractive for her age. I remembered now how I had experienced that moment of sexual excitement when she had once told me, in her very middle-class accent, how 'fucking boring' her job was. I had often read how difficult it was for middle-aged divorcees, especially those with children, to meet new men. Perhaps, I mulled, she had been finding it difficult too.

'Rosemary,' I said, 'I'm very grateful to you for coming for a drink tonight. I've really enjoyed it, in spite of, er, the circumstances. I appreciate you probably don't get a chance to go out much in the evenings. But I was thinking that, if you did get a chance to go out one evening, you and I could, er, perhaps go out somewhere for a quiet meal together?'

There was a silence, and then her mouth twitched. 'Are you asking me out, Alan?'

Well, that was certainly why I had included the word 'quiet'. I had read somewhere that inviting a woman for a 'quiet drink' or a 'quiet meal' was a way to indicate that you were looking for a date rather than a natter with a friend. 'Er, yes, I suppose so,' I said, not entirely comfortable with her direct question, but not seeing any way to avoid having to give a direct answer.

Rosemary laid her hands on the table, tilted her head slightly, and gave me what I can only describe as a sweet smile. 'Alan, I'm gay,' she said.

For a moment I wondered if this was her polite way of saying no to a date, without hurting my feelings. But, no, I remembered very quickly that she wasn't a student in a nightclub who wanted to get rid of some random creepy guy without making him angry. This was Rosemary, who had worked alongside me for years and who always hit the ball straight down the line.

'But you …'. Christ, first I nearly said, 'But you were married.' Then I nearly said, 'But you don't look gay.' However, I was a modern enough man to know that I mustn't make either of these comments. If truth be told, though, they were to my mind the obvious comments to want to make. Rosemary had been married, to a man, for a long time, which did raise some interesting questions in anyone's book. And, while of course I knew there wasn't such a thing as 'gay behaviour', I had never caught a hint of Rosemary leering at any of the secretaries.

I was still thinking of the most appropriate reply when Rosemary continued: 'You really didn't know?' she asked.

'No, you've never mentioned it.'

'You've never asked,' she replied with a quiet laugh, in a way that reminded me of the jokey childhood exchange 'I'll show you mine if you show me yours'.

'So do, er, other people know?' I meant people at Doveley's, naturally.

'Well, the Diggers do of course.' I must have looked bewildered. 'Members of the firm's Diversity and Inclusion Group,' she went on. 'They were very helpful to me when I came out, and I now try to give something back. A few other people know as well. I don't go shouting it from the roof tops, but my personal life does sometimes come up in conversation at work and I'm not going to lie about anything. So Hayley and Lucy know, of course.' She paused. 'And so did Helen.'

Sometimes I really did feel like I was living in a parallel universe. When I was at the pod I shared with Rosemary, Hayley and Lucy, the overwhelming majority of any conversations involving the four of us were work-related. Now I had this sudden vision of Rosemary, Lucy and Hayley discussing Rosemary's lesbian love-life every time I got up to go to the printer. Completely ridiculous, I knew, but I really felt as if I didn't know any of them. But I had stopped dwelling on this as soon as Helen's name was mentioned. That was even more of a surprise. Either Helen had kept this information about Rosemary from me during our relationship, or it was, how could I put it, a relatively recent development on the part of Rosemary. I angled desperately for a way to find this out without sounding like a sexual deviant (*Tell me, Rosemary, when did you first sleep with a woman?*'). But I didn't come up with anything in time. Rosemary drained the last of her white wine, placed the empty glass on the table, and brought our conversation to a very definite end:

'Well, as you said, Alan, it's been a very enjoyable drink, and I hope it's been of help to you. But I do have an online Tesco delivery to be in for, so I am going to have to shoot off now. Perhaps we can have another chat over a coffee some time?'

I wondered if, because of my faux pas, I was being down-graded from a 'drink after work' person to a 'lunchtime coffee' person. However, we walked companionably enough back towards Mill Road and its busy shops, and then we went in our different directions – me to the multi-storey, Rosemary to the train station. In spite of all its surprises, I had enjoyed our drink – and I felt it had helped put a few things into perspective. However, in terms of my investigation into Helen's death, it did feel a bit like one step forwards and two steps backwards.

*

As had become my custom, when I got to the multi-storey, I cast an eye into the passageway in which Helen's body had been found. I imagined again what the scene would have looked like on the night she died. Her broken body must have been carried out of the passageway, probably on a stretcher. But now, only a few weeks later, life was going on at the scene of her death as it always had done. Cars and pedestrians were going in and out of the multi-storey just as if no tragedy had occurred. I bet I was the only person there, I thought, who remembered that Helen had died only a few yards away. And no one other than me, I felt, cared in the slightest what had caused Helen to jump … or to have been pushed.

As I drove home slowly in the midst of the evening rush hour traffic, I thought through the implications of what Rosemary had said about Helen not liking Sam. OK, Rosemary might in theory be mistaken about this. However, it seemed unlikely, given that Helen had, for God knows what reason, known and trusted Rosemary enough to ask her for advice. And, assuming Rosemary was right, that must mean that Sam hadn't been involved with Helen after all. And if he hadn't been involved with Helen, there would have been no reason for him to kill her, or indeed for her to kill herself over him.

In which case what on earth had Sam's car been doing parked outside Helen's house? If he and Helen weren't having a relationship, even a casual sexual fling, why would he want to park his car there so early on a Saturday morning, and most probably over the Friday night as well? I supposed there might be some kind of valid reason for him to do so, perhaps involving a client or a mutual friend. But, if so, why had he denied being there with his car? It made no sense at all.

I continued to wrestle with this question all evening, but went to bed not having come up with any kind of plausible explanation.

32

Thursday

I had spent much of Wednesday at the Cambridge Innovation Park North, just off the A10 in Waterbeach, the former garrison town latterly renamed a new town. Like many people in Cambridge, I had steered clear of the town when it was full of squaddies, but now it was starting to look like quite a reasonable place to work or to live. To the surprise of the people I was meeting, I turned down the chance, after we had finished our business, to avail myself of the site's plush facilities and amenities. I preferred to drive straight back to my flat on the other side of Cambridge and concentrate uninterrupted on a new distribution agreement I had been sent to review.

I was therefore no further forward with my investigation when I arrived at the office, just after 9 a.m., on Thursday morning. Rosemary wasn't due in until after lunch, so at least I had the chance to settle in before having to deal with any embarrassing aftermath of our conversation on Tuesday evening. I saw Sam at his desk, but avoided catching his eye. Hayley and Lucy were both already at their desks, leaning towards each other in their chairs and taking turns to whisper into each other's ears. When they saw me walking towards our pod, they immediately stopped whispering and looked straight ahead at their screens. Why did everyone always seem to be talking about me, I thought.

'Did you have a nice drink with Rosemary on Tuesday after work, Alan?' Hayley asked, in her usual louder-than-necessary voice, before I had even finished logging on.

'Er, yes, very nice, thank you,' I said. How the hell did Hayley know that we were going for a drink, I thought? Did Rosemary tell her? Or did Lucy tell her, in which case did Rosemary tell Lucy first? Or did Rosemary tell them both at the same time, as part of some girly gossip session. Christ, were they all discussing me yesterday, with Rosemary laughingly telling them that I had asked her out and hadn't even known that she was gay?

As a distraction, I tried to immerse myself in an e-mail which had come in overnight from another university client in a different part of the country. They were asking for advice on the extent to which some consumer protection regulations would apply to certain of their students in a particular scenario. Students who were being asked to spend tens of thousands of pounds on degrees of indeterminate quality, and who had been asking what were they actually getting for their money. Normally this sort of thing was meat and drink to me. However, the way I was feeling that morning I couldn't be bothered to do more than acknowledge the e-mail and promise to give the in-house lawyer my considered opinion 'as soon as reasonably practicable'.

'Alan, Sam is asking if you can have a word with him straight away, please.' This was Hayley again. Instinctively I spun round in my seat to look over at Sam's pod, wondering where he had gone to in the short time since I had arrived. To my surprise, though, he was sitting motionless in his usual chair, looking straight at me, although unusually there wasn't a trace of his trade mark smirk on his face. 'I've booked you both a staff meeting room,' Hayley went on.

Great, I thought. Sam can't be arsed to walk twenty metres to speak to me; he has to get Hayley to do his dirty work for him. He must be trying to make some kind of point. OK, I said to myself, let's see what he has to say. By the time I had got up, Sam was already in front of me heading downstairs on his own towards the meeting room on the first floor. Clearly, he wasn't in the mood for any of our usual awkward small talk. Once we were seated in the meeting room, he didn't waste time on any pleasantries either: 'Alan, I've had a call from Tom. He's furious. Max Blake's father phoned him late last night. You know how important a client he is. He said that you have been pestering – his word, pestering – Max. Insinuating that he is up to no good. What the hell are you up to? I told you there were no money laundering issues for you to worry about.'

This was the first time that Sam had ever spoken to me in this way. In fact, I had never heard him speak to anyone like this before. After his outburst he just sat there glaring at me in silence. His entire face radiated coldness. Part of me felt like bursting into tears like a little boy. Another part of me wanted to punch him in the face. I did neither. I said: 'The thing is, Sam, I know you told me to leave it alone. But I found out something else about Max that was worrying me.' To my embarrassment I heard a pleading note in my voice, almost as if I was begging him not to be angry with me.

'You found out something else? What are you talking about?'

I was dreading this next bit, but I realised I had no choice. 'Er, Lucy told me that Max had been delivering something to one of her housemates.'

Sam was now looking at me as if I was an idiot.

'Apparently it was a regular thing,' I went on. Sam still said nothing. 'It sounded like it might have been drugs.' There, I had finally come out with it. I didn't dare leave it there, though, for fear of what Sam might say. 'Her housemate said it was something expensive and, well, it sounded like she was on a high afterwards. It all sounded very suspicious. Especially after the money-laundering stuff that Helen was worried about.' Just in time I stopped myself saying that Sam could ask Lucy himself if he didn't believe me. That would make me sound like a primary school kid telling tales to the teacher. Instead, I concluded with what I desperately hoped would be a magisterial flourish. 'I felt I was under a professional obligation to try to find out the truth.'

Sam licked his lips. I could see the dilemma he was now in. His instinct would have been to tell me to ignore what Lucy had said, and probably also to bollock me for good measure. But if I was right, and there must be at least a tiny chance I was right, he was lining himself, and the firm, up for a load of trouble if he dismissed what I was saying out of hand. Especially now that I had brought up the words 'professional obligation'. Getting something like this wrong was striking off territory for a law firm partner. Possibly even something deserving jail time.

I decided to press on while I had Sam on the back foot. 'Of course, I didn't say anything about drugs to Max,' I said. 'I'm not stupid. I just made a comment about him having been seen at Lucy's a couple of times, and how it was a small world, etc. I can show you my WhatsApp message if you like. If that makes him fly off the handle to his father, well doesn't that tell you something?'

Sam only hesitated for a few seconds. Like most partners in law firms, he prided himself on his ability to make decisions when in a tight spot. 'It tells us nothing, Alan,' he replied, 'except that you seem to have a habit of rubbing people up the wrong way. Frankly, I would be pissed off if I was Max. I'm going to pass on to Tom what you've said to me, and I'm sure he will give it proper consideration. But, in the meantime, I'm telling you to leave Max alone. Is that understood?'

So that was Sam's plan. To bollock me, and to cover his own back by passing the responsibility for dealing with my allegations to Tom, the firm's MLRO. This was absolutely typical of the man. It was on the tip of my tongue to ask him what he'd been doing parked outside Helen's house on the Saturday morning before she died. He'd lied to me about that, and he'd also clearly lied to Julia. How I would love to see him try to squirm out of that. Rosemary had dismissed the idea of Sam being involved with Helen, but now that I had Sam's smarmy face in front of me I was becoming convinced again that she was wrong. OK, Helen might have pretended not to find Sam attractive, but she would be far from the first lawyer to badmouth a partner she was secretly jumping into bed with. It could often be the best way to avoid arousing suspicions within a firm. How Sam would hate it, I thought, if Julia found out what he had really been up to. He would face humiliation, and possibly even divorce and financial ruin. With luck, his two children would never speak to him again. That would be reward enough on its own. But if only I could also show that he had killed Helen, that would more than make up for everything he had put me through over the years.

Of course, I didn't let any of this show. I was much too professional for that. 'I won't contact Max again,' I said. 'If he contacts me, I'll let you know straight away. I'm sorry for what happened, Sam. I was just trying to do what I thought was right.'

Even I could tell that this last bit sounded pathetic. How I wished I had the courage to face the man down. It wasn't just the fact that he was a partner that stopped me from punching him in the face. If truth be told, I was also scared of what he might do back to me. As a small child, I had developed the ability to punch bullies once, very hard, on the nose and then to run away while they were on the ground. I could hardly do the same with Sam.

My words were enough, though, to bring the meeting to a natural end. Sam would have felt that he had put me in my place, and that he could pass any difficult decisions to Tom. We left the meeting room together and walked back upstairs together in silence. As before, there was no pretence of amiable small talk. Sam hadn't tried to conceal what he thought of me, and he must have guessed what I thought of him – even if he would have had no idea of how much I knew. Once back on the second floor, we separated and returned to our separate pods. Hayley must have suspected that something had happened, because for once she made no comment, sarcastic or otherwise, about the meeting.

*

After I had sat down, I realised that my heart was beating hard and my hands were trembling. I tried to calm myself down by doing some routine administrative tasks, then I forwarded Lucy an e-mail from a client and asked her to do some initial research into a question I had been asked about the commercial agency rules. Soon I had recovered enough to start thinking rationally about the meeting with Sam. What was interesting was that he had made no mention of me having bumped into Julia at the gym. This indicated that Julia had kept our encounter from him. If she had told Sam about it, he would have asked her what we had talked about, and she would have told him that I had been asking about the whereabouts of his car on that Saturday morning. And if she'd told him that, then as sure as night follows day Sam would have found a way to tear a strip off me for that too. But why would Julia not have said anything to Sam about meeting me, even in passing? It would only have been natural for her to mention that she had met the former boyfriend of the woman whose eulogy Sam had recently delivered. Perhaps the answer was that she didn't trust Sam, but didn't want to know the truth of what he was up to. If so, then I felt that it was in her own interests to be told the truth about where her husband had been that morning. It might cause her and her children grief in the short term, but that was surely better than allowing Sam to get away with it. I needed a way, though, to let Julia know what I had found out.

I remembered what Rosemary had said about knowing Julia personally. She hadn't said how well she knew her, but she had made that cryptic comment, when we had touched on the subject of Sam's marriage, about not being surprised if he was looking elsewhere. That suggested she must know Julia pretty well. This gave me an idea which I mulled over for the rest of the morning. The possible consequences scared me, but I couldn't come up with an alternative. Hayley and Lucy were still at lunch when Rosemary arrived for her afternoon shift, and I decided to strike before I lost my nerve:

'Rosemary,' I said, 'I really enjoyed our drink on Tuesday. I hope it didn't make you late getting home. You were saying, by the way, that you know Julia. It must feel slightly odd, you working here with Sam and being friends with his wife?'

'We're not close friends,' she said, 'but we move in the same circles and we're in a few WhatsApp groups together. Sometimes she sends me a jokey message about Sam, asking me what he's up to or whether he's left the office yet. Why do you ask?'

'Er, no particular reason,' I said. 'Except that I bumped into Julia at the gym the other day. I said that I thought I'd seen Sam's car somewhere, but she said I must have been mistaken. Thinking about it further, though, I know I was right. Er, I don't have her number so could you maybe pass that message onto her? It might be important.'

I trailed off, realising how ridiculous I must be sounding. Rosemary gave me a strange look, but not an unsympathetic one. 'You're up to something, aren't you? It's not something to do with Sam and Helen, is it? I told you on Tuesday that there was nothing going on between the two of them. Believe me, that is true.'

'It's complicated,' I said, 'and I know it sounds strange. But please can you just pass on the message to Julia. Don't say that I asked you to send it. Just say that you were talking to me and I happened to mention that I'd definitely seen Sam's car near Helen's house, and .....' I paused, dreading the next bit but not seeing a way to avoid it. '... and that I'm sure it has something to do with what happened to Helen.'

Well, that was certainly that. I knew that if this ever got back to Sam, I was toast. But I was so angry and upset that for once I didn't care. At the end of the day, I was only saying something which I was certain was true, and which I was convinced he had lied about. I wasn't sure if I would ever have the courage to call him a liar to his face, but at that moment I didn't mind him knowing what I thought about him.

'OK,' she said, 'but presumably you want me to say it in such a way that it doesn't look like you asked me to tell her?'

Rosemary really was a kind person, I thought. Even though she must be thinking that I had gone mad, she was trying to protect me. 'Yes, please,' I said. 'I know it all sounds odd but ...'

'Leave it with me, Alan. And, in case you are worrying, I don't think Julia will say anything about this to Sam.' She paused. 'But, just in case she does, do bear in mind what the consequences for you might be.'

'I know,' I said miserably. 'But I can't go on like this at the firm. Sam doesn't like me anyway, and at the moment I can't do right for doing wrong. If I have to get another job elsewhere, I will do.'

'Wow, and I thought you were a lifer here,' she said. 'But it's no bad thing, you know, to be open to going elsewhere. Sometimes you can stay doing one thing for too long. It can be hard to make a change, job-wise or life-wise, but once you've done it things are often better.'

If it had been me sending the message to Julia, I would have spent half the afternoon drafting and re-drafting my words. Rosemary, on the other hand, took out her mobile, spent a maximum of one minute tapping out a message, read it through once, pressed what I presumed was the 'send' button, and then turned to me and said 'Done'.

My head swam at the enormity of what I'd just got Rosemary to do. For a moment I thought that I was going to be sick. I hadn't seen what Rosemary had written, but I was imagining Sam's reaction if Julia simply forwarded the message straight onto him. He was at his pod now, and I could envisage him storming over and shouting at me in front of everyone. I did this sort of stupid thing so often, I thought in despair. Agonising for ages over something, and then immediately regretting my decision as soon as I had committed to it. How could I have been such an idiot. I had given years of my life to Doveley's, and now I was jeopardising everything. The thought of having to move to another firm, of trying to impress new colleagues who wouldn't know the first thing about me, made me feel absolutely wretched.

*

I can't really remember how I got through the rest of the afternoon. I kept looking over in Sam's direction, dreading to see some kind of indication that Julia had passed on the message from Rosemary. But, no, he seemed engrossed in whatever matter he was working on. I didn't dare ask Rosemary if Julia had replied to, or even read, her message. And Rosemary, perhaps tactfully, didn't say anything to me. I racked my brain for a way in which I could thank her for her help. I wondered if I should offer to give some tennis lessons to her kids, but I cringed at the thought of them begging their mother to make up some excuse as to how they could reasonably say no.

I left the office on the dot of 5 p.m., desperately wanting to do something which would distract me from what I had set in motion. I called at my flat for just long enough to pick up my tennis kit, and then went straight onto the club for the mid-week evening social session which started at 6 p.m. I felt totally friendless, and for once I made a real effort with the other club members, asking my match partners how they were and not taking the games too seriously. This seemed to go down well, and I had a couple of genuinely amiable chats which helped take my mind off things. I didn't really want the session to end, because as long as I was playing tennis, I knew that I was safe from any repercussions from Sam. Even he could hardly rush onto the court and start shouting at me in front of all of the other players. But, eventually, the tennis ended and I found myself back at my flat, scrolling aimlessly through various YouTube videos, imagining what Julia might be telling Sam at that very moment at their house.

The only consolation I had was that there was nothing I could do about it now. Either Julia was going to say something to Sam, or she wasn't. I had no alternative but to go into work as normal tomorrow morning, and find out then if my actions were going to have any consequences.

33

Friday

'Alan, it's Julia.'

My desk phone had rung within minutes of me logging on. Hayley was already at her desk, collating the Commercial team's monthly bills and covering letters to be signed by Sam. Rosemary wasn't due in until later, and Lucy was upstairs on the third floor providing commercial law support on another corporate deal that Jeff was running.

Sam wasn't yet in, fortunately. Walking through the office doors that morning, my heart had been thudding so loudly that I'd been sure that it must be audible to everyone around me. In spite of having used extra deodorant after my shower, the various crevices of my body were wet with warm sweat. I'd had no idea what I was going to do if Sam was already on the second floor, waiting to tackle me over what I had asked Rosemary to send to his wife. Earlier that morning, while eating my breakfast cereal at my flat, I had tried to picture myself standing up to Sam in front of the whole floor, winning admiring glances from people who would be seeing me in a new light. But now that I was in the office, I had a horrible feeling that it would only take one angry word from Sam for me to crumple before him. I felt ashamed of my lack of courage, but knew that there was nothing I could do about it.

The ringing of my phone had been a welcome distraction, but when I heard Julia's voice at the other end of the line, I felt the blood rush to my head. For a couple of seconds, I was dizzy and light-headed. A croaked 'Hello' was all I could manage.

'I've had a message from Rosemary,' she said. 'A rather odd one. To do with Helen's death. Something about you thinking you know what happened?'

I couldn't think of anything to say, but it did sound like she hadn't yet said anything to Sam. Otherwise, he would surely have told her to let him deal with it. And he would then have been lying in wait for me when I arrived at the office.

'I've not mentioned it to Sam,' she went on, as if reading my mind. 'I wanted to speak to you first. Do you really think you know why Helen did what she did?'

'Er, yes,' I said. It was now or never. The fact that she hadn't yet told Sam might mean that she was considering keeping me out of it altogether. My best chance was to tell her what I knew and what I suspected. She might then tell me what she knew and what, if anything, she suspected about Sam. I might then be closer to working out if Helen had been killed, and if so whether the killer was Max or Sam or, however unlikely, someone else. Even if Sam turned out not to have killed Helen, Julia wasn't going to be happy with the way he had lied to her about his whereabouts on the Saturday before Helen died. If I was honest now with Julia, she might be persuaded not to tell Sam how she had found out the truth about what he was up to.

I took a deep breath and launched into my spiel: 'I think I'm close to working out how and why Helen died,' I said. 'I went to the place she fell from and there was an obvious possibility that occurred to me. Since then, I've also been finding out some things about her life before she died. Things which no one else knew about. Things which even the police don't know about.'

'Have you said anything to the police, or to anyone else?'

'No, not yet. I'm not sure the police would believe me, and there's no one else I can talk to.' The missing words 'because I don't have any close friends' hung in the air. 'I was hoping you might be able to fill in some gaps. I might then have enough to be able to go to the police.'

'I'm not sure what I can add,' Julia said slowly, 'but why not tell me everything you know? We can then try and work out together what happened. Helen seemed a nice girl, and I would like to help if I can. When are you free?'

I turned my head to see if Sam had arrived. Luckily, his chair was still empty. 'I can be free now,' I said. 'Let's meet at the car park where Helen died. At the pedestrian entrance at the front.' I looked at my watch. 'How about ten o'clock?'

'I'll be there. Don't tell anyone what you are doing, though. I don't want to have to say anything to Sam until I'm ready.'

My right hand was trembling as I put the phone back on its holder. But with relief rather than fear. I couldn't quite believe my luck. Julia hadn't said anything to Sam, and it looked like she was in no rush to do so. Even if it turned out that Sam was involved with Helen, the chances were that Julia wouldn't tell him how she had found out. I felt that, at long last, I had an ally with whom I could share my thoughts and worries.

'No sign of Sam yet?' I asked Hayley. I was still nervous in case he turned up before I could leave the office.

'No,' she said. 'He's at a client's site until this afternoon. He went straight there from home this morning.' She tilted her head in the direction of my phone. 'Was that someone wanting to speak to him?'

'No,' I said immediately. 'It was someone else.' Hayley gave me a slightly odd look and I thought she was going to ask who had been on the phone. Then she seemed to think better of it and bent her head back down again to the monthly bills. I was relieved that Rosemary wasn't yet in. She would probably have noted the state I was in, and I would have had to lie to her about where I was going.

*

Ten minutes later, I was standing on the pavement outside the front pedestrian entrance to the multi-storey car park. It was less than an hour since I had parked my Prius on the first floor of the same multi-storey, but my mood now was completely

226

different to how it had been earlier. Then, I had been dreading a confrontation with Sam, and I had walked unusually slowly to the office. Now, I was impatient for Julia to arrive, so that I could tell her everything I had found out. In spite of it being a mild morning, I was shivering from a combination of nerves and excitement. The morning rush hour was over, and there was only the occasional car entering and leaving the multi-storey. I kept an eye open for the red sports car in which Julia had come to the gym on Tuesday. I had assumed that, since we were meeting outside the multi-storey, this would be where she would park. However, I had still not seen her car by 10.05 a.m. I was starting to worry that she might have changed her mind about meeting me when I heard a familiar voice right behind me:

'Hello, Alan, I'm sorry I'm late.'

I whirled round. Julia was wearing a long black woollen overcoat, with a scarf over her hair and a pair of large round designer dark glasses. She was so well wrapped up that I wouldn't have recognised her if I hadn't been expecting her. Irrationally I noted that she was hardly dressed for a session at the gym, so she must have prioritised meeting me over her regular morning work-out.

'That's OK,' I said. 'It's, er, given me a few minutes to remember Helen. I park here every day, and I feel guilty sometimes rushing between the car park and the office, not having the time to think about what happened here just a few weeks ago.'

'They found her just down there, didn't they?' she said, lifting a glove-clad hand and indicating with a finger the passageway that ran around the side and the back of the multi-storey. I was slightly surprised that she knew where Helen's body had landed, but I assumed it must have been reported somewhere that I had missed. I shuddered at the thought of a newspaper maybe having published a photograph of the scene with an arrow indicating the exact spot where Helen's broken body had lain.

'Yes,' I said. 'It's all been cleaned up now, but I saw the place where she was found and … and it was horrible.'

'And she jumped from the top floor?' Simultaneously we raised our faces to look up at the top of the multi-storey.

'That's what the police think.'

'But you don't?' I couldn't see anything of Julia's expression behind her dark glasses.

'I'm not sure. There's another possibility which occurred to me when I was up there.'

'You've been to the spot she jumped from?'

'Yes. I wanted to get a feel for what must have been going through her mind to make her jump. But once I was up there, I couldn't imagine her actually doing it. It's terrifying enough just looking over the parapet, let alone climbing over it and letting yourself fall. It's such a long way down that you are guaranteed to be killed. It's not the kind of thing you do if you are only making a cry for help. To jump from the top floor, Helen must have been absolutely desperate, more desperate than I ever knew her to be when we were together. Or ... or if she wasn't that desperate, something else must have happened.'

'Something else? What do you mean?'

'I'll show you.'

I led Julia to the pedestrian entrance and up the stairway to the top floor. There was no one else on the stairs, but by unspoken agreement neither of us said a word to the other. I could smell the usual sharp tang of human urine overlaid with chemical cleanser. Once we were on the top floor, Julia followed me to the far corner where Helen had gone over the parapet. The floor was almost full of cars, but I didn't see anyone else either on foot or in their car. The great majority of the cars would have been parked here first thing, and their owners would either be at work or at the shops.

'It happened here,' I said, leading Julia between two parked SUVs and coming to a halt just before the motorway-style metal barrier which run around the perimeter of the floor just inside the concrete parapet.

Julia shivered. 'It's horrible even to think about it. But what do you think could have happened? Rosemary said something about you thinking it was connected with Sam's car. I assume you mean when you thought you saw his car parked outside Helen's house the Saturday before she died? But I told you that you must have been mistaken. Sam was away at a conference all that weekend.'

'I wasn't mistaken, Julia. I would know Sam's car anywhere. It's got the personalised numberplate, remember. It was definitely parked outside Helen's house. Sam wouldn't have parked it there by chance. He must have been visiting Helen. And, I'm sorry to be so blunt, but a man's car won't be parked outside a woman's house very early on a Saturday morning unless he's spent the night there. Sam must have spent Friday night at Helen's. Now, I may be wrong, it may have nothing to do with why or how she died, but it definitely needs looking into. And I think the police would certainly want to know about it.'

'Are you going to tell them?'

'Yes. I know what that will mean for my future at Doveley's, but I don't think I have any alternative.'

Even now, I didn't dare mention my idea about Sam having heaved Helen over the parapet, after getting her to look down on some pretext. I still had Max in mind as the possible culprit, but Sam was perfectly capable of having done this too.

Julia sank into thought. I imagined what a terrible prospect it must be to have Sam reported to the police. At best, it would all come out about him carrying on with Helen. At worst, well it would destroy her life if her husband was actually to be arrested for murder. 'Let me just look down,' she said eventually. 'I need to understand what must have been going through Helen's mind when she fell.' She climbed slowly over the metal barrier and leant right over the waist-high wall, her hands resting on the top and her face looking straight downwards. Suddenly she cried out: 'My watch. It's slipped off.' Then, after the briefest of pauses: 'My God, I think I can see where it's landed. Down there, look!'

I hadn't noticed anything fall off her arm, but quickly I climbed over the barrier and looked over the wall right next to her. I had forgotten how high up we were and I felt dizzy at the sight of the passageway far below. 'I can't see anything,' I said. I didn't have a clue how Julia could have spotted where her watch had landed.

'It's close to the wall, just about a foot away. Next to the downpipe. Lean over a bit more.'

I leant right over until I could look vertically downwards. I could see the approximate area that Julia was referring to, but I couldn't make out anything other than the dark grey tarmac surface of the passageway with its green sprinkling of weeds. I wondered how much longer I would have to look before I could politely say that I couldn't see her watch. Then something struck me as odd.

'Julia,' I said, 'how did you know that Sam's car was parked right outside Helen's house?' I remembered how careful I had been not to say exactly where I had seen his car. There was silence to the side of me. I half-turned my head, to check that she had heard me. And for just a moment I thought she had disappeared, as her face was no longer level with mine. Then I realised that she had bent down behind me, and just as I was wondering why, I felt her arms grip my legs from behind just around the knees. Then I felt her heaving upwards and my body started to go over the wall.

'Fuck, no,' I cried out. My arms were resting on the top of the wall, with my hands around its outside edge. This meant, to my horror, that my hands had nothing to grip on to stop me going over the top of the wall. In order to turn around, I had raised my head above the height of my body, but as Julia lifted my legs up and pushed, I felt my head go back over the top of the wall and downwards. My body was now balanced evenly on top of the wall, and I knew it would only need one final firm push to send me tumbling over the wall and down to my death on the tarmac below.

'No, please, no,' I yelled in terror. I tried desperately to sink my fingers into something, but there was of course no give in the hard concrete. I knew I was only a second or so from the end. Somehow, in my panic, I managed to free one leg from Julia's grip and frantically I kicked out behind me. If I had missed, I wouldn't have had time for another kick. But, by pure fluke, my kick must have caught her right in the face. I heard a gasp of pain and her grip on my other leg loosened momentarily. I rolled sideways on top of the wall so that my face was looking upwards, just in time to see Julia lunge towards me. Her face was absolutely expressionless; her eyes still hidden behind her large dark glasses. My lower back was flat on the top of the wall, and my neck and head were hanging out unsupported over the drop. I shrieked and kicked out again at her face, conscious even now in my frenzy that I mustn't kick so hard that I would propel myself backwards over the wall. I caught her on the nose and she gasped again with either shock or pain; I couldn't tell which and didn't care. All that mattered was that it stopped her in her tracks. For a brief moment she stood absolutely still. It was all I needed. I rolled off the wall onto the floor of the car park and, sobbing and panting with fright, I threw myself at her. My fist connected again with her nose, and I heard a satisfying crunch as something gave way. It was her turn to cry out loudly. I hit her again in the same place with as much force as I could gather. This time she went down backwards and her dark glasses fell off. I was terrified of allowing her back on her feet in case she tried again to force me over the wall, so I threw myself on top of her. I wrenched off her scarf and grabbed her long hair with one hand, then banged the back of her head three times on the hard floor. The first bang made her cry out again. The second bang drew only a gasp from her. And she made no response to the third. Bright red blood was flowing freely from her nose where I had punched her – it ran down either side of her face and started dripping onto the floor. I could still hear cries of fear and anger, however, and it took me a couple of seconds to realise that they were coming from me.

Still lying on top of Julia and gripping her hair with one hand, I reached inside the pocket of my jacket with my other hand and took out my mobile. I wondered as I opened the cover whether the face recognition software would recognise me in my state of panic, but fortunately it did. I pressed '999' and as soon as I heard the words 'Emergency. Which service?' I cried out 'Help.'

'Which service, please?'

'Police. Help. Someone's trying to kill me.'

'Where are you please?'

'Help. In the car park. Please come quickly.'

I had no idea if the operator would be able to track my location from my phone, but I assumed they probably could. Julia was lying on her back with her eyes closed and breathing evenly. I didn't know or care whether she was conscious. All I cared about was whether she might attack me again. So while I held the mobile against my ear with one hand, I maintained my tight grip on her hair with my other hand in case I needed to give her head another bang on the ground.

The operator was calmly asking me questions, and I tried to reply between pants.

'Who is trying to kill you?'

'Julia. Sam's wife. She tried to throw me off the top of the car park.'

'What is she doing now?'

'Nothing. I'm on top of her. She tried to kill me though. I managed to stop her and I've hit her and I'm trying to stop her attacking me again. Please send someone quickly.'

'Police are on their way. Don't panic. Are either of you hurt?'

'Yes. I've defended myself and I've managed to hurt her.' Even in my panic, I remembered to make sure that I emphasized the element of self-defence.

'Police will be with you very shortly. We have identified your location. Whereabouts are you in the car park?'

'On the top floor. In the corner. Near the wall. Near the wall that she tried to throw me over.' Something suddenly occurred to me. 'Christ, she must have done the same to Helen. She's already thrown someone over the same wall.'

'When? Now?' For the first time there was some emotion in the voice of the operator.

'No, a while back, the woman whose body was found at the

bottom of the car park. The police thought she had jumped. But Julia must have killed her. Oh, God, Julia must have thrown her over the wall just like she tried to do with me.' I knew I was babbling but I wanted to keep the conversation going. I was still terrified of being alone with Julia.

'Police will be with you in less than five minutes. Stay where you are please. And stay on the phone until the police arrive.'

I certainly wasn't going to disobey that last instruction. I have no idea if it took the police longer than five minutes to arrive, or whether it just felt like that. At one point Julia shook her head slightly and opened her eyes, and I heard myself shouting at her to stay still or I'd bang her head again. I tried to control my breathing, but the air was still rasping in and out of my lungs. The hand in which I was holding my phone kept trembling so much that I nearly dropped it a couple of times.

Eventually, I heard a police siren outside the multi-storey. The siren quietened as the car entered the building, then gradually got louder again as the car climbed to the top floor. Somehow the police seemed to have worked out very quickly where Julia and I were on this floor, and I heard their car draw sharply to a halt with a slight screech of its tyres, right at the other end of the SUV behind which we were lying.

'Stay still, both of you,' shouted a young male uniformed police officer as he rushed up to us. Another female officer was right behind him.

'I'm Alan Gadd,' I managed to blurt out. 'I'm a solicitor. This woman has just tried to kill me. She's already killed one person, and she tried to kill me the same way. Please keep her secure.'

'It's all right, sir. We're here now. You can get off the lady.' The two police officers were hesitating slightly. I could tell what they were thinking. Here was a fit-looking youngish man lying on top of an apparently unconscious, bleeding middle-aged woman in the corner of an otherwise deserted car park, holding her hair with one hand while claiming that she had just tried to kill him. It wasn't the kind of situation, I suddenly thought with a flash of dry humour, where they were going to be shouting 'Shotgun' to bagsy the right to keep banging Julia's head against the floor.

'I'll get off,' I said, 'but please keep me safe. That's the wall she tried to throw me over. She killed Helen that way too. Helen's the woman who died here a few weeks ago.'

I saw the two officers look at each other. 'The woman who jumped?' asked the woman.

'Yes. But she didn't jump. She was pushed by Julia.'

I felt Julia move beneath me. She opened her eyes and looked straight at the officers.

'This man has just tried to kill me,' she said. 'He probably also killed Helen. Helen used to be his girlfriend.'

34

I hadn't been expecting to see P.C. Dawn Smith again. At least not in the main local police station. And certainly not on the other side of a table in an interview room. This time she was accompanied by another officer, a slightly older male detective sergeant in a shiny suit and the kind of striped tie you typically find in the cheapest price range in somewhere like Marks & Spencer.

I gathered that Julia had been taken off to Addenbrooke's hospital in an ambulance which had arrived at the multi-storey shortly after the police car. I had made sure I kept my distance from her until she was safely off the scene, notwithstanding the presence of the police and ambulance personnel. The two police officers had then driven me back to their police station. I hadn't done any criminal law since law school, so I'd had no idea if I was going to be interviewed as a victim, a witness, or a potential suspect, and whether I would end up being cautioned or even arrested. And I hadn't wanted to ask. I had, though, been allowed to get into their car under my own steam, rather than have my head pushed in under the roof as you see on television shows, which I had taken as a good omen. I had also been allowed to sit on my own in the back of the car. I didn't know if that was the usual practice if someone was suspected of a crime, but I thought probably not. When we stopped at traffic lights, I did wonder if there was the police equivalent of a child lock in place on the door closest to me to stop me jumping out; however, I didn't dare try to find out.

Julia had certainly been thinking quickly while she was lying beneath me on the floor of the car park. I had been stunned to hear her accuse me of trying to kill her, and of having killed Helen. After her allegation, I had been uncomfortably aware that her face was covered in blood from where I had kicked and punched her hard on the nose, and that there was also some blood in her hair at the back of her head where I had repeatedly banged it against the ground. Whereas, although I was still trembling with shock, I was physically unmarked.

Fortunately, as I gradually realised, the big thing in my favour was that it had been me, not her, who had dialled 999. Outside of some trashy television psychological thriller, it was difficult to imagine any circumstances where I would phone the police for assistance while in the progress of trying to kill my supposed victim. That said, the police probably didn't have many cases where the alleged perpetrator of an attempted murder – Julia - accuses the apparent victim – me - of being the one trying to do the killing. I could see therefore why the police were initially proceeding with a bit of caution. So once at the police station, I was left on my own in a plush modern interview room for about an hour, thinking idly about what was happening back at the office and what if anything Sam had learnt so far. The hardest part was not knowing how long I was going to be kept waiting. I wondered if I was being watched on CCTV while I sat there on my own, and at one point I threw in a couple of theatrical moans and clutched my head as if I couldn't quite believe what was happening to me.

*

When, finally, Dawn and her plainclothes colleague had come to interview me, I wasn't cautioned or asked if I wanted a lawyer present; which I took, rightly or wrongly, as a good sign. To my surprise, Dawn led the interview, but I assumed this was because she had already got to know me.

She began by asking for an account of that morning's events.

I explained about Julia's phone call, which she said she would come back to. Then I related how Julia had tried to kill me, and how I had had to fight for my life, unfortunately (as I put it) having had to hurt her in self-defence.

'So going back to Julia's phone call, what did she want and why did the two of you meet up?'

'We met up because she'd heard that I'd worked out what happened to Helen. What I thought had happened to Helen, that is. She'd known Helen and said she wanted to help. I was going to show her how I thought Helen might have died.'

'But you didn't think Julia herself was involved?'

'Christ, no. You don't imagine I would have met her at the top of the multi-storey if I'd thought she was involved?'

'You say she'd heard that you had worked out what happened to Helen. How did she hear?'

'Well, she's friends with one of my colleagues, a woman called Rosemary. And, er, Rosemary messaged Julia to say that I'd worked it out.'

'How did you know that Rosemary had messaged her?'

'Um, I asked her to.' My answer hung in the air, and Dawn exchanged a glance with her colleague. I could see that they felt they were getting to a crucial point in the interview.

'Why did you ask Rosemary to message Julia?'

'It's complicated, but basically there was something unexplained about what had been going on in Helen's life just before she died. Something which I felt was relevant to how she died. Something which I thought Julia would know something about.'

'Go on.'

'Well, I saw someone's car parked outside Helen's house early on the Saturday morning before she died. At about five o'clock. Someone she knew at work. Julia's husband, in fact. The thing is, her husband had said that he was away at a conference all weekend and hadn't been into Cambridge at all. I knew he must have been lying. Or I thought I knew. And the only reason I could think of for him to lie would have been if he was having an affair with Helen. And if he'd been having an affair, as a married man with a lot to lose, that might have had something to do with why Helen died. That's why I wanted to tell Julia what I knew. To get her take on things.'

'But why did you meet her at the car park where Helen died?'

'Because I wasn't sure that Helen had jumped. I'd been up to the top floor after she died, and I'd worked out how someone she had trusted might have been able to catch her unawares and heave her over the wall. Just like … well, just like Julia tried to do to me.'

When the police had arrived at the multi-storey in response to my 999 call, I had shouted out to them that Julia had killed Helen. The realisation that this must have been what had happened had come to me intuitively. It was only when, after our arrival at the police station, I had been left on my own in the interview room that I had had time to think it through more logically. I had still come to the same conclusion. It was surely outside the realms of possibility for there to have been two murderers operating in the same way in the same car park. The idea about how Helen might have been killed had come to me from my knowledge of the Brides in the Bath murder case. Now, I was remembering another famous murder case I had read about - that of Timothy Evans and Reginald Christie, both tenants at the notorious London address of 10 Rillington Place. Evans had been hanged in the early 1950s for the murder, by strangulation, of his wife and infant daughter. Some years later, Christie had also been hanged for the murder, by strangulation, of several other women. All of the murders had been committed at the same address. Evans had subsequently been posthumously pardoned, and although the complete truth of the case will never be known, the most popular view was that it was too far-fetched to believe that two murderers, using the same methods, had been operating independently of each other at the same address over the same period.

'If you didn't suspect Julia, then, who did you suspect? Her husband?' This was the detective sergeant.

'I wasn't sure. I work for the man and I don't mind admitting that I don't much like him. But I wouldn't have had him down as a cold-blooded murderer. I thought it more likely that he'd had a row with Helen, perhaps over him refusing to leave his wife for her, and that might have driven her into doing something silly.' As if killing yourself was something silly, I chastised myself silently. 'I hadn't ruled out the possibility, though, that he'd killed her to shut her up. But if he did, I'm sure it would have been in a panic rather than something he had planned,' I added magnanimously. 'There was someone else I also thought could have been involved. A client of Helen's. She had suspected him of money-laundering, and also of drug-dealing. It occurred to me that he might have killed her, to stop her passing her suspicions onto anyone else. But I guess I was wrong on both counts,' I finished mournfully.

The detective sergeant asked me more about Max, and I told them everything I had learned. I didn't bother them with my earlier musings about Rachel, Jeff and Lucy, and whether any of them could have been involved in Helen's death. I had got enough wrong already.

'There is one thing that puzzles us, Alan,' Dawn said. 'You say that you saw Sam Snape's car parked outside Helen's house early on the Saturday morning before she died. At a ridiculously early time in fact. What were you doing there? I thought your relationship with her had ended quite a long time beforehand?'

This was embarrassing. 'If I tell you the truth,' I said miserably, 'will you keep it to yourselves?'

Dawn raised an eyebrow but said nothing.

'Well, it's like this,' I said eventually, looking down at my hands as they rested on the table. 'I woke up early on the Saturday morning. I had been worrying about a lot of things at work … and … and I wondered if she was still seeing the guy in the office she'd been going out with for a bit. So, as I couldn't get back to sleep, I thought I might as well drive out there to see if his car was parked outside her house. It seemed easier than asking her directly.' Christ, this was bad. For a moment I imagined being asked about this in court, listened to by a full house of lawyers, jurors and journalists. I cringed in anticipation of the humiliation.

'You were jealous, then?' Dawn asked.

I really didn't like her use of that word. I had read too many books about murderers for whom jealousy seemed to be their prime motivation. I didn't want Dawn and her colleague thinking that I had been planning revenge on Helen for anything. 'I suppose so,' I said after a few seconds' silence. I couldn't come up with any other explanation that wouldn't sound ridiculous. However, I told myself not to blurt out something about not having done anything to harm her. That would just make me sound guilty. 'I feel very embarrassed about it now,' I muttered. 'I was just being stupid. I wish I'd never gone there that Saturday morning.' To my horror, I felt tears welling up in my eyes and I heard my voice starting to sound squeaky.

I was half-expecting Dawn and her colleague to step up the pressure, maybe to caution me or even arrest me. I was startled, therefore, when she simply said: 'We'll pause things here. Just let me have a word with my sergeant outside.'

They returned about five minutes later, and said that they wanted to finalise a witness statement for me to sign. An hour or so later, the statement was done and I had signed it, and I was able to leave the station. My Prius was still parked at the multi-storey, of course, and I had to walk back to the building where Julia had so recently tried to throw me over the parapet. I felt light-headed, as if I had been drinking. The Friday evening rush hour was at its busiest, and the city centre pavements were heaving with pedestrians. To them I must have been just one solitary, nondescript man in the crowd. None of them would have realised that I had just survived a murder attempt. None of them would have cared how I was feeling.

Strange as it seems, I had completely forgotten to ask Dawn and her colleague what was happening with Julia.

35

Almost the first thing I did when I got home was to log on to the firm portal on my laptop and check my e-mails. I had been out of the loop all day and I wanted to make sure that I hadn't missed anything important. That, at least, was how I tried to justify it to myself. The truth, as deep down I recognised, was more complicated. I was still bewildered and frightened by what had happened to me that day. I had immersed myself over the last few weeks in what I liked to think of as my investigation. I had, dare I say, even enjoyed certain aspects of it. I had looked forward to being able to expose the lies and hypocrisies of some of the people I worked with, particularly Jeff and Sam. But I realised now that a lot of it had been a bit of an intellectual exercise. The reality was very different. It was as if I had been watching a thriller on television with a glass of wine in my hand, and then suddenly been confronted with a masked intruder smashing their way through my front door and brandishing a knife at me.

Going through my work e-mails therefore brought me a degree of comfort. It was a reminder of a world which I understood and in which I excelled professionally, and where there were seldom any unwelcome surprises.

Most of that day's e-mails were routine and could be dealt with on Monday. I'd had some feedback from my big institutional client on the first few template contracts which I had sent over to their in-house lawyer for review. The lawyer was fairly junior – probably one of those who couldn't cope with the stresses of private practice and had escaped into the cushy world of public sector legal practice at the first opportunity. A world, so I heard, where some lawyers could even get time off in lieu if they had to stay late to get work done; a world, I speculated, where possibly the most difficult decision some of them ever had to make was which pronouns to include in their e-mail signatures. The lawyer I was dealing with here had made enough comments back to show that she had read my templates; but not enough to convince me that she had appreciated all the subtleties of my drafting. Normally this would have frustrated me. Tonight, though, my reaction was simply one of relief that no immediate response from me was required.

I'd also had an e-mail from Sam just before lunchtime, asking abruptly where I was. Trying to stop your fucking wife from killing me, was my first thought. It seemed odd that he had e-mailed, but then I remembered that he'd been at a client's site that morning. Sure enough, a few minutes earlier there had also been an e-mail from Hayley, saying that Sam had called my landline and that my mobile had been switched off when she had tried to forward his call on. She had asked me to phone him back as soon as I was able to. There had been no further e-mails or messages from Sam. I bet he had other priorities later on that day, I thought sardonically.

There had been nothing from Lucy, but I expected her to have been working with Jeff all day up on the third floor. She was probably already thinking of herself as a Corporate trainee, even though strictly she still had one more week with me in Commercial.

Rosemary, of course, hadn't yet arrived at the office when I had left to meet Julia. Hayley wouldn't have known where I had gone, and I wondered if Rosemary had drawn any connection between her message to Julia yesterday and my unexplained absence today.

I tidied up my in-box and sent a few holding e-mails to clients and to colleagues in other teams with whom I was working on various projects. I was beginning to realise, though, that I couldn't keep putting off thinking further about today's events.

Normally, on a Friday night, I changed out of my work clothes as soon as I got home from the office and then cooked myself a posh ready meal, washed down with a bottle of decent wine. Tonight, I hadn't bothered changing. My suit trousers were smeared with grime from the car park floor and there were dark smudges – which I assumed was dried blood from Julia's nose - on the front of my jacket. I told myself wryly that I could go and visit Hayley in her Abbey area of Cambridge and blend into the surroundings for once. I wasn't in the mood to cook, so I walked the short distance from my apartment block to the small parade of shops on the development. I hadn't eaten anything since breakfast and, all of a sudden, I realised how hungry I was. I bought a 4 pack of chilled lagers and a big bar of fruit and nut chocolate from the mini-supermarket, and a cod and large chips from the chippy next door. Back at my flat, I wolfed down the food and lager while watching the news, then switched off and sat back in my chair to try finally to make sense of everything that had happened that day.

Julia's cold-blooded determination to kill me still sent a shiver down my spine. There had been none of the stuff that you see in television dramas, where the killer explains to the victim why, regretfully, the victim must die. Instead, it had all happened very quickly and without fuss. One moment Julia had been behaving relatively normally; the next she had grabbed me by my legs and tried to propel me over the parapet. I knew that she worked out every day, but the strength she had shown still frightened me. If I hadn't reacted so quickly, and had a bit of luck as well, I would have been over the parapet and tumbling to the ground within a couple of seconds of her launching her attack. I felt sick as I imagined what the fall would have been like - being fully conscious all the way down, knowing what the end result was going to be and that there was nothing I could do to prevent it. I wondered if I would have screamed as I fell. I couldn't resist getting my phone out of my jacket pocket and doing a Google search to find out how long my fall would have lasted before I hit the ground.

I thought about Helen's death. Would she have had time to realise what Julia had done to her? Would she have known why Julia had done it? Would she have known that she was about to die? Would she have screamed as she fell?

I remembered Helen's funeral. I wondered what my funeral would have been like if Julia had succeeded in killing me. I guessed that Helen, if she had still been alive, would have wanted to come. But who else from Doveley's would have come voluntarily, because they wanted to say goodbye to me, rather than because they thought it was the right thing to do? I couldn't think of anyone except, possibly, Rosemary. Sam, I supposed, would have played the big 'I Am' and delivered a eulogy given the chance, but he wouldn't have missed me or even particularly regretted my death.

Most of all, I wrestled with why Julia had wanted to kill Helen. I could see why, having killed Helen, she might have panicked and tried to kill me. Playing back in my mind what I had said to her, it must have sounded like I was on her trail. She would have been desperate to stop me going to the police. But why kill Helen in the first place? She knew Helen from the gym, but the only real connection between the two women was via Sam. So that must be it. Rosemary had been wrong about there being nothing going on between Helen and Sam. Julia had found out about them. She had been insanely jealous. She had met Helen on the top floor of the multi-storey. At some point, either by chance or through Julia's trickery, Helen had looked over the parapet. And Julia had then done to Helen what she had tried to do to me – grabbed her by the legs and propelled her over the parapet to a bone-shattering death below.

And yet, and yet ... I could understand Julia wanting to kill Helen. The history of crime was littered with spouses who, blinded with jealousy or hatred, had killed their love rivals. What didn't make sense to me were the mechanics of how this could have happened. If Helen was having an affair with Sam, she would have been very wary of Julia. She might have had to exchange small talk with her at the gym, when the two women occasionally ran into each other. But they weren't friends, so they wouldn't have naturally ended up together on the top floor of a multi-storey late one evening. And, if Julia had told Helen that she had found out about the affair and wanted to discuss it with her, Helen was even more unlikely to meet her in a place like that. She wouldn't, of course, have suspected Julia of wanting to kill her, but she would certainly have expected a scene, possibly a slap to the face. She would surely have insisted on meeting somewhere else - somewhere safe, where if necessary she could bail out of any confrontation. And, even if I was wrong about that, I couldn't imagine how Julia would have been able to take Helen by surprise the way she had done with me. The only reason why Julia and I had been next to the parapet together was because that was where Helen had fallen. No way would Helen have put herself in such a vulnerable position with a woman whose husband she was sleeping with.

The whole thing just didn't make sense to me.

*

Eventually, the four cans of lager had their usual effect on me, and I went to bed, falling into an unbroken sleep. I spent the rest of the weekend trying, not very successfully, to distract myself from the horrors of Friday. I was already dreading going into the office on Monday. I had no idea what had happened regarding Julia, or what Sam knew or had been told, either by her or by the police. I didn't even want to think about what Sam might say to me, if he believed what Julia had probably told him. I played tennis on Saturday afternoon, and again on Sunday morning, but I found it impossible to concentrate on the games. During the Sunday club social session, one of my doubles' partners even asked me if I was all right, and if there was anything he could do to help. It was the first time someone at the club had ever shown any interest in me as a person, and I was quite touched. I was tempted, just for a moment, to pour everything out to him, but as usual I ended up instead just smiling politely and saying thank you but I was fine.

36

Sunday

The phone rang at 10 p.m. on Sunday evening, just when I was thinking about getting ready for bed.

'Alan, it's P.C. Dawn Smith. I'm sorry to call so late, but I thought you'd want to know what's been going on before you get into work tomorrow.'

'Yes, please,' I said. 'What's happened?'

'Julia was taken to hospital on Friday, as you know. Although there was a lot of blood, her injuries were fairly superficial. However, she was kept in hospital overnight, in case of concussion, before being discharged on Saturday morning. She was then interviewed under caution at the police station over the weekend, following which she was charged and bailed.'

'Charged? What with?'

'Murder and attempted murder.'

'You mean me and Helen?'

'Yes. We looked at the CCTV from Friday morning. After Helen's death, the car park operator had put in some extra cameras, in case someone else ever decided to jump from one of their upper floors. One of the cameras captured the whole of Julia's attack on you. We showed it to her, and she broke down and admitted trying to kill you. She then also admitted causing Helen's death.'

'But how did she kill Helen? I can guess why she did it - she must have found out about Helen and Sam. But how did she persuade Helen to meet her up there late at night?'

There was a short silence. I was about to ask Dawn if she was still there, when she continued: 'There was no affair between Helen and Sam.'

'But I saw Sam's car ...'

'Yes, I know you did. But you didn't see Sam. That's because he hadn't been driving it. He'd been away at a conference all weekend, as he'd told you. He'd gone by train. Julia had been driving Sam's car. Her own car had got a flat tyre. She'd been in a hurry, so she borrowed Sam's. Sam didn't even know. And her kids had been on a sleepover, so they didn't know either.'

It was my turn to pause. Almost everything I had worked out had been on the basis that Sam and Helen were having an affair. Suddenly nothing seemed to make any sense. 'But if there was no affair,' I eventually asked, 'why did Julia go round to Helen's house? They hardly knew each other.'

'I said there was no affair between Helen and Sam. I didn't say there was no affair.'

I fell silent as the implications of what Dawn had said began to sink in. Dawn remained silent too. She must have known the nature of the bombshell she had dropped. Finally, I spoke: 'You mean, er, Helen and Julia ...?' I felt like a schoolboy volunteering the only logically possible solution to a problem, while being scared that he is making a fool of himself in front of his classmates.

'Yes. Julia and Helen had been in a relationship.'

Christ. Although I had been straightjacketed into reaching this conclusion myself, it was still a shock to hear it confirmed. For some odd reason my mind flashed back to when Rosemary had told me that she was gay. My first, fortunately unspoken, reaction had been to think that she didn't look it, and that she had been married to a man most of her life anyway. But at least Rosemary was someone whom I only knew professionally. I had an excuse for my peccadillo. On the other hand, I had been sleeping with Helen. For almost a year. My mind was already going into overdrive. I remembered all the fantasises that Helen had enjoyed, sometimes involving women. She had always maintained that they were fantasies, and nothing more. But had she been lying all along? Or had something I had done made her want to turn her fantasies into reality. Or, Christ Almighty, had something I had not done, or not been able to do, pushed her in that direction? I already knew that I was going to go through hell in the weeks to come, thinking all of this through. I felt betrayed, but I also remembered her promise that she would never be unfaithful to me with another man. Although I hadn't realised so at the time, she must have deliberately phrased that very carefully.

And then another aspect of what Dawn had revealed struck me. Helen had subsequently got involved with Jeff, and he had hinted at there being something missing between the two of them in the physical side of their relationship. Did Jeff know, or at least suspect, that Helen had other preferences? If he didn't, then that would certainly be a blow to his pride, I couldn't help but think. I might even have to be the person who broke the news. I imagined the humiliation he was bound to feel. For a moment, I pictured him and me, sitting together over our pints in my new local on Helen's road, comparing notes about our mutual inability to satisfy her ...

'Alan, are you still there?'

I forced my thoughts about Jeff from my mind. Dawn was of course still on the phone. 'Yes, sorry,' I said, 'you were saying ...?'

'According to Julia,' Dawn said, 'she and Helen had been in an on-off relationship since last autumn. Helen had been unhappy in her relationship with you, but didn't know whether that was because of what you were like or because she was gay.' Thanks very bloody much, I thought. 'Helen had taken up with Jeff,' Dawn went on, 'at least partly in case the problem from her perspective had been with you. But she quickly realised that the issue was more to do with her own sexuality.'

Dawn paused, and I wondered whether she was expecting me to thank her for this back-handed compliment. Or, perhaps, even to say how pleased I was that Helen had found her true self. Well, Dawn could sod right off, I thought. 'What went wrong, then, between Helen and Julia?' was all that I said though.

'According to Julia, Helen had been trying to persuade her to leave Sam. But Julia had decided that she didn't want to. For her the relationship had been more a bit of fun. Also, between ourselves, I think she enjoyed the status of being the wife of a successful law firm partner too much. And no doubt the money that came with it. I guess the prospect of being the girlfriend of a junior solicitor at her ex-husband's practice wasn't quite so appealing. It had all got very emotional, apparently, and Julia says that Helen – who we both know had a history of depression – had been dropping hints about harming herself. It came to a head on the evening of her death.'

Dawn paused again. I threw in the 'What happened?' which I presumed she was waiting for.

'As you know, Helen was out for a meal with work colleagues at a curry house in Cambridge. By pure coincidence, Sam and Julia were also having a meal together there at the same time. When Helen went to the toilet, Sam took the opportunity to go over and sit down in Helen's chair for a few minutes and indulge in a bit of work gossip. Helen saw Sam there on her way back from the toilets, so decided to go and sit down in Sam's chair at his and Julia's table. Normally she and Julia were very discreet about being seen together, but remember that Helen had been drinking. As it happens, though, no one from Doveley's noticed them together. During their conversation, Julia told Helen that she was staying with Sam. Helen got very overwrought, and said something to the effect that she might as well jump off the top of the multi-storey. Julia therefore decided she had better follow her when she left the curry house. She must have made some excuse to Sam, of course. When Julia got to the top of the multi-storey, she says that Helen was already leaning over the wall, looking down as if she was thinking about killing herself. Julia says that she tried, in her words, to talk some sense into Helen. But Helen lashed out at her verbally, before then leaning over the wall again, as if she was going to throw herself over head first. Julia says that in a mad moment of anger she gave Helen a push, not intending her to go over the parapet. However, as we know, Helen fell to her death. Julia then panicked and left the scene.'

'Do you believe all that?' I asked. I could tell from the ensuing silence that Dawn was wondering how much to say to me.

'It doesn't matter what I believe,' she said eventually. 'It will ultimately be for a jury to decide what they think happened. However, we do expect her legal team, one of the best that money can hire, will run a defence of diminished responsibility and loss of control to the charges of murder and attempted murder. If successful, that means that she would be found guilty of the manslaughter, rather than the murder, of Helen.'

'I'm sure she did it deliberately,' I said. 'Deliberately tried to kill Helen, I mean. I found out what she's capable of when she tried to kill me. She knew exactly what she was doing. She was utterly ruthless. I reckon she was worried about Sam finding out about her affair with Helen. Worried about what it would mean for her marriage, maybe also for her relationship with her kids. Helen wasn't the type to tell tales, but Julia wouldn't have known that for sure. She saw a one-off chance to silence Helen ... and took it. I bet she tricked Helen into peering over the parapet exactly like she did to me, and then heaved her over.' Something was nagging at the back of my mind, however. 'One thing puzzles me,' I said. 'Why did Julia admit to anything regarding Helen's death? Why didn't she say that Helen lost her balance during their argument, fell against the parapet and accidentally tumbled over? Or why, even, didn't she say that Helen jumped off the top floor of her own accord?'

'CCTV,' Dawn said.

'Sorry?'

'As I said before, we showed Julia the footage of her trying to heave you over the parapet. Her intention there was absolutely clear. However, she didn't know what other footage we might already have, or be able to obtain. She didn't therefore dare say anything that we might later be able to prove wasn't true. She couldn't deny following Helen up to the top floor, or laying her hands on her as she leant over the parapet.'

'Whereas even if you had footage of her pushing Helen over the top, she could still claim that she had done it, as she said, in a "mad moment of anger", provoked by whatever she claims Helen had said to her?'

Another silence. It told me that I was right. 'I'm not a criminal lawyer,' I said, 'but I'm surprised she didn't exercise her right to silence?'

'Julia wasn't in the mood to be silent, to be honest. In fact, she was raging mad with what she saw as your interference. I won't repeat what she called you. She also blamed you for Helen's state of mind, saying that you had made her desperately unhappy for most of last year.' I waited for Dawn to say that of course Julia had been talking rubbish, but instead she continued: 'If I am honest, we were lucky that she tried to kill you in full view of the new CCTV camera, otherwise things might have been harder for us.'

I didn't care for her use of the word 'lucky' in relation to Julia's unprovoked and brutal attack on me. 'Where is Julia now?' I had to ask.

'She's at home, under bail conditions. She won't therefore be contacting you, and obviously you mustn't contact her.'

'Does Sam know what she did?'

'He does now. The whole thing seems to have come as a complete shock to him though. Poor guy. He's made sure, as you would expect, that Julia is being represented by one of the city's top criminal defence solicitors.'

I just about managed to keep quiet at the 'poor guy' bit. It reminded me of all the 'poor Jeffs' I had had to endure in the aftermath of Helen's death. I couldn't avoid thinking, though, that this might bring Sam down a peg or two. He wouldn't find it quite so easy to wear his smug smile around the second floor once everyone knew what his wife had done. Not only had she killed one person and tried to kill another; but she had also demonstrated that he didn't exactly have the perfect home life either. I wondered how Sam was going to manage the way the news spread around the firm. Was he going to make some kind of announcement, to get his side of the story in first? If so, that would certainly be worth coming into the office for. Given what Sam must be going through, I suppose I should have been feeling guilty about having these thoughts; but I have to say that I didn't. I wondered idly who was representing Julia. No one from our firm, for sure, as we didn't sully our middle-class hands with criminal defence work.

There was one thing, though, that I desperately wanted to know. 'Um, did Sam say anything about my role in what happened?'

'Not really. To be honest, Alan, I think he has more important things to worry about than you.'

So that was me being put back in my box, I thought. I had helped to bring a murderer to justice, something that the police could not have done without me; but now I was one of the civilians again. However, I decided not to show my annoyance. I still had to tread carefully with the police, as they could cause me some embarrassment if they revealed how I had come to be outside Helen's house on that Saturday morning. I could see the newspaper headlines now: *'Jealous spurned solicitor spied on the victim's house'*. People wouldn't understand that I'd had reasons for doing what I did. 'I understand,' I said. 'But who else knows what happened? Of the people at Doveley's, I mean?'

'I don't know. It will be a matter of public record in due course what Julia is charged with, but it's not for us to tell everyone. Of course, when she appears in court it is going to be a big story in Cambridge, and probably nationally. It's not every day that the wife of one of the city's top solicitors gets charged with murder.'

Indeed not, I thought. That was certainly a newspaper headline that I was looking forward to reading. If I hadn't been holding the phone, I would have rubbed my hands together in pleasure. Naturally, I was desperately sorry for what had happened to Helen. It was a tragedy that her life had been brought to a premature end as a result of a relationship that had gone wrong. A lot of people, as well as me, had been devastated by her death. Nevertheless, as long as I handled things carefully, there must be a likelihood of me being seen as some kind of hero at the firm, for having flushed out a dangerous killer and enabled her to be brought to justice. I couldn't claim to have suspected Julia, of course, but there was no doubt in my mind that if I hadn't undertaken my investigation she would have got away with her crimes.

*

After Dawn had rung off, I remained annoyed with her for quite a while for not having thanked me properly for my role in capturing Julia. I also felt annoyed with Helen. After returning to her own table in the curry house on the night she died, she must have made a deliberate decision to make it look like I was to blame for the upset which Julia had just caused her. No one at the table would, I realised miserably, have been surprised to hear that I had apparently contacted her when she was trying to enjoy a night out with her friends.

Nevertheless, I went to bed experiencing, for the first time in ages, a pleasurable anticipation at the thought of going into the office the next day. I had toyed with the idea of sending some witty reply to Sam's e-mail from Friday asking where I was; but nothing had quite worked, so I had decided against that. Instead, I spent some time planning what I was going to say to people at Doveley's once the news about Julia became common knowledge.

37

Monday

It felt strange on Monday morning parking my Prius in its usual spot on the first floor of the multi-storey car park. For some reason it hadn't really been a problem for me to continue to park there after Helen's death. But now that the multi-storey had nearly been the scene of my own death, I wondered if I would feel more comfortable in future finding another car park. As I came out of the pedestrian stairway at the front, I couldn't stop myself from turning my head to the left and looking into the passageway which ran down the side of the building, and then round the back to the place where I would have landed if Julia's attack had been successful. Even now, three days later, the memory of what she had done made me feel slightly nauseous.

Nevertheless, my spirits had recovered somewhat by the time I reached the office. I strutted through the front doors, saying a cheery 'Hello' to the receptionist and asking a couple of hovering trainees from Property if they had had a good weekend. I felt an inch or two taller than normal, and unusually confident enough to initiate conversations with people I barely knew. There was a full-length mirror on the wall either side of the reception desk, no doubt to give an impression of extra space, and automatically I checked my reflection to see if I looked any different. Although I knew it sounded childish, I couldn't help asking myself rhetorically how many other lawyers at the firm had ever caught a murderer in the act.

When I arrived on the second floor, Rosemary, Lucy and

Hayley were already all at our pod, doing their usual start-of-the-day jobs. They said nothing, though they all gave me the kind of look that is normally reserved for a lawyer who has been fingered as having screwed up on a file, but who doesn't yet know it himself. It was my first inkling that today might not pan out how I had expected.

'Morning, all,' I said. 'Sam not in yet?' I had noticed Sam's empty chair at his pod.

'No, not yet,' said Hayley. She looked a bit uncomfortable. Lucy and Rosemary were listening, and I had the impression that they knew what she was going to say. She went on: 'You know he was looking for you on Friday? He seemed quite annoyed. He phoned here first, and then your mobile was switched off when I tried to forward his call to you. He said he was going to send you an e-mail asking you to call him. Did you get back to him in time? I think the client he was visiting wanted some urgent advice on a patent infringement claim they are being threatened with.'

If I'd had a beard, I would have stroked it in pleasure. 'As it happens, Hayley, I didn't get back to him. Something else more important cropped up.' She looked startled at my unusual boldness. 'Did anything unexpected crop up for Sam later that day?' I asked innocently.

'You haven't heard then? Yes, his wife Julia had an accident during the morning. We had a phone call from the hospital at lunchtime. She was taken there with head injuries. I don't know how she is. I sent a message to Sam before I went home on Friday, but he hasn't replied. But that's obviously got nothing to do with you not being contactable in the morning, when he was trying to get hold of you.'

I felt like a kid at the pantomime. I wanted to shout out 'Oh, yes, it does'. But I decided to play it a bit more matter-of-fact. 'Actually,' I said, 'the two were connected. I'm not sure how much I should be telling you at this stage, but I guess you will find out soon enough. Anyway, the reason why Sam couldn't reach me was that Julia tried to kill me on Friday morning. I had to defend myself, and that's why she ended up in hospital. She also killed Helen, by the way.'

If I had ever wondered what it looked like when someone's jaw was said to drop, now I knew. Three times over. Hayley's, Rosemary's and Lucy's mouths all opened wide. They could almost have been a trio of singers about to burst into a chorus. But instead of a song, there was absolute silence. I couldn't honestly say that there was any admiration in the looks they gave me, however, and to my dismay I realised that I might actually sound mad. They might, I thought in sudden horror, be wondering if I had attacked Julia for some random reason, perhaps as a way to get back at Sam, and if I might potentially also be a danger to them. Quickly I moved to reassure them. 'The police know everything,' I said. 'Julia has been arrested and charged with murder and attempted murder. Sam has arranged for her to have legal representation. That may be why he's not in yet.'

Rosemary was the first to break the silence. 'Helen and Julia. Were they a thing?'

She may now have only been a professional support lawyer, but she could still show the sharpness of thought that would previously have stood her in good stead as a fee earner. Lucy and Hayley clearly didn't have a clue what she was talking about. But, of course, I should have expected Rosemary to work it out first. Rosemary was gay herself. Various people at the firm knew she was gay. She was on the firm's Diversity and Inclusion Group, after all. Helen had come to her for advice on a personal matter. It was therefore now obvious to me what that personal matter must have been. And Rosemary also knew Julia personally – she had told me that they were on some WhatsApp groups together, and that they sometimes messaged each other privately. Why on earth hadn't I drawn the obvious conclusion when I had learned all this from Rosemary?

'Yes, they were,' I said simply. 'Did you not know?'

'No.' She still looked shaken. A bit like a dog owner whose delightful puppy has just bitten the postman. 'I knew about them both, of course. And I knew they moved in the same circles. Even in Cambridge, it's still quite a close-knit community. But I had no idea that they had become involved with each other. Poor people.'

It was all very well to be surprised, I thought, but I wasn't sure why Julia was getting Rosemary's sympathy. No one, I noted, had asked me for details of how Julia had tried to kill me, and how I had managed to overpower her and hand her over to the police.

Hayley was still following every word of our conversation, but I noticed that Lucy was banging something out very quickly on her keyboard. A few seconds later my desk phone rang. I saw from the number displayed that it was Jeff.

'Alan, what the hell's going on. Lucy says that Sam's wife has been arrested for killing Helen and attacking you?'

'More than just attacking me. Trying to kill me, actually,' I corrected him. 'It's true, I'm afraid. Helen and Julia were having an affair. At the same time as Helen was seeing you, it would appear. I assume you knew?'

'Of course I didn't know.' I was getting used to long silences on the phone from various people, and here was another. I waited patiently. 'But, Christ, a few things do start to make sense,' he went on. I could imagine what he was thinking, given what he had admitted to me in the pub. 'I can't believe it though. Why did Julia do ... what she did?' To my surprise, I heard a catch in his voice, as if he was close to tears. After another short silence he went on: 'I'm sorry, Alan, I can't take all this in. We'll talk later.' And his phone went dead. I couldn't stand the man, and I wasn't going to waste any pity on him. But it did occur to me that, under all his 'player' braggadocio that the women seemed to fall for, he might have a more human side that I had never seen.

'Alan.' I spun around at the sound of Sam's voice. I hadn't seen or heard him arrive. There was no hint of a smile on his face; he just looked weary. 'A word, please, if you've quite finished. Downstairs. The usual room. Five minutes.' He turned on his heel and walked out of the door onto the corridor which led to the lift and the stairs.

Hayley was agog. I could tell she would have given anything to join us downstairs. Lucy clearly didn't want to get into conversation with me. She bent her head to her screen and started tapping away as if it was just another Monday morning. Rosemary mouthed a 'Good luck' at me. I went downstairs to the staff meeting room and sat down facing the door, waiting for Sam to arrive. I wasn't quite sure what approach he was going to take. I wasn't naïve enough to expect a full and frank apology for his wife's attack on me, or to be congratulated on having brought a dangerous killer to book. But I expected him to show some regret for what had happened, and to check that I was OK. After all, it isn't every day that a boss's wife tries to throw one of his employees from the top floor of a multi-storey. I was prepared to be magnanimous, saying that I knew it wasn't his fault and that I was sure it wouldn't stop us working constructively together in the future. Sam arrived a couple of minutes after me. He shut the door but remained standing on the other side of the table, his arms by his side.

'You fucking cunt, Alan,' were his first words. 'I bet you've really got off on this, haven't you? Creeping around and spying on people. First Helen, then me. Then everyone else who you've either resented or who you think might be having more fun than you. I've heard what you've been like with Jeff, and Lucy, and Rachel. And no doubt with others I don't know about. And that's just people here. What about Max? The son of one of our best clients and you've basically accused him of dealing in drugs. You're a shit, an absolute fucking shit.'

I was completely blindsided. I hadn't seen this coming. To my horror, I felt my cheeks flush and tears well up in my eyes. It was so unfair, I thought. Sam was just using this as an excuse to tell me exactly what he had always thought of me. All pretence of professional veneer had gone; he really didn't like me or respect me.

'I only did what I felt I had to do,' I mumbled. 'For Helen's 'sake.' I dug a fingernail into the soft palm of a hand, praying desperately that my voice wouldn't break or a tear run down my cheek.

'For Helen's sake? It was for her sake that you spied on her in the middle of the night? For Christ's sake, man, what sort of person does something like that?'

This wasn't a question I felt I could answer directly. But I did know that if I hadn't made that early morning drive out to Helen's house, I wouldn't have seen Sam's car, and Julia would probably never have been arrested. I couldn't find any beneficial way of pointing this out to Sam though. I decided to change tack: 'Regarding Max, I only did what I thought was my professional duty. I've not contacted him again since you asked me not to.'

'Professional duty? Bollocks. You and I both know that there's only one reason why you had it in for Max. He fancied Helen and you didn't like that. You were digging around for some dirt that you could throw at him. That's how you operate.'

I didn't say anything. I could see how some people might think there was an element of truth in what Sam had said. There was no advantage in me saying that, if Max had been the murderer, I might have been able to bring him to justice.

Sam went on: 'I don't need to tell you this, but I might as well. Max was being bankrolled by his father. His father was funding the office purchase. Max didn't let on to you and Helen, because he wanted people to think that he was making a success of his business off his own back. As he is doing, no thanks to you. He's a decent guy, in other words, who has some pride and likes to do the right thing.'

Unlike me, is what you mean, I thought miserably. The tears in my eyes seemed to have dried up, but my lower lip was trembling and I couldn't meet Sam's eyes.

'Max is also helping out his sister who owns a local wine merchant business. He sometimes delivers cases of wine to her Cambridge customers. As a favour for her, because he's that type of man. All perfectly above board. I had the embarrassment of having all this explained to me by Max's father. I felt, one, a complete prat and, two, as if in some way I had betrayed their family's trust by even asking questions. So thanks for that too, Alan.'

I felt like I was a duck in a shooting gallery at an old-fashioned fair. The only part of my investigation that Sam hadn't had a rant about yet was the Ely lease which Helen had done for Piers's company. Well, that at least had turned out to be a red herring. I thought I had better say something back to Sam, but nothing suitable came to mind. I could hardly ask him how Julia was, after I had punched her in the face and repeatedly banged her head against the ground. And I couldn't really ask him how he was coping; because I'd already had the answer. Clearly, he had decided that he wasn't going to accept any blame for what Julia had done, and in fact was going to blame me for much of what had happened. Now wasn't the time for an objective explanation from me about how I had enabled the capture of a violent criminal who would otherwise have gone free.

I thought of another angle. 'I'm sorry for what's gone on in your life, Sam. It can't be easy.' His only response was to glare at me from behind his Buddy Holly glasses. His hands were still by his sides, as if he couldn't make up his mind whether to put them in his pockets or around my throat. I wondered which he found more distressing. That his wife had killed one person, and tried to kill a second. Or that she had not only been shagging a younger person at his place of work, but someone who was a woman, with all that entailed as a threat to his manhood. Nowadays everyone was, thankfully, fine and dandy about people being gay, but that wouldn't stop malicious gossip within the firm about Sam not being able to keep his wife satisfied. The same was true for me and Jeff, of course, but Sam would get it worst as the partner who basked in running the second floor. I didn't need to be told, though, that this wasn't a subject that the three of us would be exploring together over a companionable drink any time soon.

'Er, was there anything else you wanted to discuss?' I asked. 'Hayley said you had been trying to get hold of me on Friday morning about a patent infringement claim when, er, ...'

On reflection, this would probably have been better left unsaid, although to be fair to myself I was giving him a chance to tell me if there was a client issue that needed urgent attention.

Sam looked me hard in the eyes. 'Just get out of my fucking sight, Alan,' he said. 'Oh, and tell Hayley to cancel your partnership business case meetings with me until further notice. I think both of us will have more important things to worry about for quite a while to come.'

And that was that. Sam left the meeting room without another word, and headed for the stairs down to reception, no doubt on his way out to attend to some matter arising out of his wife's arrest. I traipsed miserably back up to the second floor, passing two partners on the stairs from the Corporate team who both completely blanked me. In normal times they would have had the courtesy to throw me a 'Hello, Alan, how are you?' as they passed. But today I might as well have been a piece of dog shit on the carpet, for all the notice they took of me. So that's how it's going to be, I thought.

*

Back at my pod, Hayley and Lucy were making an ostentatious point of being hard at work with their heads down and eyes on their screens. They would have seen the mood that Sam was in when he came over to summon me downstairs, and would have guessed why he was angry. They would have seen me return, no doubt white-faced, from the meeting. They wouldn't want to be seen to be taking my side against Sam. Hayley had to work with him every day, and Lucy was about to move upstairs and had no skin in the game with me. There was therefore no cheery enquiry from Hayley as to how the meeting had gone, nor one of Lucy's expressionless but typically slightly sarcastic quips.

I saw that Jeff had sent me an e-mail asking if we could meet up after work for a chat. I deleted it without replying. I wasn't going to give the little sod the chance to offer me yet another handshake.

Rosemary gave me a sympathetic smile. She was definitely a good sort. But she came to the office each day to do a job, to earn enough money to give her and her children the life she wanted away from work. She wasn't going to get involved in office politics. She fought her battles elsewhere.

I realised that I had no more battles to fight at Doveley's. Helen was gone. Her killer was gone. My partnership prospects were gone. I would have said that my friends were gone, except that I didn't really have any to start with. I supposed I still had my clients. But, as the partners at Doveley's always made clear to their fee earners, clients were the firm's clients and not their personal ones. In any event, I didn't think I would be taking any clients with me when I left. Not because the firm would be able to stop me, if the clients insisted. But because, if I was honest, I didn't expect the clients would want to come with me anyway. I never had the impression that any of them actually liked me that much. I did a job for them; they paid me; we then forgot about each other until the next time.

I left the office at 4.55 p.m. Before even any of the secretaries had dared to log off. I was making a point. I knew that I wouldn't be employed at Doveley's much longer. I had given them hundreds, probably thousands of hours of unpaid overtime during my many years there. I wasn't giving them any more. Effective immediately. Sam hadn't returned to his pod, but everyone else on the second floor watched in silence as I headed for the door. It would have been the only time they had ever seen me first out of the door at the end of the day. As I walked along the corridor and then down the stairs, I assumed that they had all started talking about me the moment the door closed after me. Some things, at least, never changed.

THE END

... but please read on for the author's afterword

AFTERWORD

When you have lived and practised as a lawyer in Cambridge, there are certain problems in writing a novel about a lawyer who lives and practises in Cambridge. Especially when using the first-person narrative. And even more especially when the narrator is not, perhaps, the most admirable of people.

Some readers may wonder if the story or any of the characters are based on real events or real people. Others may wonder if the author identifies with the narrator.

Well, on the first point, I can categorically state that they are not. Doveley's, the firm where Alan works, is described in the novel as occupying a space, overlooking Parker's Piece, between the sports centre and the swimming pool. Anyone trying to visit this location will discover that no such space exists. This is because Doveley's, and the characters who work there, and all of the other characters and businesses in the novel, are entirely fictitious; as indeed is the story itself.

Of course, readers who know Cambridge will recognise the names of some of the landmarks of the city. Having decided to set the novel in Cambridge, it seemed pointless to give invented names to well-known landmarks ('Smith's Piece', anyone?). Besides, I hoped that, to borrow a turn of phrase from the late, great P.D. James, throwing in a few genuine place names might be a cunning way to add authenticity to fictitious characters and events. Some readers may therefore be familiar with a few of the streets up and down which Alan paces or drives, or some of the general locations where he visits clients. However, any attempt to search for the two pubs in which several scenes are set, or the particular street on which Helen's house is located, or Alan's tennis club, and so on, will be fruitless; all are figments of my imagination.

As for the author identifying with the narrator: I am fairly confident that my wife was joking when she asked if I had really spent our twenty plus years of marriage having the same kind of thoughts as Alan about everyone I met and knew.

Actually, the character of Alan has its genesis in a long-time interest of mine: crime novels in ordinary middle-class or professional settings in which the protagonist is some kind of social outsider. Not necessarily a criminal, and someone who sometimes even tries to do the right thing; but who has certain character traits which at best make it difficult for him (and it usually is a him) to fit in with the world he inhabits, and at worst drive him to think and behave badly.

Alan, therefore, would not fiddle his expenses; he can be presumed to do high-quality work for his clients; and he wants to show his gratitude to Rosemary by giving her children some free tennis lessons. But his self-righteousness and lack of self-awareness are such that he has surely done well just to survive so long in his job. And in the case of his main romantic nemesis, he is too blinded by bitterness and jealousy to realise that Jeff is (putting his alleged womanising to one side) actually a pretty decent guy, probably also a pretty decent corporate lawyer, and perhaps even the sort of man (and lawyer) that Alan subconsciously wishes he himself was. Few people, I suspect, would choose to have a pint with Alan. But I hoped there would be a wish to see him succeed in uncovering the truth behind the sudden death which is at the heart of the novel, even if his motives for doing so are almost completely selfish. I could have written the novel in the third person, but in the end decided that a first-person narrative was more appropriate.

As to whether life will get better for Alan after his next career move, well we will have to wait and see. But in the meantime, if you enjoyed this story, please consider leaving a review on Amazon.

Finally, I would like to thank those people who provided comments on an early draft of this novel, and in particular Keith Aggett. Keith published his own first full-length novel ('Mixed Messages') last year, and was kind enough not to be offended when, inadvertently, I intimated that if he could write a novel then I thought that I certainly could. Of course, any shortcomings in the final version of the novel (including the poetic licence I have undoubtedly used in relation to certain aspects of police procedure) are entirely my responsibility.

Printed in Great Britain
by Amazon

17893264R00161